To Dave
The cleverest man I know
All the best
Chris

CAPSTAN AND CHALKIE
SAVE THE DAY

CAPSTAN AND CHALKIE SAVE THE DAY

Chris Haxby

Book Guild Publishing
Sussex, England

First published in Great Britain in 2011 by
The Book Guild Ltd
Pavilion View
19 New Road Brighton,
BN1 1UF

Copyright © Chris Haxby 2011

The right of Chris Haxby to be identified as the author
of this work has been asserted by him in accordance with the
Copyright, Designs and Patents Act 1988.

All rights reserved.
No part of this publication may be reproduced, transmitted,
or stored in a retrieval system, in any form or by any means,
without permission in writing from the publisher, nor be otherwise
circulated in any form of binding or cover other than that in which
it is published and without a similar condition being imposed
on the subsequent purchaser.

All characters in this publication are fictitious and any resemblance
to real people, alive or dead, is purely coincidental.

Typeset in Baskerville by
Ellipsis Digital Limited, Glasgow

Printed in Great Britain by
CPI Antony Rowe

A catalogue record for this book is available from The British Library.

ISBN 978 1 84624 626 5

Author's Note

Retirement is not easy; trust me, I know. I was a primary school teacher until I became ill with anxiety and depression. After a time medication moderated the effects of these conditions, but a more complete solution lay elsewhere, deep within. Reading definitely helped keep my mind occupied; walking was good too, as was going to the theatre; and booking cheap mini holidays online was fun, especially when plans turned into reality. So, what, you may therefore wonder, was there to complain about? Well, in order to be able to offer an answer I would have to say that 'complaining' is not the issue here. No, the problem lies elsewhere, and it is to be found in the nature of time itself, which is indeterminate, so the only solution to this issue lies in the imagination and power of the mind; that is, in finding ways to fill all those minutes, hours, days and years usefully, which in my case meant avoiding the perils of daytime television. It is a complex issue, and for a time I was reasonably successful in this task, but only for a time.

Then one day, when I was at the end of my tether, I met Joe in the Blues Bar. At the time he was reading Roger Penrose's *The Emperor's New Mind*. 'Do you understand that?' I said as he looked up and stared in my direction. 'Oh yes,' he said, 'I'm actually comparing and contrasting how algorithms in digital computers have changed as new technologies evolved.' Really! This was someone I could talk to, I felt, as I'd always been interested in science and I liked the idea of asking him questions which I'd like answers to. Unfortunately this was his idea of a busman's holiday – he told me he had a PhD and had been a computer programmer, so I quickly appreciated why he didn't want to talk about scientific issues; but I still remained confused. After all, why was he reading Roger Penrose's book if he wasn't still interested in these subjects?

'I've written a book, but the publishers won't print it,' he said by way of explanation. 'Writing is what I'm interested in. I want to be a famous novelist. My book is set in Harrogate, and I'm certain that people who live in the town would read it, but so far I can't get anyone to print it. I've therefore had to rewrite part of it, and I've also had to revisit my past, to check up on one or two things. That's why I was reading that book.'

Anyway, over the next few hours we proceeded to talk about nothing in particular, but I could tell that he had an obsessive personality and that he was also 'driven'. Some of his issues turned out to be kind of serious ones (if he was ever going to be happy), and over the next few weeks I started to take notes. But when the story was almost completed he simply disappeared and I never saw him again.

This is his story.

Prologue

Bradford – 1960s

'These places are not fit for human habitation,' the cruel and heartless politicians said, 'they have to come down.'

'But they are our homes,' replied the local people, and they pleaded to be left alone.

But it was to no avail: they were sent packing, to flats on top of one another in a wilderness otherwise devoid of life, where the main road cut through next to them like a knife.

Their homes were left empty for us to play in. And soon they looked as if they had once been bombed by the Luftwaffe in the Second World War.

Life was never the same again. The old neighbourhood was gone.

Even now all that is left is an empty space.

Joe

Nigel's Masterstroke

'The problem with the last twenty years, as I see it, is that a lot of people have mistaken having a status symbol with having status. Status refers, of course, to a person's social position (and their job), but I believe a person's status is more relative than that, so I think my definition is more meaningful. Quite simply, people are either talkers or listeners. I'm a talker, not only because I like being the centre of attention, but because others naturally listen (they always do). It is therefore the power of my intellect and the strength of my personality that gives me my status. What do you think about this?'

Silence.

'My problem hasn't therefore been lack of status, it's been lack of opportunity. I've always had a certain status, but in this world, where money speaks and everything has a price, I've had to go further. So, I've had to exercise the power I possessed. Otherwise I would never have overcome the submissive mediocrity that engulfs many. But I wouldn't have done it if I didn't think I had an option. You do understand this, don't you? Even Melanie Griffith in the film *Working Girl* had to do the same thing, otherwise she wouldn't have been noticed either.'

Silence.

'In my private life I'm courteous and considerate. But I had to reject the conventional route, so sometimes you have to break the rules. "Let all the dreamers wake the nation" was a line in the theme song in that film, by the way, and I think it's very appropriate. I too want to be honoured as a man who was independent in character and someone who could think for himself. After all, there will always be a need for creative action. So, you are now reaping the rewards.'

'Yes, we are. Now, can you please tell me what you've done to our computers?'

'Well it's quite technical, so I will try to explain the principle like so: I've used a procedure that is referred to as Euclid's algorithm for finding the highest common factor of two numbers. This is well known by all computer programmers, but I have inserted an imaginary number into the procedure and I have instructed your computers to carry out a systematic procedure. Your computers, in other words, are trying to find something that can't be found, and because it's a little bit like trying to find the final digit in pi – more and more systems will be devoted to solving this task over time, unless I stop it. In effect, I've injected the ultimate virus into your computer networks, and I can transfer this virus into any computer network I choose. I have the power to turn this virus on and off at will, and you can't do anything about it. I will bring your business to its knees if necessary. So, are you going to accept the new reality?'

Joe's Note

So this was how Nigel became the gang leader of Bradford West. In the annals of history, the takeover and unification of the Queen's gang was considered unique, and the alleged conversation you've just read was often re-enacted during festive celebrations, to the amusement of sycophants far and wide. So, as far as this story goes, being unaware of this event partly explains why there already exists, when Chalkie actually meets Nigel for the first time (as he does shortly), a fundamental difference between Capstan's perception of Nigel and Ronny's, which is in fact much closer to the truth, because it is based on far greater knowledge of him. Ronny knows, for example, all about the evil that lurks within some adults, whereas Capstan doesn't. He therefore failed to appreciate the full implications of his actions so far, even though he was aware that his partner would be no different to a lamb in a field of foxes, if things didn't go according to plan. Nigel's family history was the other serious factor here. Capstan wasn't aware of his father's – or more importantly his grandfather's – history (his grandfather was his most important influence) and this was also why he underestimated Nigel. There is a fable, I believe, which involves a scorpion, who, whilst carrying a fox safely across a river on its back, stings the fox in mid-stream. When asked, just before drowning, why he did it, he replied: 'Because it is in my nature. I couldn't help it.' Nigel acts on his instincts in a similar way.

His grandfather started off as a farm labourer in Pateley Bridge, then, in the 1920s, he worked on the construction of Scar House Reservoir, where he was known even by his fellow workers as a hard man. It was widely believed he killed a man following a dispute over a girl. The man simply disappeared. Nothing could be proved, however. Later he was even made a foreman. His guiding principle regarding women was always find 'em, fuck 'em and forget 'em, and in this regard he was very successful. The men never intervened and basically let him do as he wished. (I suppose you'd have to say that they regarded him as an alpha male, so he was probably responsible for the robust birth rate in Upper Nidderdale at that time.) Working conditions in Scar House Village, however, were relatively good, especially when compared, for example, with Pateley Bridge, so he eventually took some responsibility for one of his sons – William (who became Nigel's father) – as this allowed him to live in one of the workers' houses. These were state-of-the-art places which even had hot and cold running water, as well as electric lighting and many other facilities, and it seems that his grandfather stayed there until the dam was completed in 1936; but one night, soon after, he disappeared. He'd gone drinking and didn't return. So William and his mother then moved to Bradford, where the latter worked in Drummond Mill.

William's mother died of typhus or some similar disorder in 1953, a year before William married a local factory girl, and Nigel was born two years later. He was a bolt out of the blue. William at this time was a thief, a petty burglar and the local hoodlam, but he was nowhere near his father's class in terms of hardness – he was too frail for this – so he was therefore considered second rate by many, as well as a lost cause. His wife left him in 1960 and various kind-hearted people in the neighbourhood then helped look after Nigel, but this all changed on his grandfather's return, which was considered a mixed blessing by many. Blood ties are very strong, though, and once his grandfather recognised characteristics in him that resembled his own (these had somehow bypassed his son), he raised him up in his own likeness. William meanwhile spent increasingly lengthy periods in prison.

In time Nigel resembled the limestone carved by water, wind and rain at Malham, in both look and manner, and his reputation preceded him wherever he went. By the time Capstan arrived in the neighbourhood he was well established and was the leader of the neighbourhood gangs, that had united behind him, and his grandfather was considered, by those of similar disposition, the 'godfather' until his death in 1976.

Parallel Universes

There was a fine rain falling. Clouds seemed to be gathering and the street had already acquired the appearance of a grainy black and white photograph, so Capstan and Chalkie went indoors, into an unusual setting, as neither had met in Starbucks before, but both welcomed the coffee. They sat in the corner, next to the window, at the only table available, and they looked like two large crows on a bird table designed for sparrows. The preliminary discussion that ensued did, though, provoke an unusual outcome. It started after Capstan had picked up the local newspaper and started reading the responses to an article that apparently had said that Harrogate was 'characterless and tacky'.

'Look at this! My word, it's stirred up the locals,' he said as he passed the newspaper over to Chalkie. He then sipped at his coffee and smiled to himself as he waited in anticipation for Chalkie to say something. 'No, I'm not having that,' Chalkie soon said, after speed-reading two of the most lively letters (and after looking over his shoulder to make sure no one was listening). 'This isn't pretentious waffle, nor do I feel privileged to live here,' he said as his eyes widened. 'It goes without saying that Harrogate is a nice place to live, and if I was a philosopher I'd even say that this was a self-evident truth – so I don't understand why people are so angry. What's the big deal, Capstan? The lady's only expressing an opinion.'

Capstan had expected this response, but was nevertheless delighted. He himself had been surprised at the ferocity of the language, but not at the sentiments expressed, as he knew people who lived in nice places were always very protective towards their surroundings; Britain, after all, remained largely green and pleasant for this very reason. Nevertheless, he also thought that a few of them behaved like children inside a sweet shop, and this continued to disappoint him.

'Do you know that there isn't a bus to Bradford any more?' he said. 'It may as well exist in a parallel universe, as far as these people are concerned at any rate, or in a separate dimension. It's only eighteen miles away, but I bet you that the people who wrote those letters have never been there in their lives. Even Travelodge customers said that Bradford was the worst place they'd ever visited. Goodness knows what *these* people would say if they were forced to live there. They'd riot. That's what they'd do,' he said. 'Remember even J. B. Priestley said it was an ugly city to look at. Nevertheless, that doesn't stop me being a proud Bradfordian!'

Chalkie smiled; he had listened politely as they exchanged glances, and in the silence that followed a fantastic thought had occurred to him, so his thinking had become as sharp as a knife's edge. The meeting was intended to clarify and confirm their plans (Charlotte had already started working at the Perseverance – the pub with the giant angel, and the arranged rendezvous with Nigel and Ronny), so it was, in Chalkie's mind, already surpassing all expectations, and it was all down to something that Capstan had said. Chalkie's eyes stared in contemplation, whilst Capstan sat patiently waiting. For once their roles were reversed: it was Chalkie who continued being reflective, so much so that Capstan thought his mind had become stuck, like a computer's when a virus invades, but this was understandable, because it was Chalkie who was going to be in a much more vulnerable position. Anyway, he indicated with a slight nod of the head that he was ready to begin.

'You know I've been finding out about the history of clowns,' he said, in a tone of voice that conveyed a sense of internal anxiety. 'Well, I've discovered that there are different types. Did you know this?' While he waited for a response from his partner he hoped that his powers of persuasion were still in good working order as he considered what to say next.

Capstan nodded. 'Chalkie, my friends are trapeze artists, you know this,' he said. 'Come on, tell me – what's on your mind? I can feel something's coming in my direction. What is it? Spit it out.'

'Well, I've now decided that I'm going to be a "character" clown. I'm going to be a policeman with a moustache, a wig, big ears and baggy black trousers,' Chalkie replied. 'I've also decided that one of my speciality acts will be playing a game of football with a dog. I will act this out when I meet Nigel.'

Capstan had thought Chalkie had something of the look of a mad dog about him ever since he'd sat down, but this time he was completely taken aback, as he knew this was only the tip of the iceberg (so there was more to come), but he managed to keep his facial expressions under control and remained silent. This was, after all, going to be an idea that was opaque in the extreme, so as he looked at his partner he tried to smile. His immediate intention then was to lean forward and say something, but instead, in a rather cowardly way, he thought, he changed his mind. Instead he looked about him to make sure everyone around them was behaving normally (which they were) as this gave him some time to think; but when he noticed that Chalkie was screwing up his face, and even looking slightly scornful, Capstan sat back with a feeling of relief in his stomach, as he waited patiently for his partner to continue. When he did, his plan nearly blew Capstan's socks off.

It started obliquely, but there was nothing surprising in that, Capstan thought. He often started off by talking about a programme he'd seen on the television, and this was no different; but there was something different in the air this time, and it was genuinely intriguing. The programme he was talking about was on *Horizon*, and it was entitled 'Is Everything We Know About the Universe Wrong?' Capstan knew that science was something Chalkie had always been interested in (especially quantum mechanics), and he had listened to him talk interminably before, about interference patterns in single photons which happen, apparently, yet shouldn't. But this time he felt much more confused and unsettled, especially when he started talking about dark matter and dark energy, which he did next. Soon Chalkie was in his element, and as there was nothing he could think of that could halt his flow, he tried his best to piece together the strands Chalkie was introducing, but this time he couldn't because the sentences were arriving too thick and fast for that, so he could barely keep up. 'He'll soon run out of steam,' he said to himself, as he waited for this particular balloon to run out of hot air. But it didn't.

'The universe is really a multi-verse. It's the only thing that makes any sense,' Chalkie said as he ventured into new territories, which even Capstan noticed was all becoming a bit odd. So he tried pulling a face to show how confused he was becoming, but it was to no avail: Chalkie was in a world of his own. 'Our universe needs more gravity than it actually has, so it gets this from thousands of parallel universes, which are only a millimetre away from us,' he said, and his eyes suddenly lit up, so much so that Capstan thought he looked like a mad scientist from one of those old 3-D movies. 'I bet you didn't know this – it's actually pretty unbelievable,' he said. 'And the more you think about it, the more unbelievable it becomes,' he added. 'Well, to encapsulate everything I've just said,' Chalkie then finished, like a comedian who'd just come to the end of a very long joke, 'I've decided that I'm not going to be an ordinary run-of-the-mill type of clown. Instead, I'm going to be a clown that comes from a parallel universe! What do you think?' he asked at last.

Being completely nonplussed it was, of course, difficult for Capstan to know what to say, though he was pleased to be given a chance to speak at last. But when he did, he was interrupted by Chalkie coughing and he realised that Chalkie still hadn't finished yet. His question had merely been a rhetorical one, and so, like a member of the House of Lords, he sat back and politely listened.

'I'm going to develop a tic and I'm going to act strangely. I think I'll start walking backwards whilst doing things in reverse, and things like that,' Chalkie said. 'Maybe I'll even do a funny walk like John Cleese. Yes, that'll go down well. I'm going to be a clown who comes from Leeds, but from a Leeds that exists in a different dimension. All the things I do will distract Nigel, and with luck and good acting, he will really believe that I am a real-life clown. So Capstan, tell me, come on, I want to know what you think. Tell me,' he said, finishing at last.

Capstan had two immediate thoughts that rushed to his mind after listening to this. Only fools rush in, though, so before saying anything, he steadied himself. But it was no good – his first thought remained, despite his desperately searching for alternatives. It was this: *God, what have I done! Why did I of all people mention parallel universes?* His second thought was unchanged also, and was even more disturbing. *Chalkie you're a true real-life clown. Are you mad? They'll eat you alive!* But he refrained from saying either. Instead he took stock, and before he knew what had happened, he said, 'Chalkie, it's brilliant. But can you pull it off?'

They went for a walk afterwards. The rain was still falling but they hardly noticed. Chalkie was as talkative as ever, but this now hid the unease he was feeling. Capstan had picked up on this, and he also noticed that Chalkie had started to fidget. He was aware that Chalkie knew his plan was exuberant and extravagant, but it wasn't this that was causing him so much anxiety. It was the thought of entering the dragon's den that was leading to so much distress, and Capstan knew this.

'We'll be only a stone's throw away at all times,' Capstan said. 'You do know this, don't you? What could possibly go wrong? Friends will be all around.' Chalkie appreciated this as he knew it was true, so he told Capstan all about the acting he had done whilst studying for his degree. 'I was once a licentious old man in a Greek tragedy. I was even awarded a goblet afterwards for my performance,' he said. 'Being a clown will be a piece of cake compared to that!'

They'd walked a long way, but had hardly noticed their surroundings. When they were alongside the Stray, although they were surrounded by trees and grass, they both felt they were walking in an enclosed space full of intimacy, and even though they walked on, past some of Harrogate's more picturesque landmarks, they hardly noticed them either, as their main focus remained the affection they felt for each other. Chalkie had already visited Bradford and had familiarised himself with Manningham (he'd even visited the Queen's, the pub where a rival gang hung out), and Capstan was in the process of coordinating plans with the Bradford police. So all in all, both were happy with their day's work, and with all the planning they had done. Then Chalkie went home to reassure his wife – a visit to the hospital was planned and they had to decide if they wanted to know if they were going to have a boy or a girl – and Capstan rang Charlotte.

'Hi Charlotte. How are things going?'
'Very well . . . It's been interesting, Capstan, but I'm pleased, I must say, that's Roy's been around – he's an intimidating presence and the locals have stopped trying to chat me up, so I feel more relaxed now. Otherwise I seem to fit in – people just talk normally. I know this much though: this part of Bradford is a world away from Harrogate, and I can hardly believe some of the things I've heard. I've also dropped some rumours, just as you asked me to, and they seem to have wormed their way into some of the conversations.'
'Roy's a big guy – he's going to be important in this operation, as are you. Anyway, have you met Nigel yet?'
'I certainly have – and his friends. I call them the Bash Street gang. They're amazing. Some of them are tall, others small, and two of them look as if they're made of stone. One of them even looks like a respectable businessman. When they talk everything is always positive, and they're always laughing at each other's jokes. I don't think they're scared of anyone – except maybe each other. The other day Nigel said that he's not cruel, only truthful, and when he sat back in his seat and pulled at his neat tie knot he glanced across at me and I felt like I was a piece of bacteria in a test tube. Then he held out his arms and embraced his friends, and told them, "This is the extent of my business", and

all his friends brimmed with glee. It was terrifying. Then Plug, his best friend, stood up and spoke, and he was almost as frightening, "To be as good as us means we are probably all bleedin' intellectuals. I mean, we aren't slogging ourselves for peanuts, are we?" he said. And then they all went next door. They always do when they're all gathered together. And they always make sure they shut the door and aren't disturbed. It's very eerie, Capstan.'

'Yes, Nigel needs acolytes. Thanks, Charlotte, that's all very interesting. So, do you think we could put a bugging device in there?'

'Well, there's not much in there, it's mainly empty space. Plaster keeps falling off the walls and ceiling, but it might be possible. I'll check it out.'

'Well, be careful.'

'I will.'

'And they know that you like cocaine?'

'Yes, they do.'

'Outstanding work, Charlotte. Well done. I will speak to you soon.'

'Bye, Capstan.'

Ronny meanwhile had been pleased by the speed of his son's recovery, so he'd sent him off to stay with an old fairground family in Scarborough. He'd also been able to sort things out, to some degree at least, with Capstan. His dreams had been shattered, and he knew that, in the world he'd found himself in, he was now no different from a lion in a cage. He was someone who'd only had one real chance in life, and this was now gone. He was going to jail, but this didn't worry him especially; other issues preyed on his mind and worried him far more. He knew that his horizon was dark and full of menace; nevertheless, he remained full of optimism when he thought about his son, who was strong in both mind and body.

The circus had gone. The owners had actually told him to take a sabbatical, but it was generally recognised that his days in the ring were now over, so he'd settled himself in the local caravan park before moving back to Bradford. His son Lenny's habitation capsules were a popular attraction and he was seeking new investment from influential local businesses, whilst trying to make hay before the clouds descended once again.

Ronny had dreaded ringing Nigel, but when the time came, he simply told him that Lenny had fallen on his head. 'Do you mind if we postpone the meeting?' he'd said, as he shuddered quietly to himself and bit his lip, but Nigel's response had surprised him, and for a short time at least he even thought that the fire that burned inside him may even have died down, but this was merely an illusion. 'Of course I don't. How is he?' Nigel had said. 'It was only a matter of time before you dropped him. Don't worry about it.' And even though Ronny hadn't been able to make head or tail of the conversation afterwards, so an element of anxiety remained, he was just starting to forget all about it when Nigel turned up, completely out of the blue. The morning had even started promisingly – he'd tidied the capsule and was about to go out when he'd felt his presence and his heart had sunk.

'I've always been able, simply by staring at the back of people's heads, to make them turn around,' Nigel said as Ronny stared at him in such a way that his heart almost stopped beating, but he managed to step aside to let him and his large hound in, without any outward appearance of alarm. 'How are you? Great capsules by the way,' Nigel said as he looked around with a grimace etched on his face, which unnerved Ronny even more – so much so that the latter realised at this point that even though he was much stronger than Nigel, he was now in his grip. He felt like a small boy, and he trembled. 'What brings you to Harrogate?' he asked, as innocuously as he could, even though he knew perfectly well what had, and as he waited for the reply he watched the other man intently and remained still and silent. But as Ronny felt like a cockroach waiting to be stamped on, he quickly averted his stare.

'Why is there so much empty space in the middle of this fucking place?' Nigel asked at last, in a tone that showed he was annoyed at being asked such a silly question as why he was there. 'I mean, what values do the fucking people in Harrogate have? You could build a small village in all that space,' he said. 'Now tell me why you moved,' he said, as he placed his hand on Ronny's shoulder in such a way that Ronny felt himself melting. 'It took me a while to find you. Your capsules would be much better if they were nearer the town centre,' he finished.

Ronny didn't want to give a long explanation, as he knew that this would annoy Nigel, so he tried to explain as briefly as he could why he had to move. 'The Stray is a protected space,' he said at last, but as Nigel wasn't listening he stopped in mid-stream and allowed Nigel to speak. 'Come on, let's take my dog for a walk,' the latter said as he raised his dog up, as if it were a piece of wood.

It was a very unsettling couple of hours. They went up to the pine woods, where Nigel's dog ran backwards and forwards, sending dust into the air whilst chasing a small branch thrown by Nigel, and Ronny noticed that there was a permanent dark smile etched on Nigel's face. They walked along the path in between the trees and Nigel hardly spoke. There was no one else to be seen, but when Nigel was ready to talk, Ronny gazed immediately into his eyes.

'We are all a product of the neighbourhoods in which we live,' Nigel said. 'You do know this, don't you?' As Ronny knew this to be true he nodded.

'Yes, we are,' he said, whereupon Nigel immediately smiled.

'The meeting is set for midday, next Thursday. It's at the usual place, so just make sure you're not late,' he said as he reached into his pocket and placed a small bag of cocaine in Ronny's hands, which Ronny took without saying anything. And once Ronny had departed, he then sat and meekly watched the tree tops moving in the stiff breeze, before walking home.

Ronny sat in the shadow of his armchair before ringing Capstan later on. 'The meeting is set. Nigel's been in touch,' he said. 'Is everything going to work out?'

'It will, old friend – the planning is almost complete. I've seen Chalkie and things are looking good,' Capstan replied, and Ronny was reassured by his positive response.

So the place for the first meeting was now set. The planning was cast in stone, but Ronny wasn't sure which stone was harder – the one in his heart, or the giant angel carved in stone that sat above the bar.

The Meeting

'A week flies when you're having fun!' Chalkie said whilst eating his hamburger in the station's canteen. He'd spent hours refining his act and Capstan was impressed.

'It's authentic. It's going to work, I can feel it. Now remember: take your cues from Ronny at all times,' he said.

Chalkie's problem, though, was of a different order. He simply wanted to know what Nigel and his friends would be thinking during the meeting, so he wasn't really listening to Capstan. He'd thought about this a lot and he wished he too had a magic mirror like the one Nicholas mentioned in his diary, that could show him what was going on inside other people's heads. It was also the first week in November and this didn't help either, as November was his least favourite month, so the chill in the air matched the chill in the pit of his stomach. But everything that could be done had been done, everybody had been briefed, and it all now depended on the outcome of the meeting. The weight of worry was pressing firmly down on his shoulders.

Ed meanwhile had been standing in the doorway, unnoticed. He was quietly chuckling with delight. Wisecracks were now an everyday occurrence in the station.

'Why the fuck did you have to tell Ed about parallel universes?' Chalkie asked Capstan as he turned round and saw him for the first time. At that, Ed, true to form, bowed his head politely in his direction, and then waved to him with both hands, whilst pretending to sing a song. 'I mean, Ed of all people. You know what he's like, he'll never let up now. "What's life like in the outer rim?" he said to me the other day. "Have they let Adolf Hitler's grandson out of his cage yet?" was another of his remarks. "I believe he was spotted planning the Second World War with his co-conspirators in a fallout shelter under the city hall in Berlin." Someone is even running a competition to find the joke that's bound to make a criminal fall off his chair in laughter, for Christ's sake!'

Capstan had listened politely but he was also somewhat embarrassed, because he'd joined in with the wisecracks too. But as he didn't have the heart to tell Chalkie this, he just said, 'I just thought it would lighten the load for you,' and without waiting for a reply he added, 'It's time to go. Are you ready?'

Capstan led the way through the arched entrance, and Chalkie followed with his clown outfit crammed into a large rucksack. Ed followed behind, and they were given a rapturous farewell as they left the station. Ed and Christine started singing, 'Make 'em laugh, make 'em laugh,' and everybody joined in, but half an hour later, as they reached the outskirts of Bradford, the world was suddenly very different. The large mills on the horizon became cubist in nature to Chalkie, and the contrasting shapes and tones created dark echoes in his mind, so any feelings of calm he'd previously experienced quickly dissipated. Although Capstan still felt confident, Chalkie was becoming filled with self-doubt, so much so that he wondered how it had actually come to this. He even wondered if it was all a dream, one he was looking forward to waking up from; but it wasn't, as he'd already pinched himself to check. Nevertheless, he still felt he was having an out-of-body experience because his mind seemed to be floating in the ether. For a time this was a pleasant experience, but then reality dawned. So he ended up merely wishing he was back in Harrogate. He was usually in control, even when dealing with tragic cases like that of Nicholas.

'Concentrate on the trivial to begin with,' Capstan had told him, 'and then you'll be fine. You're a trained copper, remember that. Your own subconscious will do the rest. Trust in it.' These words went round and round in Chalkie's brain. 'Now remember, Ronny will introduce you, but if you can't think of anything to say, look around and say something like, "Who's the dame under the angel? Is she taking confessions?" Charlotte also has some repartee up her sleeve apparently, which she'll use if she thinks it will help . . . Jesus, I'd love to be a fly on the wall,' he finished in a voice that was gentle and almost melodic.

Chalkie's dusty clothes combined nicely with the dull pallor of his face as he walked away from the car ten minutes later. He walked bristly down the side road towards the Perseverance public house, and he was feeling more confident now the time had arrived; his long legs were an asset, he realised – so it was definitely possible that they'd believe he was a clown. He also had a picture of his funny walk implanted firmly inside his head, so a slight smile formed as he reached into his pocket for his red nose, which he put on when he was directly outside the pub. He knew everybody was already inside.

He saw heads immediately turn as he entered. 'Fuck me, the clown's arrived,' Nigel said as Chalkie walked in, his legs outstretched. Every nerve in his body was on fire, and he could feel their piercing eyes. He even hoped that none of them had X-ray vision, such was his unease – for this scene, he realised, wouldn't look out of place in a comic book.

'So, here goes, there's no turning back now,' he said to himself as he looked up at the ceiling, and as everybody watched him, he made his legs perform a double twist in the air; then he curled up into a ball and hopped over and introduced himself to Nigel.

'Hi, I'm Bobby. It's a pleasure to meet you and all your friends,' he said as he wrinkled his eyebrows, looked around, snapped his fingers and bowed on a bent leg. 'But before I say anything else, I just what you to know that you shouldn't believe anything that reprobate over there has said about me. There are lies and there are damn lies,' he went on. Then he looked around to see what everybody was doing, and because they were all actually looking at Ronny and smiling he was relieved, because his act seemed to be working. 'Ronny doesn't discriminate,' he said whilst waving his hand wildly in the air, so his calm voice and manic motions contrasted nicely. 'The reason for this is simple,' he continued.

'It's because Ronny simply doesn't recognise the truth. He wouldn't in actual fact know it if it bit him on the nose!' And in a voice that was stern and authoritative, he then said with a final flourish, 'Thank you for letting me introduce myself to you. Ronny's told me so much about you all.'

When he looked around after he had finished his heart was in his mouth. A silence had descended over the proceedings, and he wondered what he had done wrong, so he sat without moving a muscle, whilst waiting for a reaction. When the silence continued, he felt a sense of dread, but then the penny eventually dropped and he realised that it was simply the abrupt ending that had caught everyone by surprise, so the gap in the proceedings was simply that – a gap. Smiffy stood up moments later, and Chalkie's spirits immediately lifted.

'Bravo, what an entrance!' Smiffy said. 'Come and sit next to me. Wench, bring him a pint,' he said to Charolotte, but when there wasn't a reply he turned to look for her, and when he couldn't see her – she had temporarily disappeared under the counter, trying to hide the smirk that was across her face – he called out, 'Where the hell are you? Come out, come out, wherever you are,' as everybody laughed.

Charlotte meanwhile had waited a moment before standing up. She did this for dramatic effect, so even though she still had a wide smile on her face, she quickly recovered her composure. She knew the time was right for her to do her thing: she brought over Chalkie's drink and then sat on his lap. 'Do you have a girl-friend? Or is the lump in your trousers for my benefit!' she asked, looking directly at him before giving him a kiss on the cheek. And as she left to loud laughter Chalkie immediately called out, 'Who's the doll? I like her, but I'm a married man . . . unfortunately.'

It was all very cheesy of course, but at the time Charlotte felt that Chalkie had dealt with the situation really well, and when she thought about it in more detail, she felt she had too. Everyone there knew Marlene Dietrich had said something similar (in the spoof Western, *Destry Rides Again*), but because this was a spoof on a spoof the whole thing seemed even funnier than it actually was, so the atmosphere had become a much more relaxed one, and when Chalkie talked about his act it even became jovial for a time. But then Nigel intervened and everyone went quiet. He had the presence of an unexploded bomb. 'Chalkie can perform the rest of his act later,' he said. 'First, though, we've got things to discuss, so will everyone now shut the fuck up?'

Chalkie realised that he'd never heard the word 'fuck' spoken so quietly, but he appreciated that it wasn't necessary for people like Nigel to raise their voice, as it wasn't his voice or even his stern features that give him the power he possessed. So without a further single word being uttered, everyone followed Nigel into the next room, and Charlotte watched them intently as they walked through. She thought they all looked like rats following the Pied Piper and her heart sank as an enormous sense of foreboding enveloped her.

Charlotte's fears were, unfortunately, well founded, as Chalkie and Ronny didn't reappear shortly thereafter, but neither, for that matter, did Nigel, Plug or Johnny Handsome. Everyone else merely walked passed her as though they didn't have a care in the world. Once they'd left she immediately rang Capstan, and the police arrived in an instant. It was an impressive response, and at the time she didn't know how this was possible. But even though their arrival had been swift, there was still no trace of Chalkie and the others. The fire door at the back was open, and even when the police questioned everyone later, no one said they had seen anyone walking away, although one witness reported seeing a van outside.

The gang members were, however, rounded up quickly. Most of them were simply drinking in a nearby pub, and as all of them appeared calm, it was clear that none of them would tell the police anything. They'd only been in that room for a short time anyway, so what was there to tell? All they had to do was stick to the same story, and as this is what they did, things quickly

THE MEETING

deteriorated, and the police were left baffled. 'It's no good,' the inspector told Capstan after a couple of hours, 'we can't find him. We've looked everywhere.' Then, six hours later, Ronny was thrown out of a moving car. He was battered and bruised, and the pain remained inside his head, but once he'd calmed down Capstan was called to the police station where he was being interviewed. Capstan spoke to him on their own.

'The meeting started off reasonably calmly,' Ronny said. 'There was a menacing presence – there always is when Nigel is around – but it appeared, to me at least, that Chalkie had been accepted. I heard Nigel say he was looking forward to his 'new venture', but nothing else untoward happened – in fact, everything seemed to be going all right,' he continued. 'Chalkie's act had gone down well, Charlotte had been amusing and things were relaxed, but this period of calm didn't actually last that long. I could tell that things would soon change and turn nasty.'

Capstan was curious at this point, so he raised his hand to stop Ronny going any further. 'So up to this point Chalkie was okay?' he asked.

'Yes. Well, at least I thought so,' Ronny replied.

'What happened next then? And what changed?' Capstan asked. But then he realised that he needed to leave Ronny to describe events in his own way, for more clarity.

'Well,' said Ronny, 'the room was full of expectation. Everybody knew, when they walked into the back room, that Nigel had things on his mind, but it appeared to me also that some there knew what was going to happen next. There were a lot of sideward glances taking place, albeit in between some reasonably friendly banter, but this all changed when Nigel stood up and said, "Raise your glasses. Join me in a toast: to Harrogate." This wasn't unexpected, of course, but what happened next was. When he added in a menacing way, "What a fucking place," everybody immediately repeated what he'd just said in unison, and then they all started nodding vigorously in appreciation until silence descended again like a cloud and things then really did become bizarre. It was as if he was a puppet master and everybody was having their strings pulled by him.

'Nigel was now in his element,' Ronny said. 'So when he raised his arms slightly, the atmosphere became electric. His eyes were his control mechanism. They seem to flash like laser lights on a jet fighter in a black sky and I couldn't take my eyes off them – nor, it seemed, could anybody else. I remained watching them until they dimmed, and Chalkie, I noticed, did the same thing. But when Nigel turned to Johnny Handsome and said, "This is going to put *your* talents to the test – it's about time we put them to good use," everyone started laughing. They were all rolling around, pointing their fingers and slapping their knees, but Nigel remained unmoved – his whole body remained rigid and still. But then, when he stroked his slick hair afterwards and said, "I'm not being cruel, only honest," the laughter really became hysterical, so I looked across at Chalkie at this point and I could tell he was as baffled as I was, and I felt very uneasy.'

Capstan had listened carefully, gradually becoming horrified, as Ronny recalled what had happened. And even though there wasn't that much more to tell, he let Ronny continue. It was already clear that Chalkie had been grabbed, even before any plans had actually been discussed. This had been reinforced by the limited information they'd been able to gather from the bugging device, as it was only as Ronny began to stand that he'd apparently heard footsteps behind him. 'After that I felt a stinging pain on the back of my head and everything then went blank,' he'd said.

In an empty room, Capstan was trying to work out what had gone wrong, but he soon realised that this time he couldn't. He didn't know, for example, whether they knew about the bugging device. He didn't think they did. But more serious than that – who told them about Chalkie? Capstan had no answer to either question, and even though that was depressing, there were three things that were even worse, and that were causing anxiety to flow through his body like a jet stream across an ocean.

THE MEETING

First – how was Chalkie? This was an obvious concern. Second – why had he underestimated Nigel? How was this possible? And third – how on earth was he to tell Carol about what had happened? Jesus, he thought. What can I say to her? She trusted me.

He knew Charlotte was inconsolable, but she was safe and wasn't to blame for any of this. She had planted the bug successfully, but it hadn't worked very well, unfortunately, due to its position. It was planted in a cupboard under the sink, which was the only safe place, but it wasn't of much use there; nevertheless, it had remained untouched. A resounding *thwack*, and then a loud thud followed by a yell which sounded like 'Fuck you, you wanker' were all that was clearly audible. Thereafter, everything went silent. Nigel's plans were therefore unclear. They all knew that they involved drugs in Harrogate, but surely they were now in disarray? Capstan didn't know what had gone wrong, but it now seemed clear that Nigel knew the police were on to him. He knew he'd be furious about that, and he couldn't bear thinking about it.

Nigel's plans for supplying drugs to Harrogate were actually well advanced, and support staff had already been briefed. They involved, among other things, supplying poppers in bottles to young people at weekends in the pubs and nightclubs; cocaine in paper wraps to people walking home across the Stray during the Christmas period; ecstasy pills to dancers on New Year's Eve, and to workers at office parties; and heroin for addicts at reduced rates in a Boxing Day sale.

There were various aspects and different levels to his plans, but basically Nigel knew that no law could stop people wanting to get high at weekends. He'd even read in the newspapers that 98 per cent of clubbers used drugs, so he knew for a fact that drug-induced dancing played a significant part in modern culture. 'Intoxication is one of our strongest desires, and I'm merely carrying out a public service,' was one of his favourite sayings. He saw himself as an Al Capone figure, and *The Untouchables* was one of his favourite films. 'It just needed a different ending,' he'd told Plug. 'Why, the good people of Harrogate will thank me,' he said to him soon afterwards.

The most terrifying aspect of the plan, though, involved targeting sixth-formers in some of the town's schools. Johnny Handsome's role in this was important. He already had a variety of cigarettes laden with various illegal substances which would be made widely available throughout the neighbourhoods, especially over the Christmas holidays and at weekends. 'Once they become attracted to me, they'll be putty in my hands,' he'd told Nigel a week before the meeting was scheduled.

'It's the only good thing to come out of this fucking mess,' Nigel said, once Chalkie had begun to regain consciousness. His operation had now been compromised, so he was in a vengeful mood. 'It was a work of art. My plan was a fucking work of art,' he said as he slapped Chalkie across the face when he opened his eyes. 'Harrogate coppers – who the fuck do you think you are? Do you think you're all Superman or something? How dare you enter *my* neighbourhood!' He sounded so exuberant that Chalkie's insides immediately felt as if they'd shrunk.

It took Chalkie a little while to regain his composure, but when he turned his head to look around for the first time he soon realised that he was able to recollect quite a lot very quickly. He quickly summed up at least part of his situation, but as reality gradually dawned he then shivered involuntarily, and even though he wasn't religious he had an urge to pray. He knew he'd not been abandoned, and that Capstan would be doing everything possible to find him; nevertheless, he'd never felt so alone in his life. Things, however, were about to get a whole lot worse.

'Hold out your arm, you mother fucker,' Nigel said, and when Chalkie refused, his arm was grabbed and then forcibly held out in front of him. Nigel was perched directly over him, with eyes that appeared black and huge, and Chalkie felt like he was a goldfish in a bowl desperately trying to peer out, because he suddenly knew what was about to happen to him. At first he hoped that it was merely a distorted image he was seeing, but he soon realised it wasn't: the scene was real, and when his eyes scanned the rest of the room, he saw the three men who were holding him down.

'We've been waiting for you to wake up,' Nigel said, 'as we want you to be fully aware of what is about to happen to you. Now do as you are told. The sooner you accept the situation, the better it will be for you. After all, there isn't anything you can do to change it.' He said this in such a calm manner that he could just as easily have been describing a cricket match. 'Resistance is futile,' he said. And Chalkie watched him intently as a wicked grin formed on his lips. Resistance had indeed proved useless, so instead Chalkie breathed deeply, became still, and prepared for the worst. 'I'm going to fucking kill you, Nigel,' he said at last, but it was just hot air.

Nigel had backed away, all the while blowing kisses at him, and then Johnny Handsome appeared. He was holding a syringe and was pushing the plunger down so liquid squirted out of it. 'Know what this is?' he asked, when it was directly next to Chalkie's face. 'Heroin, and it's all for you. Soon you'll be chasing dragons on a wild stallion,' he said gleefully. 'When injected into a vein just under the skin, the effect can be electrifying. I think it will be for you. This is hot shit. Trust me – it really is,' he said.

After a surge of adrenaline jolted him, Chalkie felt the liquid rush through his body like a giant wave. All he could do now was meekly lie back on the bed as he felt his eyes glaze over. He then watched in horror as a bony arm, with fingers as sharp as scissors, slid across his body like an ice skater across butter before slicing into his delicate flesh. Blood poured out, and Chalkie realised that the hand had grasped his rapidly beating heart, so he screamed out in terror as it replaced his healthy organ with one which had worms wriggling in it. The landscape had suddenly changed beyond recognition.

An immediate sharpening of emotions was followed by a sense of euphoria, and bright lights flashed like bolts of lightning inside his head as a man with a partly severed hand, with all its fingers missing, killed victims on an aeroplane before it crashed in the Alps, which then turned into a strange field when the aeroplane had come to a rest. It was a terrifying vision, but then it turned into a peaceful and almost pleasant dream which involved driving down the mountain on a ski motorbike, until it suddenly dipped into a deep hollow. Suddenly he was flying towards a tree, and moments later he materialised inside the trunk. The tree had swallowed him, so he felt himself moving through it and felt he was a fattened turkey being prepared for slaughter.

Meanwhile, Nigel, Johnny Handsome and the others had already left him to his dreams that would continue to turn into terrible nightmares. They knew this was only the beginning of his anguish. In a battered and bare room, furnished with only a toilet sink, he was alone.

Six weeks earlier . . .

Trapped

Sergeant Eddie 'Capstan' Blake was a man who loved chocolate cake. He'd always loved it. As far back as he could remember, at any rate. So it was a thrill to see the delight in his young daughter's eyes as he sprinkled on the hundreds and thousands – the final ingredient. It was a recipe that had survived over a long period of time. Once his grandmother was adding the same final touches, or at least something similar, and just thinking about it made him deeply appreciative of the past. He was only making a chocolate cake, but he was doing it with his daughter, and that made him want to cry. 'Natasha, be patient,' he said, but it was of no use: her eyes were already the size of ostrich eggs. As she climbed off the chair she looked up as she cut into the cake. 'Thank you Daddy,' she said as he gave her a slice. 'Oooomm, it's delicious,' she cried out, and it was. The icing was all shiny and the middle was all crumbly. Afterwards Natasha walked up to him and gave him a big hug and a kiss. And this time Capstan had to wipe away a tear.

When he walked into the living room his wife was talking to their eldest daughter about the article in the local newspaper. It was entitled 'Admissions to schools – we're starting afresh'. He was slightly relieved, therefore, when the phone rang. 'Capstan, I know it's a little bit early,' the voice said without introduction, although he knew who it was, 'but we've just been contacted by a local alarm monitoring centre as the key holders can't be reached. The alarm is ringing. Apparently the CCTV system is also monitoring someone walking about outside. The owner lives in London at present – he's a pretty important guy apparently, so we need to get someone there a.s.a.p. There's been an incident out of town and no one else is available right now.' So after kissing his two daughters and his wife goodnight, Capstan set off. The incident was on the other side of town, but even that wasn't far. His partner was also being contacted and would be waiting for him outside his house.

Capstan was happily married, but there was one bone of contention between him and his wife. It concerned their children's education. He was born in Bradford and therefore thought of himself as a socialist. He'd seen how low aspirations and fewer opportunities in general basically meant many communities (such as those where he'd come from) were experiencing a Dickensian level of poverty. Policing in Harrogate was a relative walk in the park in comparison. So he felt that the whole education system, that was clearly biased towards the more able and talented, was deeply unfair, and getting children into the schools their parents approved of, was, in his view, slightly undignified. However, they had played the system too, so he therefore felt uncomfortable discussing such issues, even with his eldest daughter Emily, who was about to start the new term in the secondary school of their choice.

All of which explains why he was happy when the call came through. The prospect of talking about, for example, Leeds United's excellent start to the season with his football-fanatic partner Constable Christopher 'Chalkie' White, even though he himself wasn't particularly interested in football, was a much less troubling issue all around. Kicking a bag of wind around a field was good work if you could get it, he'd say, rather than the standard 'footballers are overpaid, nobody is worth £100,000 a week – it's immoral in my view'. But he didn't like to deflect issues he felt strongly about. 'Emily, we're a family, you must always feel free to talk about anything,' he said to her regularly.

As he pulled into his partner's street, Chalkie was outside his house waiting for him. 'We've only just moved in and Carol already wants a new kitchen, even though there's nothing wrong with the one we've got,' he said as he climbed in and before he'd properly sat down. 'We liked the house; it's why we chose it. It was the last thing I expected to hear,' he continued as he reached out to shut the car door. Capstan thought this was funny. He might have a degree but he still has more than a few things to learn about women, he thought, so he decided he wasn't going to give him any advice on the matter. Where was the fun in that?

Capstan was black haired and thickly built. He was reflective and a deep thinker. He appeared laid back in nature, but wasn't. Many of his friends at the station could testify to that. He won the 'Art of Rhetoric' medallion every year. There was also a tone of authority in his voice, so when he spoke people tended to listen. Always. There seemed to be a reason behind everything he said, so when asking them questions, he was able to put suspects off their guard, as well as a great many other people from time to time. His partner, on the other hand, was tall, lanky and more outgoing by nature. He was more impulsive and maybe quicker witted. He could tell when situations were turning ugly and he was very good at defusing aggressive situations with his rapid, and sometimes very funny, verbal responses. When they worked together there were never any awkward pauses and very few periods of silence. Everybody liked working with Chalkie, but Capstan did especially. They were still on Knaresborough Road and already he'd brought up a recent incident that he'd been involved in.

'It's true,' Chalkie said, 'anything that can happen, will happen. A driver flipped his car completely over whilst coming out of a supermarket! He hit a bollard and drove up it as if he were driving up a ramp,' he said. 'It happened in the middle of Harrogate. Can you believe it! We're all ruled by chance,' he said. 'Why, we could at this very moment in time be heading towards a madman with a loaded shotgun. Think about it,' he said as Capstan blinked in disbelief. Chalkie's speculative nature was a thing of wonder.

It was a lovely end to the day: the shadows were long, and the light was luminescent. As the temperature dropped, the colours of the trees appeared somehow richer and deeper. Harrogate always appeared very calm and peaceful by the Stray. The Prince of Wales roundabout was quiet also, and Capstan and Chalkie were soon approaching the house where an incident of some kind had been reported. On the outskirts of town they turned down a rutted road and passed an impressive gated entrance with manicured lawns. 'The difference between the rich and poor in this town is amazing,' Chalkie said. 'I've never been down here in my life. Crikey!' he exclaimed. 'Everybody in my whole street could quite easily live in one of these houses!' Even from some distance away they could already hear the alarm bell ringing. As they approached the front door a powerful exterior light dazzled them.

'CCTV cameras had obviously recorded an incident of some kind,' Capstan said, 'so any madman carrying a shotgun would surely have scampered off, and very quickly too, I reckon. I think we're safe.' And they both started laughing as they went to look around.

They hadn't got far before being startled by what they saw. At the side of the house a window had been broken, and round the back more windows and a patio door had been smashed too. So they halted briefly whilst Capstan reported the vandalism to the station, then they took out their truncheons and stepped in cautiously. They went through a conservatory and then into the living room, whereupon Chalkie cried out, 'Bloody hell, look at that,' as if he'd just seen a ghost. 'What did I tell you? What did I tell you?' he said. 'Anything that can happen *will* happen.'

Capstan was more restrained, but no less surprised. The television had been smashed, and it seemed some tables had been randomly hit with a hammer of some kind, but what really caught their attention was the message that was written in large red letters on the wall above the mantelpiece: RAPIST! YOU SHOULD HAVE BEEN LOCKED UP FOR WHAT YOU DID.

As it appeared, at first glance, to have been written in red lipstick, Capstan took it as a warning, or a prediction of some kind.

'I'll call forensics and then find out what the CCTV surveillance cameras show,' Capstan said. 'The Kaiser might want to take charge tomorrow, so let's show him what mere mortals can do tonight.' His voice conveyed more than a twinge of bitterness, Chalkie noticed. He too knew that seniority took charge in the more interesting cases. They also both had a feeling that the night might be a long one. The famous copper's instinct. 'So go easy when you search the place,' he added.

Chalkie looked around as he set off. The living room was elegant but understated, he felt. Even though the furniture and fittings were clearly expensive, he was slightly disappointed with the overall effect. There was a lot of space, and abstract sculptures sat forlornly on various tables for reasons he didn't understand. The entrance hall, dining-room, study and the 1950s-style kitchen were stunning, though, and showed a level of sophistication that was deliciously snobby and even salubrious. Money had been put to very good use in these rooms, he thought. His wife wasn't here, thank goodness. There was also no evidence of vandalism in these or any of the other ground-floor rooms, although footprints clearly showed someone had been in them recently.

Upstairs there were three large bedrooms (two of them had en suites), a bathroom and a room that was used for home cinema. All the bedrooms, including the main one, which was full of luxury fitted wardrobes, mirrors and other expensive items, were untouched. The intruder had either run out of time or simply hadn't been interested in these rooms, he thought; but this wasn't the case in the room used for home cinema, as very expensive equipment was lying everywhere on the floor in various states of disrepair. Chalkie knew quite a lot about technology and recognised a high-definition memory-stick camcorder, a hard-drive camcorder, a state-of-the-art plasma television, a laptop, a DVD recorder and a Blu-Ray disc player and speakers – and that was just for starters. The white pull-down screen was ripped, and DVDs had been thrown against the wall.

'Can you smell the money, Chalkie?' Capstan asked later. He was pacing to and fro in the hall whilst Chalkie sat on a chair.

'I can see what money can buy!' Chalkie replied. 'I've never come across half of the stuff in this house before. I didn't know most of it existed. He has enough recording equipment upstairs to make the whole British film industry green with envy,' he added in an exuberant but uneasy tone of voice, and he acknowledged Capstan with a smile, for he already knew what his colleague was getting at.

Forensics was on the way and pictures of the intruder had already been sent from the monitoring centre. It appeared from first impressions that the intruder wasn't bothered by the prospect of being identified. Quite the opposite appeared to be the case, in fact, for at one point he appeared to wave and even smile at one of the surveillance monitors. Fingerprints were clearly evident also, so if he'd been arrested previously, or even cautioned, he would be brought in for questioning within the hour. Meanwhile the two officers were waiting to contact the owner to see if he knew who the intruder was. They were already intrigued by this state of affairs and were also deeply suspicious.

'You need a keen sense of smell, but it's always there in houses like this,' Capstan continued, still on the theme of money. 'Sometimes it can be a pleasant aroma, like the smell of grass that's been recently cut, or the smell of cut flowers in a shop. I've met rich people who have simply worked hard to attain their riches and have been burgled, for example. But it can also be a stench and as strong as the smell of animal decay on a warm day in the countryside. This house has a stench to it,' he said quietly, but in a tone of voice that contained cold and ruthless overtones.

Chalkie stood back in silent admiration while Capstan continued to display his formidable powers, gained over many years.

'These people understand its real power. Sure they've a lot of purchasing power – they can buy beautiful things, for example, which also have a power all of their own,' he said, 'but it's more than that. Money enables them to live a life without limits. This is the real issue for them. They think that everybody else is addicted to a kind of blandness, brought about partly by having had periods in their lives when they've had no money to spend. Some people are bland, it's true, but most of us aren't,' he said, 'because most of us appreciate what real happiness is or can be.'

Chalkie thought that Capstan could be a little long-winded sometimes. Sometimes he took things too much to heart. 'Capstan, you're going to have a nervous breakdown – you keep on worrying about things you can do nothing about,' he'd said on more than one occasion. But he knew it was in his nature to do this. He held Capstan in high esteem. If he ever had kids he'd ask him to be their godfather. So he listened carefully to what Capstan was saying, even if he couldn't get a word in edgeways. 'Experiencing a child's delicate innocence in a simple smile, for example, like the one I experienced earlier when my daughter and I were making a cake together, brought a tear to my eye. Happiness or contentment, though, means millions of different things to different people, and as long as harm isn't done to others, all are equally important. As long as people empathise with each other there isn't a problem. Without it we are all just animal carcasses!'

'You've got the wrong nickname, you know that, don't you?' Chalkie said as he clapped his hands together.

'I know,' Capstan replied. 'It was given to me by one nameless individual at the station. She was my partner and the nickname came to her, she said, after she'd listened to my objections to the smoking ban. 'Capstans were cigarettes without filters, she said. And the name stuck.'

Within the hour the call came through. The caller was Mr Mark Torch.

'So, you've seen the pictures. I believe you recognise the intruder?' Chalkie began.

'Yes, I fucking well do. He's a little runt called Nicholas Torch. He's my adopted brother. He's a freak, in a freak show he'd be the biggest attraction. He's vermin on two legs. He's a piece of shit. He's an oleaginous slime ball. He's a glutinous scum bag, a . . .'

'Yes, thank you sir. I think we get the picture. Do you have his address, by any chance?'

'What the fuck is he doing in Harrogate? He shouldn't be anywhere near a place like Harrogate. Harrogate's a place where decent, hard-working people live. And what's he done to my house, for Christ's sake?'

'He's caused relatively minor damage to some doors and windows. I'm afraid he's also broken most of your very expensive recording equipment, your television and a couple of laptops. But I'm sure your insurance company will adequately reimburse you.'

'The shit-head. Wait till I get my hands on—'

'His address, sir. Do you have his address?'

'It's somewhere here, I suppose – I'll just find it for you. But I wouldn't pay him much regard if I were you.'

Chalkie wrote down the name and address, along with the telephone number Mark Torch had given him. He handed it to Capstan, who was standing next to him with his mouth open wide in amazement.

'Thank you – we'll attend to the matter right away,' he said.

'Attend to? Attend to? What the fuck does that mean? Arrest him – arrest the myopic little fucker before he does any more harm to decent people. You do know that he's mad, don't you?'

'Mad, sir?'

'Yes, mad. He's as mad as a fucking hatter. My father had to have him locked up in a lunatic asylum when he was eighteen.'

'Thank you, sir. As I said, we'll attend to the matter. We'll do everything that needs to be done. Will you be able to arrange for someone to make the property secure, or would you like us to do that?'

'I've already done that, thank you, officer. Roger Goulding is on his way right now.'

'Okay sir. Thank you, you've been very informative. We'll be in touch.'

Afterwards, neither officer knew how to respond, so they stood for a while swaying slightly, like tree saplings do on a windy day. They were men of the world, but they'd both been shocked by the vitriol. 'What does oleaginous mean?' Chalkie said at last. Capstan didn't reply; he was thinking about ignoring strict procedural matters. He wanted to go through the house with a fine-tooth comb. 'The intruder may be mentally ill,' he said, 'in fact that may even be likely. But even so, that man is one serious mother fucker!' he said, pointing to the telephone.

They both appreciated that there was rarely smoke without fire, or, as Capstan would say, rarely an effect without a cause, and it was possible, even if they broke with protocol and went in search of it, that there might be some incriminating evidence lurking somewhere. But they both doubted that there would be. Even if Mark Torch had raped someone, he was too clever to leave behind anything that might incriminate him. So they asked forensics to see if they could find any in the course of gathering evidence. And that would mean that any decisions would then be out of their hands.

Capstan this time made the call to Scarborough. After the preliminaries, the conversation, which was of a completely different nature, went as follows:

'There's been an incident involving Nicholas Torch. He's broken into a house owned by his adopted brother, I'm afraid. He's caused quite a lot of damage and he's also defaced one of the living-room walls.'

'Oh no! Oh, I'm so sorry. I should never have left him alone for the last two weeks, but he said he'd be fine. He said he'd be okay.' Pause. 'He told me that being left alone for two weeks would do him good. He's such a lovely person, you know. We believed him. We all thought it would do him good. Whenever we rang he said he was doing fine. It's my entire fault.' Pause. 'I'm so sorry.'

'How do you mean, sir?'

'Well I'm his nearest relative. It's a long story, but in a nutshell I'm his legal guardian. His best friends Charlotte and Roy went to the Greek islands for their honeymoon two weeks ago. Along with them, my wife and my son who lives in York, we all help look after him and make sure he's okay.' Pause. 'Can I ask what he's written? I'm afraid I have a pretty good idea already.'

'Yes. He's written "Rapist! You should have been locked up for what you did."'

'Sergeant, he's planned it. He's planned the whole thing. Oh no! You need to get over to his caravan as soon as you can. He's going to commit suicide. I think he's either dead already or soon will be. I'm setting off immediately.'

'Chalkie, you're a harbinger of doom,' Capstan said as they set off pell-mell to Nicholas's caravan.

'It might not be that bad,' Chalkie replied, in hope rather than expectation. The signs weren't good, however. Harrogate always looked serene at night, but under the calm exterior, things were often less straightforward and more complex. Chalkie had already experienced some quite challenging situations in his career, but nothing like this. This was as real as it gets.

They entered the site and all seemed normal enough. But as they approached Nicholas's caravan they could see that the lights weren't on, and the curtains weren't closed either. 'It doesn't look good,' Capstan said.

Both men, feeling uneasy, got out off the car and approached on foot. The door to the caravan wasn't locked either, so they went in, expecting the worst. But the first impression was favourable and their moods lifted. The space inside was neat and tidy; it was in fact quite a pleasant place to live.

'If this is the residence of someone who is mad, it is a very well ordered and peaceful madhouse,' Capstan said with some relief.

'Thank the Lord for that,' Chalkie responded. He had never been involved in a suicide. Seeing a dead body would have brought home to him how frail life can be. But Nicholas was nowhere to be seen.

Next, of course, was the search for clues. Where was he? What was he up to? And what might he have left behind? But as something had already been triggered in their subconscious, they soon noticed the two documents and letters lying on the coffee table. They'd been placed there so they'd be easily spotted. 'Oh shit,' was Chalkie's response to this. One of the letters was addressed to Uncle Alf and the other one was addressed to the police. 'Fuck me,' he went on. Then they sat down and Capstan hesitantly opened the letter addressed to the police, while Chalkie looked on. He then read it out loud:

To Whom It May Concern:

Firstly I am sorry to have put you to so much trouble. I will almost certainly be dead by the time you read this. A man can only die once, it's true, but a small piece of me had been dying each day and this has been the reason for this act, which has been planned in advance. To use an analogy: if I were a motorcar I wouldn't pass my MOT. I often felt that, whilst I was walking normally on my two feet, everyone else, when I looked around, was walking upside down. It felt like I was living in a parallel universe, with Alice maybe – in Wonderland. It was a dizzying thought and worse than vertigo. I was the reflection inside a mirror, looking out as it were, at you all. I always appreciated that the real situation was the reverse one, but this doesn't invalidate my reasoning or beliefs, which are and were generally sound. I do suffer from bi-polar but was never as mad as Mark liked to assert. Although killing myself doesn't exactly add any credence to this view, probably. Mad people only harm others. This is my opinion anyway and it is the one I'm taking with me.

I'd stopped taking my tablets, but this hadn't modified my behaviour and suddenly made me suicidal. I'd just become very good at keeping the real reasons for my depressive events secret, so no one should blame themselves for my action. I think, in actual fact, that most people are actually calm when they kill themselves, but that's another issue. My real problems have always been cumulative ones: a build-up of everyday issues and the gnawing away, deep inside me, that was making my life too difficult. These feelings weren't easing either; they were in fact gaining strength. I suppose like waves do on a windy day. Wanting to pour hot chip fat over my face wasn't the issue either. I am a very gifted thinker, I can tell you this now, and I am not into self-harm of this nature: I'm not crying out for help, I've been helped a lot in my life, so I knew this wasn't an adequate solution to the problems I was experiencing.

The MAJOR issues concerned Mark, Mark and Mark. Firstly he'd raped Charlotte. I was very unwell at the time, but I still can't live with this fact, especially as he's never shown any remorse. I really thought that I might find the DVD tonight but didn't, but I still believe he has it. I also believe he will rape someone again, so something had to be done to try and stop him.

Secondly, I can't live in a world where powerful people like him feel they can do what they want. Mark will always exert an influence over me, he knows it and I know it. It was an unbearable thought. Maybe my death might modify his behaviour, especially now that the police are involved. It was, after all, one of the reasons for writing the diary. But I still doubt it. He feels untouchable.

The third major issue concerned Charlotte. At present

she is on her honeymoon and she is not aware that Mark is moving to Harrogate, so I dread to think what it will do to her if she bumped into him one day. If Roy then saw him, he'd probably want to kill him also. Either eventuality is possible and would ruin their lives. Charlotte, in particular, couldn't cope the second time round, with any confrontation of this kind. I therefore ask you to help them in any way you are able.

The diary in front of you is for you to read. A copy has already been sent to Mark and it should reach him tomorrow. I suppose you could say that it is a very long and detailed hate letter to him. (If nothing else, he will fully appreciate how much Charlotte and I hate him.) The diary isn't REAL but it contains MANY things that are true, Charlotte being homeless in York is just one of the many examples I could give you, and it was written for a purpose. Writing it was the happiest time of my life; in one respect anyway (I 'lived' it – in my dreams at night). I have also sent a copy to Uncle Alf. I love Charlotte and always have, so the diary is a special kind of love letter to her also. I know that this comes across very clearly. I hope she isn't bothered by it. I don't think she will be. I don't know if Charlotte would like a copy but I hope she will. Anyway, I'll let you and Uncle Alf decide about that.

Lastly, since Father died, Mark decided to stop my allowance. Uncle Alf and Auntie Gwen were going to buy a caravan for me to live in, near them. Tell them I love them and that I'm sorry.

Thank you and best wishes,
Nicholas

P.S. I hope Mark won't be able to harm Uncle Alf in any way. Surely everyone would consider my acts to be the behaviour of a mad man who killed himself.

The two officers were stunned and bewildered, but also nonplussed. They sat in silence for a time, open-mouthed in disbelief. Then Capstan informed the station and an all-points alert was put out. Nicholas was clearly a man trapped in his own thoughts. They felt he was trying to repair something that had probably happened and was terribly wrong, but ultimately couldn't. 'I've never read anything like it – and I've been on the force a long time,' Capstan said. Just then they were informed that a body had been found. It was almost certainly that of Nicholas.

'He made it easy for us,' the police officer on the radio said. 'He'd made his whereabouts known on the train. He was carrying a bottle of whisky in his inside pocket and seemed intoxicated. The witness thought he might be on drugs. "He appeared both calm and distressed," she said, "and his mannerisms were unsettling also. He was talking to himself or to someone imaginary in front of him, and his facial expressions were a mixture of smiles and scowls." When he got off the train at Knaresborough he started walking down some steps towards the river, apparently. He must have waited for a short time before walking back onto the viaduct. There he placed a coat and mobile phone on the wall and jumped off. The witness had walked back to the station, as she felt there was something that was not quite right about him, and she saw him jump. She's in a terrible state.'

The two officers had never met Nicholas, but they'd both felt deeply sad when this news came through. Suicide was always very upsetting, but after reading his letter they felt they knew a part of him. They wondered if he'd felt he was incomplete in some way. Maybe he'd felt he even didn't really belong in this world; but in other ways they felt he had lived in a world full of bright light, whilst they felt they lived in shadow. Pragmatism or idealism – take your pick. Most of us would probably choose the former. Maybe Nicholas had no choice in the matter, and this may have been one of the issues he'd been grappling with, but they knew one thing was for certain: Mark Torch was more than a rod for his back. He was a black cloud who'd suffocated him. And goodness knows what he might have done to Charlotte.

'Well, that's it for tonight then,' said Chalkie. 'I won't forget this night in a hurry. He's left deep footprints inside my head, that's for sure. There was nothing more we could have done, but it doesn't feel like that. It feels like we should have done more somehow. I suppose our elders and betters will take over tomorrow.' And it was whilst reflecting on this point that Capstan made a vital decision. 'Chalkie, go and look around the house. Look for anything unusual. We might have missed something. Forensics would have rung us if they'd found anything. See what you make of Roger Goulding also, when he turns up. I'm going to stay here and read Nicholas's diary, whilst waiting for Alf Turner. As well as hearing the tragic news he's going to have to identify the body. Nicholas told us to read it. I'm going to read it now. Maybe I can pick up something that may be of use. Maybe Alf Turner can help also.'

Afterwards Capstan felt that this was one of the most important decisions he'd ever made. Was instinct involved? Who knows. It was certainly a combination of a few things, but Capstan liked to think he possessed a certain propensity in this department. In retrospect, though, he realised that luck had played its part as well: a lorry had spilt its load on the northbound carriageway of the M1 and would delay Roger Goulding's time of arrival. This meant that Capstan felt under less pressure, and he would therefore have more time to reflect on the night's tragic event, whilst reading the diary. The time spent doing this was the crucial step: it enabled Capstan to formulate the theory that would help achieve some level of restorative justice for Charlotte and Alf Turner, and give some meaning at least to Nicholas's death.

Author's Forgotten Insert

Joe had written three different versions of the diary, and in many ways all of them were strange accounts. Mark was undoubtedly a cunning and resourceful man, but if I'd written it I would have given Nicholas more power, for all he does, after all, is fire blanks, so I was considering pulling the plug. Nicholas, I thought, should be much angrier than he actually is, especially as he only has two weeks to live. He should turn green occasionally, like the Incredible Hulk. He should destroy more things in Mark's house, also. And even though the game of British Bulldog was amusing, and a useful way of obtaining mixed-media materials, the diary therefore didn't quite grab my imagination as I felt it should. So thoughts of crawling through a radioactive swamp, next to the castle where the princess was imprisoned and guarded by a dragon on the top of a sheer mountain, grew in my consciousness, as I considered how it should be changed. And as I read it for the last time, I even felt that a literary agent wouldn't accept it in its present form either, so there was no more to be said. But then an idea formed, and for a time I was pleasantly diverted; and as I thought about it in more detail, the more I liked it and the more absorbed I became. Yes, blackmailing an agent, by carrying out a similar procedure to the one Nigel used, was the way forward, I realised. Yes, that should do it, I thought. Then I'd get my book published, that's for sure. And by the time I'd dotted all the i's and crossed all the t's, I'd even determined how the finished conversation would go:

'Thanks for the email. So, are you going to recommend my book to a publisher?'
'Yes, we are.'
'Writing's a craft. I've put hundreds and hundreds of hours into writing it so far, I think Capstan and Chalkie are

great characters, Mark is an excellent villain, a 'sleaze bucket' according to my friend, and I can't wait until you meet Nigel. He makes Mark look like a pussy cat. So, what do you think?'

'Well, I've not read the whole book yet. But I've enjoyed it so far.'

'So, you can now see that Nicholas's diary is about mental health, and that the passages in Mark's house are a metaphor for his mental disintegration?'

'Yes, I can.'

'The diary is an allegory also. The greed of the bankers has destroyed the economy of the country. And Mark is a greedy man who acts in a similar way. After all, the "noughties" were an era of greed.'

'Yes. We are now reaping what was sown back then.'

'The other main theme of the diary is of course *love*. It's a sad and quirky love story and is all about "heart". Nicholas doesn't belong in the twenty-first century, he belongs in the sixties, and if he had the chance he would carry out a peaceful revolution. So, there's no violence. He's harmless. But I did listen to what you had to say, so I added the game of British Bulldog.'

'Yes, that was a good addition . . . Now, can you please tell me what you've done to our web pages, and what you've done to our computers?'

But as I poured myself another whisky I too realised that Nicholas was an eccentric, and someone who was very similar to my grandfather, being a man who could fiddle about for hours in his shed at the bottom of the garden whilst doing nothing in particular with tedious regularity; so his endearing and protective tenderness began to seep into my own consciousness, and while dwelling on this matter I began to change my mind about the diary, especially when I thought about the oppressive hierarchies which had in his particular life left him to gather moss. So, I wasn't sure if blackmailing a literary agent was necessary. Confused, I then sat back and finished off the bottle of whisky.

Also, I'd become conscious of what a famous scientist once said, and this had annoyed me as I thought about it. He said, 'The man who regards his life as meaningless is not merely unhappy but hardly fit for life.' But as I wasn't going to be lectured on this by someone who'd disowned his own daughter, and as the light filtered through the window and cast long shadows, and as I realised that this was the place where I was one day going to die, I began to appreciate that it was his idealism that gave him a meaning to his life. Charlotte was also a princess (she was almost perfect and all I do is change her into a brunette), and as I thought about it all, and as I took a last swig of the remaining whisky in my glass whilst looking out of the window at my small garden, and as I reflected on my own life and realised that to me the world often seemed too grim to write about, I thought about what I'd now actually change, if rewriting the diary was down to me? And as it turned out, it wouldn't be much.

The world of reality was self-devouring. It was even becoming devoid of love, where even mutual love seemed impossible, so the only alternative to entering into a world of nothingness was to ensure that my book was published, as aesthetic experiences are the only escape for people like me in this world. My book will at least provide some of those, I thought. So before falling asleep I wrote this insert. Yes, I was going to press forward, and yes, I was going to ensure through foul means or fair, that there would be a positive outcome to that night's interesting monologue. Nicholas's diary was also going to remain unchanged.

Twisted Logic

or:

The Life and Times of a Princess (the Good), a Scumbag (the Bad) and a Madman (the Ugly)

or:

The House that Died of Shame

by Nicholas Torch

Day One

Hello brother. No, that's wrong. Hello, dear brother? Yes, that's better. Anyway, it's time to tell you that holding a grudge (as I do) has given my life . . . a purpose. It is with this in mind that I've started writing to you. Other issues will become clearer soon enough. Please bear with me. I often wondered if you cried when Father died. Well, did you?

When I was away Father only wrote to me occasionally. But when he did, it was always very clear how proud he was of you, and how insensitive he was to me. I didn't think he knew you very well, but when I started to think about it I realised why. He was always working, so how could he? It was very clear, however, that you were both becoming staunch defenders of privilege. Once you'd reached the top of the ladder you were determined to cut away the rungs, so nobody else could. When I asked him about this, Father said, 'It's the genes dear boy. Cream always rises to the top.' That was convenient for you both, I thought. Genes, yes, they are responsible for everything. I realised after this that I was always a lost cause, and you should be in no doubt that I always resented it. Forgotten memories? How very convenient! It was these same forgotten memories, in my opinion anyway, that explained your rise to the top!

You forgot easily. Or was it harder than that? I know that you also received therapy, but it always appeared to be a game to you. 'Freud is God,' you said on numerous occasions, 'and we are all his children.' To me, though, the issue was more straightforward, and it was simply this: women raised an excitement within you that went beyond what you could tolerate, so you acted solely on instinct. I was right about this, wasn't I? Blood ties are very strong though, so I understood why you received the help you did, but only to a certain extent, for what you did was unforgivable.

Of course my own abnormal development was a problem, as was my idealism, and I always appreciated that I wasn't what you all had in mind when I was adopted. Nevertheless, I could have been helped much more. I didn't realise then that respectability was so important, but of course should have: it is a prerequisite for a family with such aspirations. Up until then I believed we were all equal, but I couldn't have been more wrong if I'd tried. Once you and Father had made up your minds about me, you all cheerfully turned your backs, and the realisation that all my painful memories would remain with me for ever barely seemed to raise a flicker in the consciousness of any of you.

A little later

I need a period of quiet reflection – a rest, in other words – before continuing, for I am, I have to say, excited. The plan will become clear soon enough. First, I'd like to bring to your attention my school days. I appreciate that I'm being a little self-indulgent here, but if this early period of my life had been a more fruitful one, my life might have turned out differently. I may even have led a worthwhile life, and been a cause for celebration. If this had been the case, I wonder what would have happened to you. How would your life have turned out?

There is a special spark in young people, but in my experience many children are never given enough oxygen to breathe. The creative flame is therefore a very dull one; sometimes it is hardly noticeable. I can't say I wasn't noticed; unfortunately I was a horror child, but there wasn't anything authentic happening in my life at the time. There was nothing I did that was exciting or that was good, so no creative processes were being activated inside my head, that was for sure. I was being held back at school, just as I was at home. I believed in what were utopian values, but I appreciate that my behaviour was awful and inexcusable. I was never, though, schizophrenic. I was wilful and opinionated. I even appreciate that I must have left a trail of debris in the teachers' minds, and in Miss Hillary's mind in particular, but I didn't deserve *that* label.

As an infant I was perfectly normal and realised that lying was important. All young children do. When Mother asked me what I thought of her new dress I said, 'Mummy, you look like Snow White in it. It is beautiful.' She was going to an important garden party at the time if you remember, and she actually looked like a dandelion, especially when she put on her yellow hat! I remember painting daffodils with symmetrical stalks because the teacher liked them better. "They are so much prettier," she said. There was the time also when I soiled myself in the classroom because I was too scared to ask the teacher if I could go to the toilet. I always believed what the teachers said too. 'God sees everything,' the teachers told us. If we didn't behave ourselves I therefore believed that a giant hand would appear from nowhere, or from out of the sky, and smack us.

All things change, however, and for the worse in my case. 'You were lovely when you were five' became 'Nicholas, where on earth did that come from? I've never heard language like that in my life!' I certainly remember saying to the head teacher, 'I don't fucking believe in God any more,' as I was carted off to his office and smacked. And after that things really did get worse. I was uncontrollable, and I cringe, even now, when I think about it. I started gouging out big holes in the toilets with a screwdriver I'd pinched, and I remember emptying powder paint over as many desks as I could one dinner time. Another time I remember swearing at Miss Hillary. I said to her, 'These dinners are a fucking disgrace.' This time, though, the wheels came off, along with everything else. When I refused to eat the rhubarb crumble I was suspended.

This broke Mother's heart. I know this. She wasn't well – the cancer was spreading – and I completely broke down. I was different somehow and felt helpless. I didn't know what to do about it. I knew I was hypersensitive and resented being told what to do all the time by people like you. You were awful to me. But I also knew that I wasn't capable of causing anybody any actual physical harm, so I think I was still hopeful. I was twelve and you were nearly seventeen, and you felt the world was your oyster didn't you! You were sexually active and I was just beginning to realise that different rules were operating. You'd always be forgiven for your mistakes, but I wouldn't be. So I was sent to a Special School.

The therapy I received was based on modifying my behaviour. I was given graded exposure to events that had caused difficulties earlier and was given strategies to cope. These would enable me to become more amenable and less intransigent. I was given the opportunities for creative expression and I recorded my experiences in a sketchbook. Then they analysed what I'd done. They encouraged me to look at the world with fresh eyes and to learn how to step back from it. Soon I started to make good progress, even though I still had depressive and morbid tendencies, but this progress didn't last long. I became sullen again, and less responsive, and they didn't know why.

They knew Mother had died but still believed the situation at home was a good one. There were lots of friends and family about who appeared supportive, and there was even a wood at the back of the house to play in. But young people can be sophisticated when they have to be, and I don't believe that this is properly recognised, or understood. The strategies I learnt were based on concealment; they were developed and deployed to protect you, of course. I was scared of you and knew that no one would believe me, and that they'd always take your word against mine. So you got away with murder. I kept some of my own interests secret though. I couldn't blame you for everything. I liked Goya's pictures of mad people and some of David Cronenberg's films too. *Shivers* was great, for example. But my behaviour always deteriorated after I'd been at home and even this suited your purpose, especially when Father started working away from home after Mother's death. The therapists didn't know about this either, and your own behaviour was a complete mystery to them. Then your relatives turned against me, and then everybody else. What do I remember about your friends? Well, where do I start? I was a freak in their eyes. And as for your girlfriends: what can I say? I only saw them in horizontal positions! They were never in the right position to judge me.

Day Two

I didn't sleep every well last night. Writing this diary isn't going to be as easy as I'd first anticipated. I'd been waiting to start for ages, and what happens when I do? I get writer's cramp. Or is the correct term writer's block? Whatever, the usual bad dreams didn't help either I suppose, as I'd been tossing and turning for ages, so I quickly dressed and set off on a walk through the empty streets of Harrogate. I was confused more than anything else this time, though. When I'd reached Christ Church, however, I realised I'd unwittingly discovered the best way to proceed. Had the hand of God lent a helping hand? I wondered. Start with the walk! That was it. Start with the here and now. So here I am in Harrogate – yes, I felt sure that would shock you, and I'm here to tell you that I've planned with Charlotte – yes, Charlotte is here too – a dramatic resolution to this hitherto sad journey of ours.

I wrote prodigiously in my teenage years (or my early 'blue' period as I like to call it, if Picasso doesn't mind – I was largely isolated from 'the banquet of life'), but I know I remain a novice at it in your eyes. However, I do believe, even without a formal education, that this diary will be at least satisfactorily understood. You may even admire it. If you do I would be pleased. This diary's purpose is important. As well as conveying important information it is intended to change your behaviour! Is this possible? Who knows? Anyway, it goes without saying that it has to be well written and succinct if it is to have any chance at all. If it isn't you might throw it in the bin with all the other rubbish and then where would we be? The events it will describe may even allow a form of closure for us both, but especially so for Charlotte, and if all goes to plan there will be nothing you will be able to do because you have a reputation to protect! If you report us to the police you will suffer torment and ridicule. I would be interested in what action your relatives would take, and also in the effect it would have on the business if you did. So, enough said. How many surprises can a man handle in such a short period of time? Well, prepare yourself for more. We've hardly started!

It was bizarre how we met. When any strange or unlikely things happen people say it was fate or what goes around comes around. I don't believe it was either. When I met Charlotte it was simply a chance event. We were watching *Blithe Spirit* at the Harrogate Theatre – which proves my point I think. This is a play about a man who is haunted by two people, as you are! Few of us appreciate the importance of coincidence or how likely unlikely things happen. It is all down to the laws of mathematics and complex probability formulae. Nevertheless, that meeting changed our lives for ever and I am forever grateful.

Charlotte stood very still. This was the first thing I noticed about her. She had the grace of a ballet dancer but looked, on closer inspection, as if she'd been made by children in a sculpture lesson. She was the colour of ash covered in scratches and small bumps. When I looked into her eyes I thought they were wide and blank, and wouldn't have looked out of place in a goldfish. So seeing her for the first time in a while was quite shocking to me. She was beautiful still, but also very fragile. 'Charlotte,' I said as we embraced, 'what's happened to you? I thought you'd gone to university.'

At first it appeared that she didn't know how to reply, but then she lowered her head slightly and smiled. 'You should have seen me a few years ago!' she said. Her face then became drawn and anxious so I stepped back slightly and was filled with terror, as I thought about what she'd just said. I could tell she'd suffered a great deal and I now knew why. So over the next two hours we slowly teased out from one another the strange and very difficult events of our lives. 'Being raped,' she concluded, 'wasn't just a terrible trauma; it changed my personality as well as destroying my relationship with my parents. I became withdrawn and started taking drugs. I packed in university and became homeless in York.'

So Mark, how are you feeling? Without remorse probably, being someone who has three personality disorders in my opinion. Yes, three! But psychopathy was always the most serious of course. By the way, I bet your motto 'only the strongest survive' still remains, doesn't it? Anyway, about a year ago we moved together into a small ex-laundry worker's cottage in the town. Our relationship is a platonic one, but we care for each other deeply. She still takes tablets for anxiety, but she is much better than she was, and she isn't now quite as afraid of the dark.

The next topic to bring up, not surprisingly, is my own mental health. I remember vaguely being sent to the psychiatric ward at the time of her rape. I remember being aware of what had happened to her, but I knew I wasn't in a fit state to do anything about it. This, of course, I now realise, had terrible repercussions. So what happened to me? Well, I think I know. At that time you would have been able to get hold of various medicines. Your friends had connections, and as Mother was a doctor you'd know what to get hold of, so I think you were sprinkling various chemicals onto my food and into my drinks. After a period of time this would have had a serious effect on me. Certain MAO inhibitor drugs, for example, can cause excessive stimulation of the brain, especially when they are used in conjunction with certain foods, I believe. Cheese is just one example, and as I loved cheese I ate lots of it, so it was no wonder that I soon started trembling. Soon after that I even remember seeing things that weren't there, and then I experienced feelings of agitation and downright anger. So from then on it would have been easy for you to convince Father that I was suffering from psychotic episodes, especially once I'd started shouting and raving. Anyway, friends, family, social workers, Romans and countrymen then gathered around like vultures, and with the consent of the doctor I was sent to a psychiatric hospital.

There, I was immediately given tranquillisers, but they were soon not deemed necessary. Can you believe that! In the meantime frantic arrangements were taking place. I was given a generous allowance from Father and was then sent, as you know (with my consent), to Scarborough. Auntie Gwen and Uncle Alf (her second husband and great big cuddly bear) agreed to be my new nearest relatives, but it was Uncle Alf who did really. My prognosis was hopeful:

'Nicholas has a borderline paranoid personality disorder. He doesn't trust people and feels hostility to anyone, including himself, who acts inappropriately. He suffers from bi-polar but responds well to his medication. The tablets block certain nerve endings and hinder agitated responses. He should therefore only need to see specialists in outpatients. He will still need to be routinely assessed and will need a controlled environment with limits, controls and rewards, but these can be relaxed over time. We do not feel he is a danger to other people so he should, in time, be reasonably free to do as he wishes, as long as he continues to take his tablets. In the meantime, a caring environment, lots of exercise and a well-balanced diet with lots of vitamins will enhance his progress and development.'

Well, the next two years had its ups and downs as you can imagine. Auntie Gwen and Uncle Alf were very patient and the sessions at outpatients were positive too. I became interested in philosophy and read about how the two hemispheres of the brain interact. This helped me understand myself and I appreciated talking to my therapist about it. I didn't become too involved in it, but it certainly helped. The last year in particular has been good. My strengths have helped Charlotte and vice versa. Together we are more complete somehow.

Day Three

'At one time so much ceased to matter,' Charlotte said whilst drying the dishes, 'but now it does.' This was the first time she'd really started to talk about her dark-age period. I remembered it so clearly. I also remembered watching as she dried every knife and fork before putting them in the drawer. I never did that, I just threw all the cutlery into the drawer in one go and didn't even dry it. Not only did Charlotte dry each piece of cutlery, she sometimes even breathed on some and then wiped them again with the towel, until they looked new. 'I felt no pleasure when taking a hot bath,' she said whilst doing this, 'or from the smell of bacon sizzling in a frying pan. I never bought flowers or went walking on a sunny day. I preferred to hide under the bed covers or behind drawn curtains, so I spent hours curled up on that settee. I'll never forget it. It was a dishevelled old thing and very appropriate for the time. My, how I used to scream! You should have heard me,' she said with a sigh. Then she looked directly at my eyes. Whenever she did this I always felt she could see right through me. 'Just thinking about it now makes me squirm,' she said, and she shivered like she did when she saw a spider. I remembered saying to her, 'Talking about it is a good thing – it shows how far you've travelled.' I could still never get her to truly open up about her time in York, but this was the start of her opening-up process and I remembered the conversation so clearly.

Later, in the living room, she went on to talk about happiness. 'It can't be pursued,' she said. 'It just appears. It might be a simple smile, the first one in months; there may even be a sudden lifting of the spirit, which you can feel in the lightness of your footsteps, and it might only last for a fleeting moment, but you recognise it even though it has gone so quickly. Later you might notice yourself humming to a favourite song; suddenly you're actually glad to be alive, and you can't believe it. The dark moments come again of course. I often felt that the world was devoid of human warmth, especially during the night, but over time you learn how to cope.'

Occasionally, later on, I found myself joining in. I'd told her that I found even making a cup of tea impossible. Sometimes I felt as though a knife had been plunged into the side of my body, and the sun wouldn't appear on these days either. Sometimes the curtains lit up and shapes started to dance, but I too tried to cope. Usually I tried not to say too much about my problems because my situation was a different one. Charlotte's problems were solely down to you. She was totally blameless, whereas I wasn't.

Anyway, goodness knows what might have become of Charlotte if Lady Luck hadn't intervened (as she is prone to do sometimes in this mathematically ordered universe of ours). She might even be dead! One day she met a woman in a café in Harrogate. The place was full, apparently, so she sat near the window on the only spare seat, and she found herself talking to the woman next to her. Margaret was her name, and she was setting up a small business dealing in holistic products and skin treatments. She was looking for a reliable assistant whom she could trust and work with, and Charlotte, it seemed, fit the bill. Margaret's business started well and grew very quickly. In a short time she started showing her products around the county.

They set up various connected events, but I'm not exactly sure what this entails. Charlotte's actually at one of these right now. She's with Margaret in Whitby and I miss her when she is away, but it's fantastic to see how much more confident she is these days. The pay isn't good, but Margaret gives her as much as she can afford, and she receives the odd bonus from time to time. The job isn't, of course, mentally challenging, but Charlotte remains grateful for the work.

It is hard to put into words the difference having someone in your life makes. My eyes fill up with tears sometimes when I watch her sleeping, or see her mind working furiously when she is arguing. One subject always raises her shackles, naturally, and it concerns you. One subject can always be guaranteed to cause her to shudder and become agitated. All I have to say is, 'Look, Charlotte, now that we've got each other, our lives have meaning. So why don't you let me carry through our plan by myself? You aren't needed, you know. I'm perfectly capable of doing it on my own. As a matter of fact, it would be easier if I did do it by myself!'

Her mannerisms were always the same when I brought up this subject, they never changed. First she'd stare, and then she'd screw up her face so that her nose twitched, and then she'd say, 'Look, Nicholas, will you stop bringing this up? I don't just want to be there, I'm *going* to be there, okay?' I understood why she was so keen to be there, I really did. I'd want to be there if I'd suffered like she had, but I was always trying to make sure that she knew what she was getting herself into. I know you filmed it. Or rather, your sicko friend Roger did. You filmed me once, if you remember, also. So I know you filmed Charlotte. You did your *Lord of the Flies* version in the wood, and even though you'd say it was only fooling around, it made a lasting impression on me, I can tell you.

Day Five

I was busy all day yesterday so I couldn't attend to the diary. I know it was remiss of me, but there you are. First I was asked if I'd do a spot of gardening for Mrs T. She lives next door and is a lovely old lady. She's a dying breed, if you know what I mean. This country doesn't produce her type any more. And then I was called upon to do some brick-laying for Roy the builder. I'm meticulous apparently, and although it was only a garden wall that needed replacing, I always work hard and give value for money. I started late, for reasons that will become obvious, so didn't finish until evening. Roy seeks me out when he is overstretched and I'm very grateful for the odd labouring job. Working adds some variety to my life, and I enjoy being in the outdoors.

The front gardens are small, so a little effort makes a big difference. I planted a couple of dwarf rhododendrons in our garden and some early-flowering violas, so there is a splash of colour from late March until October. Mrs T just leaves me to get on with it, so I've done something similar in her garden. She gives me the money for the flowers and I plant them where I like. She is always so grateful. She actually has a large family but she likes to help me when she can. She can talk for hours, but she is a good listener as well.

Her mother came to Harrogate from the North East. She worked in the hotels as a servant. Her father worked in the large laundry at the back of the house. Her uncle attended to all the fires in another hotel as well. 'He was an irascible man,' she said. 'When his pecker was up, there was no stopping him. Once, Agatha Christie stayed in the hotel. "She was nice enough," he said "but you'd think she was royalty." He'd say it over and over again. I suppose he was typical of people of that time: plain speaking, hard-working and decent.'

Mrs T's house has a slight musty smell, but is full of interesting things from the past, and she loves showing me her old photographs. 'That's my husband – oh, and there's Bill,' she'd say, and so on. And they'd all be smartly dressed, which is surprising when you think about it. No one wears a tie at the seaside or when going for a walk any more. I wonder why not?

She is very interested when I talk to her about depression. Yesterday we seemed to talk for hours about it. She made a pot of tea and put out a lovely spread of food. When I'd told her previously about the hospital she'd said, 'Oh my.' She didn't understand how anyone so young could get like that. But when she listened she'd hardly moved in her chair and you could hear a pin drop. Sometimes she'd be sat stroking the cat too. 'In my day, everyone was just too busy,' she said. 'We hardly had time to think, never mind get depressed! I can understand it if old people feel like that, especially if they are in pain and can't move easily, but even then there are always chores that need doing!'

She can understand loneliness though. She never gets lonely, she says. 'I never bleedin' get the chance. Someone is always around. They are all too bloody nosey.' But she knows many who have died, and for a time she bowed her head slightly, as if in prayer. Then she perked up and said, 'What's the definition of old age?' She'd asked me something I'd never considered before, and I was intrigued to say the least. 'I don't know,' I said. She then paused before saying, 'Crossed-off names in an address book,' and I was immediately taken with that definition. When I did manage to get away I thought about it a lot. People should listen more to the old people, I thought.

During the evening my attention was taken by an interesting story in the local newspaper. North Yorkshire, according to the 2008 Place Survey, whatever that is, is one of the two best counties in England to live. The other one is Dorset. Regarding Harrogate, it said: Harrogate isn't stuck in the past. It's vibrant and charming, faster paced and more cosmopolitan than the rest of the Yorkshire Dales. And it hasn't lost its friendly face. I mentioned it because I know you've bought a large house here. Yes, Uncle Alf told me. He tells me quite a lot these days.

Harrogate is a nice place to live, for sure. The Stray gives it a pleasant open feel and some of the shops are certainly exclusive, but I'm not convinced by the friendly bit. The people who were born here seem friendly enough, but there is a shortage of work within the town and this, even you must agree, creates its own problems. I'm not convinced either that many young people are asked their opinion in surveys anyway. Since living here I've read a bit about its history. I think history matters, but it does appear to me, at any rate, that the history of Harrogate concerns the privileged few. The poor seem to have been airbrushed out somewhat. When the railway reached Harrogate, for example, there was an influx of both rich and poor, as Mrs T's example shows. If you do come though, I'm sure you won't be socialising with many working-class people. Your money will be spent in places where most people don't go.

Anyway this reminds me of a joke that is quite popular up here:

Question: *What does Harrogate have in common with a wounded bull?*
Answer: *It charges too much!*

I'm not sure you'll like Yorkshire humour though.

All in all, I'd say today has been quite an anxious day. But rather than hide in the shadows I've confronted my demons – by heading them off at the pass, as the cowboys would say! I intend going down to Nidd Gorge tomorrow. Strangely, a bike was left behind when we moved into the house, so I'll go down on that. It's an odd-looking thing I must say. It's not really a road bike, and it's not a mountain bike either. I suppose you'd have to say that it is therefore a 'middle of the road' bike!

If I go I promise not to get run over!

Day Six

The morning passed without incident. There was nothing to report. I suppose I was lingering, if the truth be told. I'd intended setting off quite early but was feeling dispirited. I'd a lot on my mind. Then Charlotte rang out of the blue. She was in high spirits and she cheered me up somewhat.

'You'll never guess where I am,' she said.

Okay, I thought, I'll play along. 'Now let me see,' I said mischievously. 'I know, you're on a rocket ship, and you're going to the moon for some cheese.' There was a pause after I'd said that, and then I heard a slight sigh.

'Look who got out the wrong side of the bed. But you're nearly right,' she said in a slightly withering tone of voice. 'Look lively, brace the mainsail. I'm with Margaret, and we're on a yellow boat to Staithes. I'm drinking wine and Margaret's already on her second gin and tonic.'

'Blimey,' I said, 'is it a pirate ship? Are you in search of rum?'

'Maybe on the return journey – that is, if we can still stand,' she said. 'Are you all right? You seem a bit down.'

'No, I'm okay,' I replied. 'I suppose I'm just missing you.'

'Well, I've got some bad news for you. Uncle Alf has just rung, so I'll be staying in Scarborough for an extra day,' she said.

'Fine,' I said. 'Thanks for ringing. You've cheered me up. I'm setting off for Nidd Gorge. See you when you return.'

So shortly afterwards, but still with some trepidation, I set off on the bike. I'm not a very good cyclist at the best of times (short levers for one thing), but a heavy heart made the short trip, which is actually downhill to begin with and then along an old railway line, unmemorable to say the least. However, when I arrived my spirits lifted somewhat. Nidd Gorge is a very beautiful place. I looked down at it from the massive viaduct which used to carry trains northwards on what must have been a stunning journey. Except for the odd person out walking the dog, it was surprisingly quiet too. I was glad about this, for I had come to think and ponder. You opened Pandora's box and I was planning on shutting it! Unfortunately, the way ahead was not easy. What were the consequences going to be for Charlotte and me? This was my major consideration, but I also wanted to think about the ethics involved. First, though, I went to have a look around. I'd not been here before.

Woods and rivers cast spells, don't they? I strode down through the tall grasses, shrub-like trees, yellow and purple flowers, bluebells and strange plants called, I think, 'lords and ladies'. These apparently give off smells that attract flies, though they weren't doing so on this occasion (as far as I could tell, anyway). There was a mix of oak, ash and beech trees on the way down, and lots of scrubby vegetation and bramble. Near the river the larch and willow trees stood out of the water like giant witches' claws and marsh marigold spread in clumps in the damp patches. It was eerily quiet, like all gorges are, but the large viaduct behind made it seem especially so. The light reflected in different intensities off the different surfaces. Overhead the sun shone through the green leaves, catching their movement in the slight breeze, at times almost blocking out the blue of the sky.

I sat on a large rock next to where a stream meanders before entering the river. The pine trees on the opposite bank soared tall and straight into the sky. I had a quick look for newts in the stream but didn't see any. There were loads of other tiny pond creatures moving to and fro and also the odd water boatman swimming upside down just below the surface of the water, while pond skaters stood motionless on the water's surface above them. Nature's diversity is truly astounding, I thought, and I was pleased how much I still remembered, so for a short time I was very pleasantly diverted. It was quite easy to imagine how, during the ice age, this river could have cut through the rock so easily. It is now reasonably placid, but the odd broken tree is still a reminder of how strong the current can be when the river is swollen. Nature certainly has its moods, I realised.

TWISTED LOGIC

I hadn't been in a wood in ages. In London the wood behind our house wasn't anything like this, though it was nice enough. I know there was only one kind of nature study you were interested in, and it didn't involve trees, so you probably hardly noticed them. So, being almost entirely alone there – the wood was usually quiet – I used to enjoy exploring and making maps of secret places. I thought of all the places that I knew well as being my own private wilderness, even empty garages and back alleys outside the wood. It was fantastic. Then, after exploring, and once I was back in the city and surrounded by noise, I'd often go to the pictures. Sometimes I'd even venture as far as Camden Market. I'd get lost for hours there in the underground corridors. It was like a maze and similar, I thought, to the one I'd been in at Hampton Court. But maybe I'm even thinking of the maze in *The Shining*, that I probably saw around the same time. But the stalls made a difference of course, and Camden Market was full of them. They sold everything you could think of, and as nobody knew where I was, I always spent hours exploring them, as I knew that, for all you cared, I could just as easily have been on a rocket ship to the moon. I'd learnt to stay away from you and was beyond your reach, for most of the time anyway.

When you first appeared I wasn't too concerned. I wasn't, I would say, easily scared. I myself had been pretty revolting at times, remember. But there was definitely something different about both of you this time. Your face was distorted and angry; Roger, holding the camera, hollered and screamed as if he'd seen the bogeyman. You were leaping and screaming also, and as you brushed against the bramble bushes they were scratching you quite badly, but you hardly noticed as the twigs snapped under your feet like lollipop sticks. You'd also painted red paint on your faces, but it wasn't funny: you were frightening, and you definitely weren't playing around.

After tying me to the tree you tugged at my shirt and tore long rips into it. You also prodded me with your pointed stick, scratching and cutting my skin; then you rose over me and started hissing and cursing. 'You are a worthless human being. A slug is more useful than you,' you said. 'You shouldn't be in a wood at all – a zoo is where *you* belong. None of us wants you around. You're a virus, a germ, you are worse than a plague of ants.' And then you said you'd like to kill me, and I could see that you were becoming out of control, so I don't know what would have happened if Roger hadn't been there. Then you just left. Roger had his arm round you. Even today that moment sickens me and I can still remember it so clearly. You never appeared ashamed afterwards. But even worse was to come, in fact. Without a controlling influence, you had been unleashed. The incident in the wood was merely the beginning. It was a portent of things to come.

Justice

I sat on that large rock for ages; my mind had wandered far and wide. But my bottom hurt and it felt slightly squashed, so I left that spot and rode to the pub. There, I stood by the stream that runs through the beer garden for a while, and then I sat down on a bench and sipped my drink. I was soon once again deep in thought.

The Godfather is one of my favourite films. Rich and powerful people have influence over all sorts of institutions, don't they – like the Church – and access to expensive lawyers and the like. Is this fair? I wondered. Of course it isn't. One favourite statistic of mine actually involves lawyers: the next generation of them will come from families who are 70 per cent wealthier than the average population, apparently. I therefore decided that the profession was socially exclusive. I know you'd say 'Good, it's how it should be' or words to that effect, but I say keep reading. When the plan is completed I wonder what you'll think then. Will justice have been done? You have no way of stopping me, by the way. The horse will have bolted by the time *you* become involved.

Then I started thinking about the word itself. Of course I

believe in just acts, but I never realised that the word 'justice' is what's known as a universal, until I first read about it when I was receiving therapy. I liked reading about the ideas of Plato especially, and still do. Universals don't exist in the real world, by the way. Just acts do, but not universals like justice. Universals exist in the supra-sensitive world, which is a world that is more real. That world seems to be a lot like heaven to me. If heaven exists, I wondered, might I go there? I doubt it, but neither will you, or for that matter, the Godfather. I thought about this a lot today and just hoped I find that DVD. Then one just act will certainly take place. Nidd Gorge is a fantastic place. It is even a good place to go to when you need to think. I even enjoyed the bike ride.

Day Seven

A busy day is planned. I awoke refreshed and was raring to go. Roy popped round last night. Yes, he literally popped round. He was popping off somewhere else also. 'Nicholas, are you free?' he said. He wanted me to trim his privet hedge for him. He had urgent business to attend to. 'Yes, I am,' I replied and that was that. It was a brief call. Builders are a world unto themselves and Roy was no exception, I thought afterwards. The work would occupy my mind and body, and it would do me good. Charlotte would soon be back and I was looking forward to her return. I wondered if she'd been seasick. The North Sea had always been choppy when I'd been on it. I once went fishing for the day. I'll never go again. That's all I've got to say on the matter. I was as sick as a dog.

When I started work I soon became immersed in my own thoughts. I thought we could go to the Dales tomorrow, and Simon's Seat suddenly came into my mind. It involved a reasonable walk up the valley, to a rocky outcrop above Appletreewick. It's a place, I thought, as I steadied myself on the ladder, where you can enjoy some of the best views of Wharfedale: dry stone walls, green open spaces swept by wind and rain, and fast-flowing streams plummeting down to the River Wharfe, which glistens like a long, thin ribbon of silver as it cradles the valley floor below. I was suddenly in my 'rose' period. What a relief! Anyway, it would be nice to spend the day with Charlotte. She has arranged leave thereafter, when plans and operational procedures will be properly evaluated, finishing touches will be added, and initial sorties will be made. Although, to be honest, Uncle Alf has already supplied us with a great deal of background intelligence already, and the plans have already been through feasibility studies. Chances of complete success have already been rated as good. If the tape or DVD of Charlotte's violation is found, there will be no turning back. Uncle Alf has hinted that he has already completed his arrangements, so the final act should be devastating – though not, it should be stressed, nihilistic. Redemption is possible. Trust me on this.

I started cutting the hedge at nine, but it still took all morning, even with an electric hedge trimmer. I'd say that once I'd got the hang of it, it was quite enjoyable work, and I found that if I cocked my leg out behind me, I didn't overbalance. In estate agent's language, I'd say that the house had a generous-sized garden. One or two people I knew passed by, as did many who I didn't. It was a quiet street, and it was surprising how many people I saw. Some emerged from nowhere, it seemed to me, whilst others shrieked and shouted, so you could hear them from miles away. I also noticed one schoolgirl standing by a wall furtively smoking.

I had a long chat with the lady at number six about her tortoise. 'It's the first time in thirty years that I've had to take it to the vet's,' she said. 'He's been very naughty. He keeps on biting my leg!' Mmmn, I thought, and I replied in a voice that was a little higher than I would have liked. 'Thirty years!' I said. 'I didn't know they could live that long!' Anyway, to cut a long story short, the vet said he'd never seen a tortoise in better condition. 'He just wants a mate,' the vet said, and a huge smile spread across his face apparently.

A little later Jean stopped for a chat whilst out walking the dog. Jack is one of the friendliest dogs I've ever come across. He's a mongrel who was nearly put down. He'd had distemper. 'He's discovered a novel way of playing rounders,' she said. 'My word, the boys get angry. Whenever he finds the ball, he keeps it in his mouth. He then walks around with the batter. His tail wags in the air. It means whoever is batting always gets a rounder! I've never seen anything so funny in my life.'

During the afternoon I tried to develop some lucky-charm ideas. It was all connected to an 'inner sanctum' idea I'd had for Charlotte. I thought that a market stall selling lucky bracelets or lucky elves might be a good idea, especially in Knaresborough, as it was once the home of Mother Shipton. She was a witch who predicted when the world will end, probably by global warming. Anyway, it is just meant to be a bit of fun. I do not wish to be disparaging about Margaret's business, in any shape or form. Personally I'm not convinced that treatments involving hot stones have great medical benefits, but I am convinced that a positive mental outlook can help heal mental scars and build greater self-confidence. Maybe alternative therapies can do this. Who knows? It all comes down to personal choice I suppose.

'Stressed out? Is the rat race taking its toll on your health? Well fear not. Buy one of our beautifully moulded wax elves. They come in all shapes and sizes. Each is laden with special aromas that have been designed to release their soothing vapours slowly throughout the day. They come complete with their own necklace in a wide range of prices. Buy one today and clear away all the pessimistic clutter in your life.'

I liked the idea, but it wouldn't appeal to Charlotte, I realised. In a witheringly sarcastic way she'd say, 'If this is an example of what you're going to be like in your rose period, I think I'd prefer it if you stayed in the blue one.'

Feeling therefore slightly chastened, I caught the bus to Knaresborough. I'll spare you a history lesson this time, but I like the town because part of it is very old. It is of course situated high up above the River Nidd. The river seems to be the great divide to some. One local told me that he hadn't crossed it for years. There is a degree of distrust – yes, that's the right way of putting it – between Knaresborough and Harrogate, but I think that they both complement one another rather well.

Some of the locals are characters, and many of them are usually proud Yorkshire men. I stood and listened to one of them talking whilst I was waiting to be served. 'The landlord in one of the pubs was selling a pint of mild for a pound,' he said. 'Anyway one man walked in and said, "Is that right – a pint of mild for a pound? What's wrong with it?" So the landlord said, "There's nothing wrong with it. I don't serve any of that crap southern beer in my pub. It's a Yorkshire beer." So the man replied, "Well, I don't know what to make of that, I'm a southerner." Then he walked out.'

You hear lots of stories like that in Knaresborough. And it's all the better for it, in my opinion. Anyway, it was quite late when I caught the bus home. Outside the house I remember having a brief discussion with the lad who lives at number eleven. 'I'm off to Europe,' he said. 'There's no work in Harrogate; and look at it, just cast your eye around for a second or two – three houses are up to let and the pavements are a disgrace. Just look at them.' And I could see his point. Every paving stone was cracked, it seemed, and weeds were growing in them all.

Day Eight

My rose period didn't last long at all. Oh well, I suppose it comes with the territory. You can't make an omelette without breaking eggs. Anyway, I entered my 'cubist' period at two in the afternoon. As far as I understand it, cubist pictures are multi-faceted and therefore complex. It seems to me that the artist has painted the same object from different angles, and somehow overlapped them all. The person looking at one of these pictures is therefore looking at different views of a 3-D object on a 2-D surface. Is this correct? Whatever, the world was becoming more complicated by the minute. It was expected. Charlotte arrived back in a state of some agitation. She'd spent a couple of hours talking to Auntie Gwen. Uncle Alf realised that they needed to talk to each other, as neither was completely in the picture. She knew a lot about my own circumstances, of course, as I lived with her in Scarborough, but she hadn't really spoken at any length to Charlotte.

She was white and still shaken when I saw her, and her eyes had shrunk. If she were a snail you'd say that they'd disappeared into her shell. At this moment I realised, once again, what a despicable human being you were. You are beneath contempt and we should stop even trying to understand you. I made her a cup of tea and waited for her to relax and unwind. I had a pretty good idea of what had happened.

Auntie Gwen was still in the loop. She was after all your mother's sister, so she was still part of the family, I suppose. She knew that deals were brokered between Charlotte's parents and your father. I use the pronoun 'your' deliberately, as he'd ceased to have anything to do with me. It was all pretty squalid stuff anyway. The money Charlotte received was meant to help cover her costs when she went to university in York. 'We all appreciated,' Auntie Gwen said, as they walked past the harbour, 'that there was rarely smoke without fire, but the deal that was struck seemed to be in everyone's best interests. Especially as Roger was Mark's alibi. He said he was in the house at the time, and that you'd given your consent. Mark was made to seek therapy, but I don't think it made a jot of difference to him. He seemed to treat it all like a game,' she said with some alarm. 'I think both Alf and I were horrified by that.' Listening to all that made Charlotte want to be sick, of course.

Auntie Gwen then talked about her son, John. She told Charlotte that you'd asked him to draw up some plans for an extension. 'It was all rather odd,' he'd said. 'It didn't make sense.

A lot of expense was involved without any real benefits in terms of added space.' He then told his parents that Mark wanted a state-of-the-art cinema to be installed in one of the bedrooms, along with some idiosyncratic features. At this point Charlotte became furious, as the terrible implications dawned on her. Auntie Gwen was silent, but Charlotte told me that she watched her as she dug her nails into her wrist and drew blood. It was clear that you hadn't changed, and that you still had turgid and obscene plans in the pipeline. Charlotte realised that you'd still have the recording of her rape, and she knew there and then that you were probably still watching it. I already knew that John had been approached by you because Uncle Alf told me and we'd both arrived at the same conclusions that Charlotte had, unfortunately.

John is an interesting character, and a very clever man. I know him well, of course. He's been like a brother to me. He's always been very kind and helpful. He listened when I talked to him and said things like, 'Nicholas, that's a good idea' 'Yes, I can see that', or 'Keep thinking, Nicholas – it's what you're good at'. Whereas all I ever heard from you was, 'Nicholas, you make me sick', 'Shut up and sit down', 'Who cares what you think?' and 'It's all your fault!' He was much cleverer than you, also. When he told you that he was overloaded with work, you believed him, didn't you? Of course you did. You hid – you literally put you hands over your ears whenever any truthful thoughts were in danger of permeating that thick skull of yours. As far as you were concerned, he was just another sycophantic relative of yours, or someone like Roger, who worshipped at your feet. John once spent an evening with you and Roger. You probably don't remember. 'He's the most self-obsessed man I've ever met,' he told his parents afterwards, referring to you. You were, he believed, a person who thought he could do anything he wanted with impunity. When he was listening to you talking about your greatest coup so far, he said he had a feeling of loathing in his stomach. He was merely a sounding board.

Describing you, Mark, Auntie Gwen said, 'He'd always had a smudge of bad inside him.' You fell on your head when you were young apparently, but Auntie Gwen didn't think that was the reason why you turned out the way you did. 'He was overindulged, it was as simple as that,' she said. 'My sister was a doctor and Jeremy was a businessman so Mark just arrived out of the blue,' she told Charlotte. 'He was most unexpected.' I was then adopted a few years later. I was supposed to be company for you, but I was more like your rag doll as it turned out. Regarding me, she simply told Charlotte that I was a naughty boy, and when she stuck out her chin and gave a big sigh Charlotte found it funny.

Both now realised that the plan was going to proceed. Auntie Gwen was a little worried at first. 'Is it a form of atavistic pleasure?' she'd asked. But once Charlotte had explained that it partly was, she then listened as Charlotte spoke. 'But Mark has to change, and this is the most likely outcome. We are convinced that there isn't an alternative,' she said. Thereupon Auntie Gwen fumbled in her bag and handed over the keys to your house, which had been given to her by John.

We now knew quite a lot about you. This is what we'd found out:

You are, undoubtedly, a very talented businessman. All your businesses, under their generic name, have performed above expectation. You have, it would seem, the trust of the banks. You are therefore able to borrow money on highly favourable terms. This means that you have an advantage over your rivals.

One year ago you gave yourself a large dividend. You split the amount between yourself and your wife, who lives in the Isle of Man, we believe. This means she, and therefore you, don't have to pay the normal rate of tax that exists on the mainland. You married her at university. It is now a marriage of convenience.

You have excellent advisors – the best that money can buy. You therefore invested some of your money in the house on the outskirts of Harrogate. It will be listed as your permanent place of residence. The house is modern and is complemented by delightful gardens to the front and rear. It is approached through an impressive gated entrance.

You feel that you are the king of your domain. You probably are. You therefore believe that you are untouchable. You surround yourself with sycophantic friends and family members. It is their job to protect and look after you. You are therefore delusional and are a dangerous man. You have lost the capacity to understand personal responsibility, and the importance of limits in your dealings with others.

Charlotte had had a difficult day, but she appreciated the help and support she'd received, and once she'd had a long soak in the bath and felt sufficiently recuperated, we walked into town. We needed large amounts of black and white poster paints, some blue, black and white oil paints, and pens and inks, brushes and craft knives, which we bought without thinking about what we were doing, and this was just as well because we argued all the way there, and even in the art shop, about which CD to buy. We planned on visiting Sandsend and Runswick Bay the next day.

'Marvin Gaye, buy something by Marvin Gaye, or if not him, at least something melodic,' I said. But the reply, when it came, was unexpected. 'If you think I'm spending good money on someone who is probably dead think again, sucker,' she said, and I wasn't quite sure if her tongue was in her cheek or not. Eventually we bought the *West Ryder Pauper Lunatic Asylum* CD by Kasabian. I didn't know why, but I'd enjoyed the argument. The outcome was a compromise apparently, even though this meant Charlotte had probably got her way.

Day Nine

'Charlotte, slice the tomatoes thinly,' I said. 'The cheese can be cut thicker when it melts, it will then ooze out at the edges.'

'Make sure the water has boiled, don't leave the teabag in too long, and add only a splash of milk – go on, tell me all that too! You really are too fussy. I don't know how I forget, but I do, it's true. I'm away a few days and I forget.'

'If a job needs doing, it needs doing well,' I said defensively. 'Have you seen my walking shoes anywhere?'

I'd already made up the picnic. I was feeling highly energetic and raring to go. Charlotte had tied her long ginger hair in a bun, her face looked relaxed – radiant almost – and her brown eyes had regained their glow. She was at her most impressive and beautiful. The weather forecast was quite good: sunshine and patchy cloud, with an odd shower later in the day.

This was how an almost perfect day began. We passed the North Yorkshire Railway steam train at Pickering station at barely nine o'clock, and were well and truly in the middle of the moors soon after. The scenery was spectacular. The countryside was, I would say, more open than the Yorkshire Dales, and we both felt a tremendous thrill of freedom, particularly as we hardly saw another car. The colours were different too, different shades of green and widespread splashes of mauve and purple. The moors were also full of dips and hollows, and we came across one or two picture-book streams. We stopped by the side of one of them to stretch our legs.

'We were born in the wrong decade, it's as simple as that,' Charlotte said. Her comments came out of the ether, but there was no surprise in that, I thought to myself, before replying as quickly as I was able.

'Our blind faith in technology will destroy us; there's no doubt about it. In the future machines will do everything for us. We'll lose the use of our legs and we'll slowly turn into jelly,' I said.

'I don't disagree, but I was thinking about music,' Charlotte said. 'I mean, all the best songs were written before we were born. Kasabian are good, but I'd much rather listen to a compilation album of music from the sixties and the seventies; maybe even a greatest-hit album of Cat Stevens, the Beatles, or even Jimi Hendrix.'

'Hmm,' I said. 'I'd add Rachmaninov to your list, maybe even Tchaikovsky, and I'd definitely include *The Lark Ascending*.'

'Nicholas, they're all too long,' Charlotte said, slightly aghast. 'The beauty of a pop song is that it only lasts for three minutes. Remember what Lewis Carroll said: "When I use a word, it means exactly what I want it to mean, neither more, nor less." If it can't be done in three minutes, it's too long!'

Well, what could I say to that? Personally I didn't think Rachmaninov's music was too long, but when Charlotte starts to build up steam there's no stopping her. By the time we reached Sandsend we'd talked about everything from women's pay in the market place to which three people you'd invite to a dinner party. I wouldn't tell you who one of Charlotte's guests would be, even if you were a friend. Which you're not, so you've got no chance. But it was embarrassing.

Sandsend is where the long stretch of sand from Whitby ends. Two very attractive streams enter the sea here. We sat on a bench watching children playing. Sandcastles were being made from wet gritty sand, and many of the children were walking to and fro to top up their buckets at the water's edge in order to fill up their moats. Buckets and spades littered the beach. Screams of laughter and shrieks of joy filled the air.

'Right,' said Charlotte, 'let's make a start.' As she rose to her feet I followed behind her and we set to work with our buckets and spades. Many of the adults stared in bewilderment as we started to dam the stream nearest the cliffs. We made two massive piles of sand at either side and collected some pebbles upstream. 'These will be our reinforced concrete,' I said.

Soon three children joined in the fun, and we all took pleasure at the sight of the walls of the dam converging. Charlotte was bossy, but full of fun, and soon a group of children had gathered to watch. 'It'll never work,' they whispered. 'The current's too strong,' they shouted. But it did work. And we all went wild running around and laughing. We then left the children to paddle in the dam behind, and saw more join in. Everyone was in their element. They added more sand and pebbles and kept the water at bay for who knows how long.

Runswick is at the bottom of a very steep hill. There are narrow paths and beautiful gardens between the houses there. The beach is crescent shaped and beautiful. Unfortunately the sun went behind a large black cloud just as we arrived, so we went to the pub for a drink. Then it started to rain and a gusty wind developed from nowhere. 'Basically,' I said, 'it's all about buying assets at the right time. Father was good at it. By the time Mark started to work with him, Father had developed and expanded into all kinds of home furnishings and bespoke furniture. It was a labour of love, I suppose, for them both.' And, for a time, I tried to present a fair assessment of your achievements. But it was difficult and Charlotte didn't appear too interested. She'd heard me talk about Father many times before, but his death still shook me, which is why I think I broached the subject. For me though, every time I think back to those days, I'm haunted by flashbacks of specific moments frozen in time. The most vivid being the look on my mother's face when I was suspended from school. That look and the way she held her fingers against her face always reminded me of the lady in that famous painting *The Scream*. Happily, Charlotte didn't want to be reminded of old wounds, so we went for a paddle in the sea, as by now it had stopped raining and the sun was shining once again.

It was as we started splashing each other and behaving like children once again that we stared into each other's eyes, and there was quite simply a look between us that hadn't been there before. This too was a moment that was frozen in time. Then we embraced and kissed. It was as simple as that. I pictured the scene from *Beauty and the Beast*. Yes I was the 'beast', and the beautiful theme song and all the words were lit up as brightly and as vividly in my mind as the Blackpool illuminations probably are in the minds of young children, after their first visit.

Afterwards we set off to Goathland for something to eat before slowly making our way back, and I kept reciting the words 'O frabjous day! Callooh! Callay!' – nonsense words from the Jabberwocky poem, over and over again to myself, as Katie Melua played. What happened later is, of course, none of your business, for our nearly perfect day ended perfectly.

Day Ten

Today and yesterday have been, quite simply, the two best days of our lives. Thus, I will remain silent on the details. Suffice to say, I can barely be bothered to write down these few words. Charlotte has gone out momentarily. Once Uncle Alf gives us a date, and it won't be long now, we will plan accordingly.

I know our particular journey is a strange one, but in one way at least we had something in common with that steam train yesterday. Shortly, we too will set off towards our own destination.

Just as the train was building up steam yesterday for its journey to Whitby, so you could say we will soon do likewise. Unfortunately we shall not be travelling through the North Yorkshire Moors. It's nearly time for action. The word play will soon cease.

Day Eleven

I awoke in a breathless panic. I put on some trousers and a shirt, and ran outside as quickly as I was able. The sky was mainly dark grey, as you'd expect, and in the moonlight I noticed the odd silver cloud, which changed the overall complexion. I breathed deeply as I looked up at the sky. This always helped, as did the relative coolness of the air at night. The relief was tangible. Sometimes an old star, like the one that always appears in the northern skies, helped too, but so did torrential rain, for that matter. The pattern was also the same: I'd clutch my stomach and wait for my breathing to steady; when it did, I realised, once again, that I wasn't going to die. I soon knew the cause of this panic attack, so I recovered quickly.

Panic attacks

Desperate people, wherever they are, will recognise these symptoms. These people will often be alone. If this is the case they may even feel that they are in outer space – no one can hear you scream out there! But it isn't always this way. Cumulative effects also wear vulnerable people down, so even a slight breeze can cause a twig to break, metaphorically speaking. In the middle of the night especially you may even see these people, when you are returning home from a party.

Regarding nightmares

When I was young I often awoke in a hot sweat. The nightmares I experienced often involved scenes from my everyday life, and they showed me how I was perceived by others. It was as if I were looking through a magic mirror so I saw myself as other people did. I was almost inside their heads.

   Sometimes the curtains lit up and people appeared on the plain part of the material, next to the patterns. It was a little like being in my own horror movie. People walked towards or away from me. Sometimes they became smaller as they approached me, and sometimes they became larger as they moved away. It was the opposite of what should happen. My brain was warping the images, like certain lenses do in a camera, but the effects were much more extreme. Father always looked exasperated and Auntie Mary always cackled like a witch: she had long, bony fingers and sometimes, in a certain light, she looked like a skeleton because her skin was so thin. She'd be pointing her fingers and screaming at me. She'd say things like, 'You are the Devil's child,' and everybody would then start nodding their heads in agreement. Often I'd be standing in a corner, with my hands on my head. I'd look angelic, I'd be wearing my old school uniform and my hair would be cut short. But out of the blue the scene would change dramatically. Suddenly a smile would appear on my face and my mouth would become as big as a dustbin – like a cartoon face, I suppose – and everyone would cower as they became first dismayed, and then terrified.

Another nightmare would concern Mother. She'd be sat in a chair in front of a hospital window. I was as usual outside, looking in, but she couldn't see me. She'd always be wearing her favourite flowered dress and there'd be an unread newspaper on her lap. But this time I'd have X-ray vision, so I can see the cancer eating away her insides, and it is always raining, so my outstretched arms are always sliding down the wet windowpane. They say you can only die once, but I died a hundred times or more when I was a teenager.

This nightmare was a regular occurrence then, but I still experience something similar, even now; but the whole scene has become much more vivid and colourful. The dots in the image have joined up and I can now see a slight smile on Mother's face. It is only a slight smile but it is definitely there, just as it is on the Mona Lisa. And I feel like I'm walking on air. This nightmare has become a simple dream.

The nightmare that caused the panic attack I'd just had was similar to the claustrophobia attacks I experienced in the mental hospital. The cause was different, even though the effect was very similar. I saw the indescribable look of terror on Charlotte's face after you'd raped her. The effect in fact resembled that of strobe lighting. Her passive face had turned into a screaming face in a series of separate movements. It was as though, after every blink of her eyes, it turned progressively into something resembling the face of a patient in a mental asylum. I therefore knew I had to find that tape or DVD right away.

Phase One

0300 hours

Charlotte was sleeping peacefully. There was a sweet and pleasant expression on her face. I picked up the keys without making a sound, and set off on the bike. I knew where your house was. I felt like I was a soldier going into battle. I felt a degree of apprehension, but also a sense of righteousness: I was going to do something that was going to hurt you. Free will exists, we all have a choice, and as I relived all those painful memories of my time with you – and as I passed the church on my right – I felt this wasn't even about right and wrong: it had gone beyond all of that. Montgomery Clift, the actor, once said that compromise is poison and worthless. I hope you and that fucker Roger understand this, I thought.

I knew that money buys location and privacy, so I wouldn't say I was surprised by the entrance to your house. I liked your iron gates because I liked heraldic decoration. The crests and shields made them look authentic, even authoritative, but I'd expected nothing less. I even rode along the short drive whistling quietly to myself.

My first impressions of your actual house were good. I liked the circular driveway, but when I started to look with a more reflective eye, I thought the whole place was more a status symbol than a home, sitting as it did, rather smugly, in an elevated position overlooking countryside devoid of river or stream. Its size was illusory too. The lawns were well tended and gave the house a pleasant open aspect, but they were too ordered for my taste and not actually that large. The all-weather tennis court was a nice addition, but there wasn't a swimming pool. The double garage and various outbuildings added no further aesthetic quality, but I don't suppose they were meant to. The security lights, though, showed off the house pleasantly enough at night, I suppose. All in all I thought it was a house that was cobbled together. It wasn't traditionally designed or exciting, as some modern buildings can be.

   The heavy wooden porch made the front of the house distinctive, and I was full of anticipation when I opened the door. Inside, the reception hall was well proportioned and had a nice airy feel, and I stood and looked around for a short while. The darkly stained oak flooring, plain walls, candle-style lights, large rug, and, most striking of all, original staircase and ornate balustrade created an immediate sense of arrival. Yes, it was an impressive room for greeting guests, and I could almost hear Father's endorsements ringing around too. 'When people feel at their ease, they open up and become more malleable,' he'd often said (sounding, albeit retrospectively, like one of my therapists). 'Beauty isn't in the eye of the beholder. Everybody recognises the innate quality of beautiful things. It's why they cost so much, after all.' He had a point, I realised. I was apprehensive a few moments ago, but wasn't now. Even I appreciated the elegance of this room.

   So I was pleased to see the lounge straight ahead. I still wanted this to be a speedy 'get in, and get the hell out' type of operation, and I was confident that this would be the case when I entered. The room was quite sparse and all the furniture was simply arranged. It didn't suit my taste, and I was relieved that there was no further stand-and-stare moment or delay! There'd be nice views, of course, if I cared to look, as the large doors opened onto the terrace, but I felt a sense of dread in this room: the atmosphere was unpleasant, it had, in fact, the presence of an unexploded bomb, and I was just glad that you weren't there to detonate it.

   I therefore headed straight towards your large LCD television (was it really fifty inches?), DVD recorder and speakers. I rifled through your collection of DVDs, but there was nothing of interest there. Then I opened up my bag and brought out my hammer. My eyes were certainly wide open at this stage, and every nerve in my body was tingling. I thought I'd been through the whole gamut of emotions in my short life, but this was a new experience for me and literally every bit of my body was tingling. I was still determined that we weren't going to knock down anything structural (even though I would have liked to), as I wanted destruction to the actual house to be avoided; but as this didn't apply to any objects in the house, I knelt directly above the wooden box in the corner, raised the hammer high, and brought it smashing down on the padlock with as much force as I could manage. It stood no chance. Then I opened up the box. Inside were a number of expensive camcorders, including the latest ones that can download pictures directly onto hard drives of computers, but I wasn't interested in them. What interested me was the DVD I'd unearthed. It was hidden underneath all the clutter. It even had Charlotte's name written on it! 'Knowing Me, Knowing You', the song by Abba, came to mind at this moment. I realised that I knew you as well as you knew yourself, and I felt sick.

The silence was painful. She was still slumped in the armchair when I returned from a walk through Valley Gardens. I had left her to her own thoughts and given her the time she needed to rediscover her composure. 'How long have you been gone?' she asked eventually. 'Not long,' I said. 'Did you know that tears taste of salt? It feels like ages,' she said. Then she sat up, gave a sigh and said, 'Thanks Nicholas, we both now know what needs to be done. No one can weep for ever.' She took a couple of steps forward and we embraced. Watching the DVD and coming to terms with the realisation of what we had done transformed her. It was remarkable. It had put much-needed iron in her soul.

The DVD was a complete recording of the rape, and Charlotte then went immediately to the post office to have it sent, by special delivery, to Uncle Alf. Her eyes were sparkling like little Catherine wheels in the light when she returned. Her response to the earlier unpleasantness was rapid and belligerent. I think we both felt we were ultimately being liberated, and Charlotte walked with a swagger that I couldn't replicate. It was still morning. I set to work and made bacon sandwiches for us both for breakfast, although it felt like high noon. I was walking on air.

So, Phase One was brought to a satisfactory conclusion.

The afternoon was uneventful. I spent it trying to understand the actual form your consumerism had taken, but tired of that pastime. Nihilism had to be avoided, so we walked into town around four. Charlotte looked at some of the beautiful dresses on display in the chic shops near the estate agents, and I couldn't decide which she'd look best in. It was either the black checked shirt and matching plain black trousers with purple sweater or the red dress with grey polka dots. I thought the large pearl necklace would suit her, as would the deep red high-heeled shoes; however, Charlotte was paying more attention to the chocolate-coloured dress, and I must admit I could see why: she'd look stunning in it. Charlotte told me afterwards that she saw a nice casual shirt I'd look good in. 'You'd look elegant and smooth, and stylish and distinguished,' she said, showing, I thought, a rather dry sense of humour.

In the electronic superstore I looked at some of the camcorders, but not having either a script or any actors meant that I wasn't that interested in them. I've never had much in common with my peers; as you know, the virtual-reality world has never really interested me either, so all the electronic gadgetry on display didn't hold my interest for long, and I soon became bored. The local newspaper briefly caught our eye (the main story was about a famous businessman who was moving to the local area), but it didn't interest us for long either. Instead we went for a drink, which became two or three. I stopped so that I'd be able complete this diary entry whilst being reasonably sober, but Charlotte had another couple of glasses of wine, and then she became intoxicated. She enjoyed forming ever larger triangles with as many glasses as she could find and started to form a pyramid with them. A psychologist might say she was subconsciously building one of nature's strongest structures so that she could knock it down to show how powerful she was, but I didn't think this was the case. In my view she was simply being 'playful'. I think she'd noticed that the men on the next table were watching her, so when these strangers volunteered to buy more drinks I wouldn't let them. There is only a very small gap between being friendly and being cruel, I thought at the time, and I still do.

On the way back home Charlotte was funny. It was only a distance of a mile, but it took us over an hour because Charlotte kept stopping to talk to me. As more and more things dawned on her, she kept saying things like, 'Wait a minute, if he thinks that is going to happen, then he's got another think coming,' and things like that.

So another eventful day had been and gone. I'd been awake for over eighteen hours. I'd been listening to *The Lark Ascending* by Vaughn Williams whilst finishing this entry, and I've been drinking just a drop of Macallam whisky, also. Uncle Alf bought me a bottle for my birthday. 'It'll do you no harm. If anything, it'll clear away the cobwebs,' he said. It's the only one I drink, because it is silky and smooth and not too harsh for my taste buds. Anyway *The Lark Ascending* is a beautiful piece of music and very evocative: it brings to mind wonderful pictures of the English countryside. Yorkshire has very beautiful countryside and the music had reminded me of the best day I'd ever had, in the North Yorkshire Moors once again. England's countryside, generally, of rolling hills, pretty villages, old barns and lovely rivers and streams is delightful. Nevertheless, the young, in my view, are witnessing the death of England as a country. And people like you, through your indifference, are partly to blame, in my view.

Day Twelve

I'd had a long sleep but woke up restless and agitated and I knew you were to blame. 'What's new about that?' you'd say. I felt slightly rejuvenated when Charlotte told me that Uncle Alf had rung. There was now an end in sight, but I still felt I was juggling too many balls inside my head. A little knowledge is a dangerous thing, but it is preferable to ignorance, I thought. Anyway, I was wondering why people do evil things. Perfectly normal people in peacetime, like bus drivers, for example, can turn into evil killers when there is a war, and I'd been trying to work out why I thought you were an evil man.

It seemed to me that men like you can't see their flaws. I realised that you probably didn't know where, or how, to look for them, but even if shown, I still thought you'd wear sunglasses if you tried. I also had to appreciate (I realised) that knowledge, or wisdom, cannot be based on personal experiences alone. The intellect has to be involved. If all your thinking is therefore based on the premise that you only do things that will produce successful personal outcomes, then this must surely mean that all your evaluation processes are entirely subjective. If this is so, I thought, it probably means that you will do almost anything to get you own way, because this is all that matters to you. And after pausing for breath I felt that there was a great deal of truth in my hypothesis, and I performed a little jig – thinking that a weight had been lifted off my shoulders. Bingo, I thought, I'd cracked it! But when I told Charlotte that I'd been trying to work out why some people do evil things, she groaned.

Anyway, back to the matter in hand. The ending we've planned for you is relatively straightforward; it is how our particular adventure ends that is easily more uncertain and hazardous, although first impressions would suggest otherwise, but we both hope you will consider *our* ending with some measure of even-handedness and intelligence, when the time comes, even though I personally think it unlikely. Remember you are only losing money. You may even realise that not everything in the world comes with a price. If you do decide to have us arrested, though, Uncle Alf will always have details of where we will be, and he will make this information available to you, without hesitation.

Rest assured, we will take great interest in your behaviour after these momentous events are concluded. Unfortunately, due to the author's wishes, I am reserving the right not to tell you how this ends for you, just yet. It would spoil the flow of the story, and would mean that we failed in one of our main objectives. I hope you will therefore continue to read this diary in the linear form presented; if you do, we feel sure it will enable you to reach a more holistic and rounded final decision.

Phase Two

Planning

You've probably been too busy to notice, but Uncle Alf has arranged for a lump sum to be given to me out of Father's estate. This has replaced the monthly allowance. I would have preferred it if I stopped receiving this money altogether, but this just isn't possible. Anyway, it is only a trifling matter – in the bigger family scheme of things. Nevertheless, I recognise the hypocrisy of my actions; I will, to some extent, be biting the hand that feeds me, and for this I am sincerely sorry.

Uncle Alf has also already made some travel arrangements for us. In September he has booked cheap flights to Athens, and cheap hostel accommodation on a couple of the Greek islands. 'It's a little honeymoon for you, now that you are lovers,' he said. 'It's a present from Auntie Gwen and me.' He is making arrangements, literally as I am writing this. He is making sure money is available to us, sending us open tickets for the trains in Europe, as well as guides to cheap hostel accommodation. Once we find our feet we will then try and find some work – in France to begin with, as Charlotte speaks French, but if unsuccessful, we'll go to Spain or anywhere really. We will always be in contact via emails.

He has also made arrangements for the tablets I need to be made available. He has taken out some form of travel insurance, and there shouldn't be a problem because the tablets are widely available (yes, other people DO get depressed!) – but here comes the surprise. Over a few months I will be trying to wean myself off them, and both Charlotte and I are optimistic about me being able to do this. Hopefully love may find a way! But if I am unsuccessful it will mean I will have to return to England. This would be the nightmare scenario, of course. Charlotte would be free to do what's best for her, with all our blessings, but what the realities would be for her are unclear, and really don't bear thinking about. *A Christmas Carol* by Charles Dickens is a wonderful story, but even we do not believe that your repentance would be total. But you never know; we may even be welcomed back!

The Calm Before the Storm

Charlotte didn't want anything alcoholic to drink, so during the afternoon we went for a walk. We walked three miles at least before sitting on a park bench beside the pine woods. It was drizzling, but warm. 'He's definitely someone who'll take a great deal of effort to look good,' she said. 'I bet he uses moisturiser on his skin; he'll use full hair and body shampoo, and those "new" crystals that are on the market. They remove dead skin, and help healing. I guarantee we'll find Mach 3 razors and a very expensive three-piece shaving set, as well.'

I nodded and didn't really disagree. Charlotte knew your looks were important to you. She also knew that your body was a source of your power. Fashionable clothes were important to you too, we realised. And this caused me some personal distress, I must say, as it made me think about my own personal hygiene, as my only luxury bathroom accessory was baby hair shampoo. And even then I'd been trying to experiment by not washing my hair regularly, to see if it would clean itself. Some experts say hair does, if left alone. But my hair always became too greasy for that. Talk about going from the sublime to the ridiculous, I thought. Maybe I should, I thought, take more interest in my own personal grooming after all – but it didn't take me long to realise that my looks weren't an issue to Charlotte. In fact, for me, looking like I did actually raised my personal esteem. Whenever I saw other lads wondering how on earth I could possibly be Charlotte's boyfriend – or friend, as I really was for a long time – I always felt ten feet tall. She was a glamorous young woman who wore modern and casual outfits, she had unblemished skin and good posture, and she was with ME.

But really I was more interested in your home items and the way you'd displayed them. These were important status symbols – expensive items all carefully selected to impress. This was, in my opinion, where your real power lay. I understood Charlotte's point perfectly, of course I did, and those issues concerning me, but there are many good-looking blokes around who are perfectly kind and unassuming, yet also take a great deal of pride over their appearance. No, you have the charm of a snake-oil salesman – it's the riches you surround yourself with that encourage people to trust and respect you. You are held in high esteem because of them. I'd already had a few glimpses of paintings on the wall downstairs, and of the porcelain bowls, ceramic stoneware bottles and figures scattered around on the contemporary furniture that was, if anything, on the sparse side, in the lounge – where there was, in my opinion, a lot of empty space – but I could see that this would stimulate levels of enquiry and people would listen to your elegant conversations concerning the importance of space, design and clutter. In other areas of the house, I thought you'd adopt a thematic approach anyway, and I was almost certain that each room would be designed differently, so I expected to see a very expensively assembled kitchen and at least one bedroom that was as sumptuous as your reception hall.

'Charlotte, let's wait and see,' I said as Charlotte was about to raise another issue about our operation tonight. 'Try not to think too much about it. Let's not let Mark take over our lives entirely,' I said as firmly as I felt I could. I could tell she was becoming very anxious. I wasn't. My life had been empty, you must remember, for so long, so I suppose I felt like a poker player playing for high stakes. Anyway, I'd already been in your house, and had already overcome that first hurdle, and that had helped. I therefore understood why Charlotte was feeling particularly apprehensive. But when I turned to look at her directly I realised she hadn't been paying attention to what I'd said, anyway. She was staring into space, and then her face suddenly lit up. She then stood up, and she was suddenly full of steely determination, clenching her fist as the thought took root.

'We can't afford that beautiful chocolate dress I so adored, but there are cheaper dresses that'll look almost as good,' she said. 'In fact, I know the one I want. It is black with a beautiful floral design in red, orange and green. I already have a maroon jumper that will go well with it. I need to buy some stay-in-place deep red lipstick, some foundation, mascara and eye shadow; I want my eyes to look sharply defined and wide. I want to look my best when we start tonight!' Then she hit the air with both her fists. That's my girl, I thought. What a girl and what a brilliant idea. 'I wish I'd thought of it,' I said, and I really meant it.

So the rest of the afternoon was comprised of shopping and loading up the car with everything that was required to enable Phase Three to proceed without any hitches. Charlotte even felt relaxed enough to go for a nap; nervous energy and adrenalin are a potent mixture, and she slept for well over an hour, whilst I listened to some opera – a compilation album of some of some of the most well-known pieces. Then Charlotte had a bath, and when she reappeared, at around six, she looked a million dollars.

We ordered two pizzas and ate them in relative silence. The moment had nearly arrived. It was, in fact, during this period of quiet contemplation that I first fully appreciated the enormity of what we were about to do. But we were eager and raring to go. The hardest part of the whole operation, I realised, would probably be writing tomorrow's diary entry. The night would stretch to the limit my ability to record events accurately. It would be, after all, a venture into the unknown. So I therefore made this silent pledge to you:

I will do my best to include all the relevant details, and I will try and present as full a picture of the proceedings as I possibly can. My aim is to make you feel that you were there with us: a ghostly presence who could only witness the proceedings, being unable to intervene.

Day Thirteen

Phase Three

Part one

We set off in the early evening, our plans involving creative enterprise the only thing on our minds, and I am pleased to tell you that our expectations were easily met. This may sound bizarre, but the night's events became more enjoyable than we'd anticipated. We didn't have any strict time limits, so the night produced some deeply satisfying outcomes.

It all started, as you'd expect, with a fair amount of trepidation. Charlotte became tense as we went in through the gated entrance and then very still. She gasped as we pulled up outside the house, but when she walked towards your front door I'd never seen a more glamorous intruder. The security lights made her ginger hair glisten, her face looked ghostly white, and her eyes were dark and luminous. The bright orange, green and red flowers in her dress were dazzling, set as they were against the black background, and I stood still and watched her for a moment, overcome by her beauty once again. But when she turned to face me, I regained my composure and opened the door. 'Onwards and upwards,' I said as I beckoned her in. 'After you,' Charlotte said, and we both set foot inside, side by side.

You must remember we'd already deactivated the burglar alarm, thanks to you-know-who. Your security measures otherwise, it has to be said, were perfectly adequate (locks on windows and anti-lift blocks on your patio doors, as I'd already noted previously).

'Nicholas, you were right, people would feel at ease straight away in this hall, it has a lovely open feel to it,' Charlotte said immediately upon seeing it.

We then intended on doing a quick tour, skimming and scanning all the rooms, but it was as we went into the room to our immediate right, the dining-room, that our eyes lit up. The black furniture and wallpaper, the large silver floor tiles, the crystal lamps and glasses, the black chandelier, the silver-plated tea service and cutlery, the golden lamps and fittings were all fabulous. The lime green string curtains were trendy and added to the modern feel of the room, but it was the life-size Terminator robot, holding a tea tray in his long robotic fingers, that practically blew us away. 'Oh my,' I whispered to myself. 'I knew there'd be surprises along the way, but this room is staggering. A servant Terminator! Mark obviously thinks he can do anything!' I said. Was I right about this, Mark? It was a magical touch and deserved respect.

'He's got some style, I'll give him that,' Charlotte said, in a tone of voice that echoed my thoughts.

We both felt that the Terminator had provided an element of sophistication, so, excited and taken aback by this development, we continued on our quick tour of the house, hoping for further inspiration to strike. And by the time we'd seen all the mannequins, clothes, books, children's toys and games, it had done. Soon we were on the right track and we knew exactly what we were going to do, especially as it was still warm and dry outside. First, though, Charlotte carried out a true act of destruction – she smashed the television screen and made your DVD recorder and camcorders inoperable with a hammer and a mallet, which she then took to all the DVDs we could find. 'That was the most cathartic thing I've ever done,' she said with a glint in her eye. 'The scumbag's dirty little games are now well and truly now over.'

We then set to work properly. First we carried all your mannequins downstairs. They were obviously dressed in your favourite clothes. We arranged them on the main lawn outside, and without looking too closely, I then placed all your other clothes in black bags. Charlotte, as you can imagine, didn't want to go anywhere near your underwear, so I was largely responsible for the removal of all your garments, but after initially feeling disinterested and indifferent, I must confess that I did then try on one or two of them; and whilst it was true to say that I liked some of the retro knitwear

(I'd been told by Charlotte many times that tone-on-tone was trendy), when I tried on a pair of your chinos, and other shirts and T-shirts in the same colour the look didn't suit me, so everything was more or less thrown into the bags from then on, and this pleased me enormously, I have to say.

Meanwhile, Charlotte had the more arduous task of carrying out all the books she could find in the whole house, and packing them into cardboard boxes (most of them, though, still remained packed in boxes and we carried these between us). She noticed, she told me, some classic fiction like *Middlemarch* and *Great Expectations*; historical books of key battles; the odd philosophical book (*Thus Spake Zarathustra* was one); lots of biographies of contemporary heroes; some modern fiction, surprisingly; books on sport; loads of old encyclopaedias and old children's annuals; sex books (of course); magazines, travel books, and so on. It was an eclectic collection.

Once we'd done this, we picked up all the pots and ornaments and placed them artfully outside on the lawns and under trees, on a selection of tables taken from all the rooms in the house. Then we removed some of the mixed-media paintings of local beauty spots, remote cottages and beautiful villages by the sea, and either hung them from the branches of the trees or placed them beside ornamental bushes. We then lit candles near them and the effect was already tremendous. Lastly we removed every item from the dining-room. It was the room nearest the front door, so this wasn't too difficult to do, especially as the Terminator also had little wheels attached for ease of movement. We placed everything as it'd been arranged in the room, but out on the front lawn, and near the mannequins, without too much effort. We then lit your thick red candles and opened a bottle of your expensive champagne from the wine cellar, sat back, took deep breaths and started to relax.

But suddenly a thought occurred to both of us at the same time, and it was fabulous! Without talking, we moved the mannequins into the background slightly, so that they looked like characters from Bob Fosse's musical *Sweet Charity* (a very underestimated film); then we fetched a tablecloth and placed it over the Terminator robot's arm and placed a book of riddles in his other hand, so he appeared to be reading it, and once we'd placed the sandwiches we'd brought on the dining-room table, along with glasses of orange squash, all the elements immediately came together. It was, of course, our madcap version of the Mad Hatter's tea party – the table had been laid out for far too many people, and the Mad Hatter would surely have approved of the book of riddles. (The sleeping dormouse also made an excellent weight for the newspapers.) *Alice's Adventures in Wonderland* and her adventures when she went through the looking glass were two of our favourite books, and we knew them off by heart. So we walked up to the table, glanced at each other and began.

'Have some wine,' Charlotte said in an encouraging tone, like the March Hare in the book. I was playing Alice, so I looked all around the table and saw nothing on it but orange squash. 'I don't see any wine,' I remarked, in a voice that sounded like I was reading the news. Trying hard not to laugh, Charlotte then said, 'Well, that's because there isn't any,' in a very squeaky voice that sounded more like a field mouse than a March Hare to me. And looking as bemused and infuriated as I was able to, I said firmly, 'Then it wasn't very civil of you to offer it, was it!' And soon we were laughing so much it hurt.

Later, we surveyed the scene, which, I can tell you, wouldn't have looked out of place on the moon. The air was still, the various lighting effects and the eclectic figures looked surreal, and their shadows produced an extraordinary sight. The champagne added to the effect, too. We were going to play some of your music, but preferred the night's silence. 'It was Uma Thurman in *Kill Bill* who said that she'd lacked mercy, compassion and forgiveness,' Charlotte said, after a long pause and much reflection. 'I think we do too. Even when I was on drugs I could never have imagined a scene like this,' she added, as she looked around and could scarcely take in the scene. 'I know,' I replied at last. 'I went down to Nidd Gorge when you were in Whitby – to try and work it all out in my head – and I think I did. I did yesterday too, if you remember? Mark thinks ideas to do with good and evil don't apply to him. What we are doing hasn't anything to do with goodness either, but some good will come out of it, as we both know. People make life impossible sometimes – I know I once made it impossible for everyone around me.'

Charlotte nodded and sipped at her champagne. 'It's just that this isn't a dream, it's the fact that it's really happening that scares me.'

So, Mark, once again you provoked a lively debate. Whilst thinking about last night's conversation, all I can say now about it now is this: don't drink alone with a Terminator in the night! I know Charlotte felt much better afterwards. The first night was only a promising start, she now realised.

Later on some of the creatures of the night appeared – first a hedgehog, and then a cat in the shadows. The cat's silhouetted curved body and outstretched tail defined it, but its cautiousness and alertness did too. Charlotte saw a fox walking down the side of the house. Its prickly fur and bushy tail was clearly visible, she said. Afterwards we both went inside and fell asleep for a couple of hours on your sofas. In the morning we split everything up into manageable portions and took your clothes and books to the charity shops before going home.

Day Fourteen

Phase Three

Part two

'When I was at school, I was, for a time, very popular with the boys,' Charlotte said. 'I was pretty and my breasts grew before a lot of the other girls' did. They were like weapons, as they gave me power; the pretty girls were jealous and the boys were always either looking at my chest or fooling around trying to impress me. I joined in their games and was a bit of a tomboy I suppose, as I liked being the centre of attention. The boys were very competitive and the biggest and strongest always fancied their chances of a quick grope. The girls were generally more passive but they loved being ogled at too, especially when their breasts grew,' she said and then paused. I think she was aware that I was looking at her breasts, which I was, so I looked into her eyes instead.

'Darwin is right about the law of the jungle,' she continued, 'and about the theory of evolution as well, probably. I could see that the strongest boys seemed to go out with the best-looking girls and vice versa. Personally, however, I believed cooperation was equally important and, like you, I probably believed chance mutations were too, by the way, so after a time the boys started to bore me. It seemed to me that they kept on living the same day over and over again! It might be okay for a lion to do this, but it wasn't a very attractive trait in a human being. So I stopped indulging them any longer, and I hung out instead with the quiet girls who went through school largely unnoticed.' Here she paused to consider, I think, what she was going to say next.

'Mark was interesting,' she went on whilst sighing, 'because he could talk about a lot of things. He knew he was good looking, and even when he wasn't with his mates he was a bit smug, but he could also be charming; he was good at English and he knew a lot, but he also seemed to know how to listen. However, I couldn't have been more wrong about that if I tried, could I? Looking back at it now, though, I suppose he was already developing into a Jekyll and Hyde character. His friends, and Roger in particular, had a lot to do with that, I'm sure. Anyway, getting to know him was the biggest mistake of my life.'

'I wasn't popular at school, full stop,' I admitted to her. 'I turned more than a few stomachs – but I knew Mark was a rat a long time before you did.' Charlotte nodded at this.

'My parents were terribly impressed by money,' Charlotte said. 'I'd say not being able to keep up with the neighbours, with new cars and so on, was their particular nightmare. Even though it was only, in actual fact, a polite acquaintance, they felt privileged to know your family, albeit in a very casual way. We lived near each other, basically – that was all – but they did see themselves as friends. Once your parents invited them to an art exhibition and they were so honoured when Mark and his dad greeted them there. They didn't stop talking about it for ages. So they liked the idea of Mark being seemingly friendly to me.' As she was fidgeting on her bottom at this point, I said, 'I know.' It was the only response I could think of.

I've included this conversation in its entirety because I hope it will make you squirm. After all, you were once held in high esteem. I'd asked her about yesterday's turn of events and Charlotte was very keen to offer a full embellishment. When she starts off in this way I can listen to her for ever. Her manner was therefore one of quiet confidence before we'd set off. It was lovely to see. We'd decided to walk to your house and to pick up some food shopping on the way, as we wanted to use your three-oven Aga. It was a chance that we both felt was too good to miss, as last night's activities had enhanced our aesthetic appreciation. We were going to use one of the ovens to make a Flemish-style beef casserole, with a bottle of real ale from your cellar, and the two electric hobs for mashed potatoes and green beans.

Your house has four beautifully designed rooms, I'm sorry to say. I'd underestimated you, once again. Your bedroom is the third such room and the kitchen the fourth, containing, as it did, the Aga, but also the 1950s-inspired kitchen units. We loved the chrome, the Bakelite handles, the beautiful badges and red knobs, and as for the Aga, well . . . words are hard to find: it is a serious piece of kit which no self-serving man with your means should be without. We didn't realise how energy efficient it was, or how sophisticated it was either, until we read about it in the book that must have come with it. Anyway, the whole kitchen looked simply adorable; even though it included the HMS *Victory* model you made and meticulously painted as a child, your painting-by-numbers *Laughing Cavalier*, and your vulgar collection of cheap clocks set in classic cars and red telephone boxes, each showing the time in one or other of the major cities of the world, which you checked weekly for their accuracy. 'Look after the seconds and the minutes will take care of themselves,' you said, if you remember. Your upstairs bedroom wasn't going to escape, but your kitchen certainly would. There was a limit to our hypocrisy. If we'd made use of a room and its belongings in some way, it was our intention not to paint or harm it gratuitously. We'd decided this last night when we placed your mixed-media paintings in your tool shed before we left. Sorry, I forgot to mention this earlier. The weather forecast is sunshine and just a few showers for the rest of the week, so all your other lovely things from the dining-room won't be harmed – well, not *too* much. Anyway, regarding the nature our actions, I think I can now say quite categorically that they won't be indiscriminate. We didn't think anybody had ever tattooed a house before – it was obviously up to Charlotte how she did it, of course – but I had a pretty good idea about the themes she'd use, even though I still wasn't sure what I'd do.

We arrived at about three and I started preparing the casserole, but it was whilst I was chopping the onions that I realised that my thoughts about your study, when I was a child, were prescient, so I asked Charlotte not to use that room as a base for her paints. I then watched her as she started planning out her version of Picasso's *Guernica* on the large wall in the hall, before stepping into your study, as I'd realised that it was almost identical to the one in London. It was a devastating discovery, and I even nearly cut off my little finger whilst contemplating this fact, but it was a room I decided I was going to break. In a way it was a shame. The storage units were sleek and good looking; the oak cabinets blended in very well and didn't look out of place at all. In fact, the room looked perfectly adequate; it was even innocuous to an untrained eye, but it wasn't now to me. These units were largely empty, but all that space would soon be much needed, and I realised that my feelings of unease were based on the fact that it was going to be your new operational headquarters, so it would be the room where all your evil plotting with Roger would take place once again.

Charlotte joined me when I was ready, and her timing was perfect. I was ready to use the sledgehammer for the first – and I hoped only – time. It was a big and heavy monster of a tool, so I made sure she was standing well clear when I raised it above my head and brought it crashing down on the storage units, and the noise was tremendous as each shelf, door, desktop and window cracked, buckled, broke and fell to the floor. Charlotte stood watching with delight. She was still initially, but she soon started bouncing up and down on the spot clapping, and her smile spread across her face, so it was lovely to see. And later, when I was exhausted and gulping for air, with arms that felt heavier than lead, I soon realised just how much could be done in one action-packed minute, so my concept of time changed there and then.

After recovering, I joined Charlotte back in the hall. She was listening to *Peter and the Wolf*, and I watched her as she filled in, with great sideward swings of her paintbrush, the outline of herself on the wall, with large dollops of black, grey and white paint. She was screaming and her hands were raised high, but when I looked carefully at what she had done I could clearly see that she'd also painted you. You looked like a bull with a human face and you had the largest erect penis I'd ever seen! Charlotte's image of herself was perched under you, so the scene was amazingly powerful, but she was so engrossed in her work that she hadn't noticed that I was standing close by, and she only turned when I said, 'Oh my!'

'What do you think?' she asked at last, when she took a step backwards to view her work.

'Picasso would be proud of you,' I said. 'It's also a philosophical reminder that acts of creativity are completely different from acts of destruction,' I added. But Charlotte merely smiled. She'd obviously still a lot on her mind, so I watched as she started painting great eyeballs which looked down at her from every conceivable angle, until the hall wall was full of black tears.

'I've seen bodies covered with tattoos but never a house. This is a house that is going to die of shame,' she said as she then proceeded to paint in some famous Harrogate buildings, in various shades of black, grey and white, with lots of people lying around whilst screaming and shouting. 'Terrible things don't just happen in wartime,' she said, 'or in gloomy places.'

It was true, I thought. Charlotte's words of wisdom once again had made me think. So why, I wondered, *do* so many people think that only bad things happen in big and gloomy cities, or during wars? And I felt sad because no one else could see what she had done. I was once too wild and free, so Charlotte's work meant something to me, but it represented a view of life others wouldn't wish to see.

The beef casserole was delicious. We'd used beef skirt rather than braising steak, and the added thyme, bay leaves and parsley combined with the beer, streaky bacon and onions made lovely gravy. Cooking it in the Aga, though, definitely improved the taste of the whole dish. A bottle of red wine from your cellar was a nice accompaniment, as well.

Afterwards, and whilst there was a pause in the conversation, I looked around and realised that even in the kitchen there was wooden furniture. We were sitting on wooden chairs, eating off a wooden table, and opposite was a wooden cabinet containing what looked to be lots of expensive plates. It seemed nearly all the rooms contained some wooden furniture at least. I wondered why this was. Then I pictured you outside looking in, and thought about this for a second or two. I said, 'Even if Mark could only see us in the kitchen, and nothing more, he'd have a fit. It would be his worst nightmare, that's for sure, at this moment in time anyway.'

Then Charlotte said, 'Everybody has nightmares, you know, it's not just you and me. Why, even the Vikings had nightmares!'

(Now Charlotte, as I'm sure you're now aware, is very capable of making surprising links. Who would have imagined, for example, a link between *Peter and the Wolf*, the painting of a bombing of a Spanish village, and her rape? So I couldn't say I thought it was totally unexpected. This was, after all one of Charlotte's wonderful qualities – she is a great lateral thinker. But it might still be surprising to you. So I've added this new paragraph, hoping that this slight pause in proceedings will help you realise just how special she is.)

'What kind of nightmares did they have then?' I asked her some moments later. And she reeled off three nightmares, just like that. The first was dying without a sword. This was relatively obvious, I thought. The second was realising you were a coward in battle. And the third was fabulous: whilst raping and pillaging in foreign lands, a Viking finds out that his wife has been having an affair every time he's away. 'Brilliant, absolutely brilliant,' I said, afterwards. 'You're my girl, you are definitely my girl.'

We then brought down most of the wonderful toys and games from upstairs. These included your train set, a Scalextric, an expensive medieval-style chess set, and your beautifully carved wooden backgammon set. We had one more visit to the Yorkshire Dales planned and knew of a place where these toys and games could be auctioned. We felt sure they'd fetch a good price. I wanted the proceeds to go to Oxfam, but Charlotte preferred the British Heart Foundation or Rape Crisis. It had definitely been a fruitful day and we felt slightly weary as we headed home. The 'Do Not Enter' sign outside the gate was a great idea, we thought as we walked past it. It contained serious warnings about the safety of the site.

Day Fifteen

I'd been tossing and turning throughout the whole night. It was clearly true that I needed a rest from writing about our adventures in your house, and two ideas entered my head simultaneously. I realised immediately that I was going to be quite insistent about them both. So I dressed quickly and went downstairs.

Charlotte told me she had been awoken quite early by a loud knock on the door. Roy the builder had called to see if I was available to do some tiling for him. Being the meticulous type, I particularly enjoyed tiling, and as you know, I'd appreciated the work previously, so Roy was probably expecting a very quick and affirmative 'Yes, he'll be ready immediately' response. Circumstances were delicate to say the least now, and when Charlotte, thinking quickly on her feet (a better sign of intelligence surely than all those ubiquitous paper qualifications) made some excuse or other and explained also that I wasn't able to work for the rest of the week, Roy left, she said, very perplexed and with his head bowed down. I'd forgotten all about Roy and was grateful to Charlotte for her quick thinking. I then outlined the plan I had for the day. I was determined and I gave it to her straight. 'Charlotte,' I said, 'it's a day for exorcising some ghosts. We are not going up to Mark's house today; we are going to York instead. We are going to fly close to the sun – we are going to grow bigger wings!'

Regarding York

The past – things you need to know

As Mother's family comes from York, it would be patronising of me to give you a historical perspective. Ever since studying in London she'd made it clear to us all that she was a Yorkshire girl at heart, so you probably know quite a lot about the place. My own experiences of the place are also quite positive. I moved into a bedsit in Acomb (an area of York) when I left Scarborough. It was my first taste of independence, and as John had also moved to York he used to pop in occasionally, just to make sure that I was okay. I still visited outpatients for the odd medical check-up; Scarborough wasn't far away either, so I felt at home in the city: help was all around, and all the signs were good.

I passed the time quite productively, and my favourite pastimes were going to the cinema and visiting the theatre. I saw, in particular, some really good plays, including one about mental health called *The Wonderful World of Dissocia*. It was miles better than *Equus*, in my opinion: I mean, how on earth can a psychotic young man pass on his condition, through transference, to his psychiatrist? Being psychotic can't be like having a cold, I thought. (It's obvious that I am no admirer of Freud, but I have brought it to your attention, merely hoping that you may think the point worthy of some consideration.)

I made some good acquaintances there also, and simply enjoyed living in a unique city. I'd walked around the whole city on the walls, a journey, I believe, of three miles. I'd climbed to the top of the minster and looked over the rooftops, and even went on a ghost walk at night. I think I could therefore say that I was intimately acquainted with the city. I'd read about the Civil War and even took part in a re-enactment near the racecourse. I fought on the Roundheads' side. It wasn't for any great ideological reasons, it was solely because they had a spare costume; even so, I think they were impressed by my performance. My death was dramatic, I thought.

Charlotte's experiences of York were the opposite of mine – in fact, they were horrific, and ever since I'd known her we'd avoided going there. If we were going to Scarborough, for example, we wouldn't even go on the ring road; we'd always take the northern route through Helmsley and Pickering. First, though, we went to my favourite café in Starbeck for bacon sandwiches. The saying up here is that breakfast is the most important meal of the day, but I also wanted to make sure that Charlotte was okay and was not too anxious, so there was a dual purpose to our visit.

She'd studied at university for six months and then dropped out. By then she was already taking drugs and was a heavy drinker and all her money was being used up in that way. She had also fallen out with her parents.

She was quiet but not seemingly overwhelmed in the café, so then we caught the train as planned. I could tell she appreciated that there was a good reason for going to York, and was okay to do so, especially as she wasn't alone. She spent the time on the train looking out the window in a reasonably relaxed state of contemplation, whereas I spent my time mulling over the stories she'd told me of her time there, and was angry! The details were sketchy because she'd been delirious a lot of the time, but some of her accounts had been very clear. Often, after drinking and taking drugs, she'd seen human heads on insects and animals, and things of that nature. She'd also told me about the indifference of the general public. 'They'd literally walk over you as they passed by,' she'd said, 'and just when you're trying to sit quietly or sleep, even during the day.' She'd apparently spent the nights in the courtyards in the snickelways.

Receiving help as a homeless person from personal support workers, caseworkers and social workers, and talking very intimately to them was also, generally, she said, very difficult, especially initially. She'd described it as like being naked without a fig leaf, and I could really empathise with this. Such help, however, probably saved her life. As did the help I eventually received. The difference here, of course, is the fact that Charlotte was completely blameless.

Snickelways, I hear you say – what are those? Well, they are simply old pathways between, under and next to houses, churches, markets and shops, in the centre of York. I bet most visitors wouldn't even know of their existence.

CAPSTAN AND CHALKIE SAVE THE DAY

The Present Day

The afternoon

We arrived at one. Charlotte appreciated my steely resolve, and we set off straight away. We headed to all the places she'd mentioned previously, so I could see them for myself. They were all situated very close to each other, next to the main roads and shops and underneath the minster's towering shadow. York's past isn't solely on display in its museums. We were experiencing parts of it all over again, at this very moment in time, in a very intimate and vivid way. I therefore knew what the term 'living history' really meant, I truly did.

'The first place I slept was just off Stonegate,' she said. Crikey, I thought, I would have seen you if I'd been a year older, as I started living in York when I was twenty and knew this snickelway reasonably well, as it was near a famous pub I used to go in, where the views of the chimneystacks and gables hadn't changed in over a hundred and fifty years. It was the place called the Coffee Yard. 'I slept there, in the yard, right under those steps,' she said. Yes, it was exactly as I remembered it, I thought. 'Sometimes I slept at a place called Tongue's Court, at the end of Hornpot Lane, which was next to a lovely church, or at Lady Peckett's Yard.' So we went to look at these places also. Neither of us spoke. I wanted to absorb as much as I could and I tried to picture myself in her position.

'The church is a beautiful place and must have provided some solace,' I said at last, 'and I can see too that these were places where you could escape the crowds, their glaring eyes and judgmental looks. I suppose you could even have pretended to be a tourist during the day, but the night-time must have been awful, even in the beginning.' I shuddered. Just thinking about Charlotte lying in these quite desolate places was an ordeal. The snickelways were all reasonably sheltered, but it was heartbreaking to think that Charlotte spent her nights there. Spending time in them during the day was bad enough. They were very quiet places where even respectable people looked as if they had evil intent in their souls as they passed through. But at night they would have been very frightening. Some of them were long and twisty and as thin as a finger. 'They are clearly places to travel through and not to stop,' I said.

'They were all close to the market, the library, Barley Hall and the Merchant Adventurers' Hall,' Charlotte said. 'The market traders had hearts of gold – they offered me bits of meat to eat, but I was never hungry. They also gave me hot cups of tea and coffee. I then either read during the day or pottered about in the beautiful churches and gardens. I was able to keep dry if it was raining, and as it was spring I never really felt cold. The Merchant Hall's garden especially was lovely – it was situated right by the River Foss, so I could relax and watch the swans there. In the beginning I even felt a strange sense of liberation because homeless people all looked the same, but this was before the visions started,' she said, and she shivered. At this moment the expression on her face hardened, and she looked at me for a long time after she had said this. She'd placed her hands on my shoulder and was a little ashamed, I think.

'Yes,' she then said, 'the nights were awful, and it wasn't long before I soon started to deteriorate. I became mad, I started seeing visions and I didn't care what happened to me. I felt like a piece of debris and as useless as an old bent and rusty nail. I left a trail of dust wherever I went. People would cross over to the other side of the road when they saw me coming. I think they felt sorry for me, but they were also angry when they saw people like me. I think I made them feel uncomfortable. Nevertheless, I was also lucky,' she said, 'because I still had a little money and I wasn't raped or beaten.'

I could tell, when she said this, that she still felt ashamed by her fall from grace. She had opened her heart once again and was nervously shifting her feet a little, but I knew she was relieved also. She knew that she could have fallen further. Her descriptions and my own experiences at this point reminded me a little of some of the scenes in the book *Last Exit to Brooklyn*, which was full of desolation, but I could also read her face so well and knew that this visit was becoming a beneficial one – for both of us. And I knew that our story was going to have a different ending. My own apprehensions concerning this visit had therefore lifted considerably. Charlotte was being so talkative. Then she started talking about Molly.

'Molly was a lot more unfortunate than me. We always met up at the end of the day, as you couldn't survive alone,' Charlotte said. 'We both knew that. Molly couldn't read, she was on drugs as well and she'd been homeless a lot longer that I had. I think she was beaten up on a few occasions, but she never talked about it. A lot of the homeless feel a certain shame. I know Molly always believed that it was her fault when bad things happened to her, as did I. To get hold of drugs she knew she'd sometimes have to humiliate herself too,' she said solemnly. 'When I first caught up with her, her teeth were already blackened, her skin was as coarse as pumice stone and I couldn't tell what colour her hair was due to the grease and dirt.'

She then talked about what happened next. 'I was lucky – it's as simple as that – how I found help was a lucky coincidence,' she said. 'I could have been in Selby for all I knew.' But I think there was a growing determination to kick the drug habit and luck really didn't have much to do with it. She'd apparently turned up at one of the hostels in York without knowing where she was and was immediately taken in. I think her subconscious memory had saved her, and that she'd found out about the hostel when she'd visited the library. 'I knew that Molly would qualify for emergency help and accommodation immediately as well,' Charlotte said, 'but when I tried to find her she'd disappeared off the face of the earth and I cried for ages afterwards. Even now I do, even though I know I wasn't well enough to help her at the time. She must have wondered where I'd gone when I didn't turn up at the usual places, but it was days before I became conscious of anything again, and a few weeks before I was on the road to any sort of recovery. And even now I sometimes miss taking drugs.'

The pain was still tangible, but she had started to appreciate that she wasn't responsible for Molly's plight. 'Charlotte, you had a duty of care to yourself,' I said, and she knew this to be true. Her facial expression had softened, and I knew a great weight had been lifted off both our shoulders. More than two hours had flown by. On our way back to the station she was even able to pass a homeless man drinking a cup of tea by a market stall without too much anxiety.

The day had therefore exceeded all expectation – so much so that decorum forbids me from continuing any further with the course of events. Except to say that Charlotte moved to Harrogate thanks partly to your father's money, and she was able to find work, which, as you know already, was down to fortuitous circumstances. Once independent, she cut her connections to your family entirely.

P.S. One further issue had been cleared up by our visit to York. We both now knew where the money from the auction of your toys and games was going.

Day Sixteen

Phase Three

Part three

'Alpha Male Needs To Hunt' – this was the headline I'd read in this morning's paper. The article explained why fox hunting, fishing, grouse shooting, deer stalking and rabbit culling should be allowed, and the most important reason was man's hierarchical status on the planet. Traditional ways of life in the countryside are important and need preserving, it said; there are conservational issues to consider as well, but the main reason why hunting should always be allowed is because of man's dominion over all other life forms on the planet. Religion has its part to play also. Animals don't have souls and therefore don't go to heaven. They therefore don't have rights.

This was all interesting stuff, I thought. I know I am very opinionated on most philosophical issues and debates, but as someone who'd never lived in the countryside, I possess an indifferent attitude to animal rights. Politically and philosophically I think human rights are important, but I have never considered the rights of animals to be *as* important. I don't like to see pets being harmed in anyway, I hope all livestock is killed humanely (I will always be a meat eater), but I still consider any ill treatment of people to be of primary concern.

Anyway, this article helped make the start to the day an interesting one. Once again my brain went into overdrive, and after much pondering I came to the conclusion that you'd be a person who'd hunt. It was an intriguing issue and it helped set the tone for the day. The article stated that hunting was also important as an outlet for man's aggression: it was better that males with high levels of testosterone killed animals rather than harm human beings! So, I had to find out if you went hunting. I was sure you'd now understand why this issue was important to me. There was one outbuilding I hadn't been into previously. I hadn't even considered breaking in to it, but now I did. It would also allow Charlotte to work independently for an hour or so.

We arrived at about one. This time Charlotte had brought with her a collection of oil paints, and as she set to work I immediately went to the cupboard under the stairs and pulled out the circuit breakers. There were labels above each one, so I could see which rooms were having their electricity supplies terminated. We were like ghosts in the machine now. I then turned off the water supply in the kitchen. It was purely a symbolic gesture, but

I felt I was taking away the house's power, and then I watched Charlotte as she started painting on the wall above the stairs next to a large window. As she circled around the hall in a predatory fashion, I noticed that there was diffused lighting all around her. It was an optical effect of some kind caused by the sun shining in, but she looked extraordinary. 'Fuck you,' she said, 'I'm not afraid of you any more.' And as she said this I'd never been more impressed. 'Nicholas,' she then said as she turned around to face me, 'I'm going to need some loose material for my mixed-media paintings. Some plaster will come in very handy.' So a game of British Bulldogs came into my mind.

We started by arranging the furniture in the living room, then we brought in from the garage the trampoline you'd kept since you were a boy, and we placed it by the end of the settee. It seemed perfectly feasible then to jump off it, swing on the chandelier directly above and land on the settee; and once I'd brought in some stepladders and placed these by the end of the trampoline, whilst Charlotte brought in every cushion she could find (she placed these in front of the settee, just in case we bounced off the settee awkwardly), we were both raring to go. Any concerns for our safety had suddenly eased. Charlotte started off. 'Watch this,' she said as she jumped off the ladder and onto the trampoline – and as she bounced high in the air she gave the ceiling a good whack whilst she swung on the chandelier. 'Wheeee!' she shouted, like a schoolgirl, before landing on the settee. She'd even managed to pull the chandelier away from the ceiling with one swing, so it hung limply by the electricity cable, as a load of plaster fell all over me. I was once again impressed. Already we had all the loose material she needed, but I took my turn. I performed a straightforward single loop in the tucked position.

The shed was locked, but once I'd forced my way inside I could see immediately that my suspicions were correct. You had certificates on the wall, a shotgun and expensive-looking fishing rod and tackle, wellington boots, walking boots, and waterproof clothing. All were neatly stored on brackets or hooks, or on tables and in baskets. The catalogue said that the fishing rod was made of carbon fibre and that your wellingtons cost £300. In a photograph you were standing beside a man of ruddy complexion who was holding up a large fish in front of a metallic-grey Range Rover. I was staggered. Possibilities appeared limitless to you, I thought, and I realised that underestimating you was becoming habitual. It was depressing in a way, but as it was our primary aim only to change the thought patterns and behaviour that were dangerous to others, I couldn't see why this hobby was any of our concern, so I left everything intact. I sat outside beside the Terminator robot and thought about these issues for a long time before heading back in to the house. I didn't talk to Charlotte about what I hadn't done, only because I knew she'd be keener about animal rights than me.

Anyway, describing the walls I'd left was impossible, once I saw the walls that were before me when I entered the house – Charlotte's unrestrained and indiscriminate actions had turned them into a strange vision of beauty. Disorganised confusion had produced something that wouldn't have looked out of place in an art gallery. I thought the images resembled an abstract impressionistic painting in a cubist style with hints of Lowry. The walls were an eclectic mix of paints and materials, in a range of different shapes, colours and textures, and as a whole, looked like a large face full of fragments and shards of glass. She had fully used a wide range of tools, and the theme of holes, gaps and cavities, linked to the style of placing the prepared materials and plaster onto a prepared surface, combined with an excellent rearrangement of mixed-media debris with her feet on the floor below, had produced an effect that was highly original. Your face looked like a giant gargoyle with its mouth wide open; and your tongue was sucking up all the matchstick people, who were being eaten alive as they marched towards you – powerless to resist.

The upstairs hall had been too modernist and sparse for my liking, and too reliant on natural materials to give depth and interest. It was elegant but too pared down and with too many quirky accessories. The sculptures were full of curves and seemed to be of people kneeling and lying, and the pottery was too bright and the colours too garish in my view, but I suppose the hall had been thoughtfully designed and some people would say it was stylish; but now it was striking and worthy of a Turner prize. 'You are a natural. You should do this for a living!' I said, and Charlotte looked at me as I said this, without moving a muscle. 'Once I realised that I wasn't being observed I felt free to do whatever I wanted,' she said calmly. 'My own anger liberated me from the fear and the boredom of my everyday existence, and because I didn't have to explain what I was doing to anyone either, I felt as free as a bird.'

This was thought-provoking stuff, and it was immediately clear to me that it was something else that needed to be considered. So I sat down and thought about what she had just said. 'It's true, being observed does change people's behaviour,' I said at last, and in a manner that made me sound as if I'd discovered a new star in the night sky. 'And I now know why I was once so horrible when I was young,' I added. 'It was because I could shock people; that's was why I told Miss Hillary to fuck off when I did.' Charlotte smiled, even though I couldn't really tell that she was smiling. She was covered from head to foot in paint and mixed-media materials. She was standing upright, motionless, and she looked like a statue. She looked like one of those characters you see on the street sometimes. They've covered themselves in paint, they don't move, and they look just like tin soldiers. You will have seen them, probably in Covent Garden.

'Remember,' she said soon afterwards, and once she'd cleared away some of the debris on her face, 'when I was raped I was also being observed. So when I was painting and using mixed-media materials, I felt I had been unleashed, so I was thrilled.' She was right again, I thought. And I could see why even happily married people need to preserve the thing inside them that is their essence. Every human being needs to understand this. Contemplation, as well as carrying out solitary pursuits – these are very important to all human beings, and I suddenly realised why men used to spend hours alone in sheds at the bottom of their gardens.

At about five o'clock we set off for home. So much that mattered had happened in the last few days, and it was not difficult to see how far we had both travelled. I think it was Alfred Hitchcock who once said that drama was life without the dull bits. I know we both concurred.

Our first serious argument

The evening had been a very pleasant one. We'd just drunk a bottle of your house red wine and I was talking about how I liked to ask questions that couldn't be answered with a yes or a no answer. It was all going reasonably well until I brought up the issue of animal rights. (Once I'd started, I then had to tell Charlotte about the newspaper report and what I'd been up to in your shed.) I started by saying that hunting foxes was a complex issue and that an opinion on the matter would have to reflect that. 'So you've not read the poem "*Hurt No Living Thing*" then,' Charlotte said, and I noticed that there seemed to be more than a fair share of indignation in her eyes, which were fixed as she stared straight ahead whilst sitting up. There was more than a twinge of bitterness in the tone of her voice, I thought also, but foolishly I pressed on regardless. You can always rely on me to do that, I thought afterwards. 'Well,' I said, 'it can't be wrong to swat a fly.' Charlotte looked at me, then she shook her head, and seemingly without pausing for breath said, 'We're not talking about flies, though, are we! A fox, like a cat, is a conscious animal.'

In retrospect I really wished I'd eased up here, but arguing until a conclusion was reached was a habit of mine and I said, 'Charlotte, a pig is much cleverer than a cat, yet I still eat bacon. In some cultures they eat dogs, but they wouldn't dream of eating a pig. Why, I would eat a cat if it had died naturally and I was starving, as would most people.' It was too late to redeem myself, of course. To Charlotte I had gone too far, and her eyes had misted over in disappointment. She was obviously alarmed and angry with me, I realised this, of course I did, but I was also a little bewildered myself by Charlotte's attitude, as I felt that it would have been wrong to keep my activities and views secret. Unfortunately I soon realised that it wasn't my reasoning that was wrong: I had made matters worse because I liked the sound of my own voice too much, and this was the real reason for Charlotte uneasiness. It was a bitter pill for me to swallow. If things were going to work out between us I knew I'd have to stop being so argumentative and so sure of myself.

Later

Charlotte seemed to be sleeping peacefully enough. It was after midnight. I'd not been able to sleep yet, so I'd come downstairs for a quick nightcap. Whilst writing this addendum I hoped I might find a solution to a very difficult problem of mine. If I didn't, I realised that I would always be by myself.

I've never wanted to be the same as everyone else. Too many men like to be in a gang. It seems they all like hierarchical structures too; but being different wasn't easy either. (Neither was finding the right balance, for that matter.) I certainly didn't want to be someone who finds fault with everything, and I knew that trying to find a middle way was a noble endeavour, even if it is one that might be too difficult to achieve. I've always been a person who thinks too much and feels too little. This is the main problem, I think. Certainly some of my personality traits remain, of course, but I don't think these are an issue or a cause for concern, as Charlotte accepts them. No, Charlotte, like most women, understands the needs of others. This is the real issue. She is civilised, but I'm not sure I am. Loving and caring for someone else is going to be the hardest thing of all, I realised.

Day Seventeen

Phase Three

Part four

The day started unusually. There was no surprise in that. I rubbed my eyes and squinted, a habit from when I was young, but my vision remained blurry. So I fumbled for my glasses and put them on. I remained disorientated for a few moments whilst I regained my bearings. As my focus returned I saw Charlotte walking towards me. She stopped when she was standing directly over me. She was barely a foot away. She was a vision of beauty and I was immediately taken aback. She was wearing a white silk blouse and a brown bouclé cardigan, skinny black trousers and black leather boots. On a scale from shameless to beautiful the look was beautiful but with a hint of restrained flamboyance. I'd say she looked as if she was going for lunch to a respectable restaurant in town with friends. So you could say I was confused and deeply worried. She had obviously made plans for the day that didn't include me.

My heart was racing as I sat up on the settee, and I was thinking for a terrible second or two that she was even angrier with me than I'd anticipated. She was giving me a quizzical look, I noticed, so I looked directly into her eyes and was enormously relieved, I can tell you, when I her mouth curled up and a slight smile developed. She'd been looking around, had seen the half-empty bottle of whisky lying sideways on the floor, noticed I was still dressed in yesterday's clothes, and was, I believe, giggling to herself. When she spoke, her voice was relaxed and intimate.

'I bet you've been beating yourself up again,' she said. 'Look, Nicholas, I'm not faultless either. Sometimes I'm not as sensitive as you think I am. Women can be cruel and heartless too, you know. Why, one day you could even turn into one of those conservative types – you already have the cardigans.' And she said this in such a matter-of-fact way that all I could do was nod my head and politely agree.

I hadn't considered this. Personally I didn't think her prediction for me was possible, but I was just relieved that things still seemed all right between us. It was true that all my therapy hadn't been in vain, I realised. Yes, it was true that I was caught in a dilemma, but I remained determined that you were going to pay for what you'd done. Anyway, it was too late to change direction now, I thought, even though my main concern remained, so I told her what I had written in the diary late last night. 'You'll soon learn,' she said. 'When you see my eyes mist over, or my voice change pitch, maybe as a car does when it changes gear, you'll soon know when to stop talking. Don't worry about it. After all, it's the differing nature of the intimacy that makes women different to men also – it's not *just* different chemicals in our bodies. When I wake up sometimes, I *still* want to rip Mark's arms and legs off.'

Her confession and her openness were a revelation to me. Receiving therapy had made me acutely aware of people's bodily expressions, facial movements and gestures. I'd learnt how they'd often described a person's mental activities, but they'd often driven me to search for hidden meanings that simply weren't there. Sometimes I knew I was in danger of becoming paranoid. Too much analysis and introspection was still something that had to be overcome. Once again it was raising its ugly head, and it had done all through the early hours, so I'd hardly slept.

'Today I've formulated a plan, and I'm just as determined to carry it out as you were the other day,' she said. She carried a slight note of warning in the tone of her voice, so, bearing in mind what had just been said, I listened carefully to her without interruption. She'd decided that she was going to paint the master bedrooms by herself today. 'Spend the day relaxing and I'll see you when I get back. I built up a head of steam up yesterday – one more day like that will do me the world of good,' she said, and because she'd suddenly spoken in such a quiet and nonchalant way, I simply acknowledged her with a polite smile. Five minutes later she'd gone.

Regarding Self-Awareness

Part One

What would have happened two weeks ago

An optician once told me that short-sighted people are more aware of any changes in their eyesight because their glasses enable them to see almost perfectly. 'There are a great many people who are not aware of any deterioration in their sight, because they have never seen the world clearly in the first place,' she'd said. It is the same with some people who have received therapy, I thought. Once you've been made more aware, it's like growing antennae: colours can appear brighter and everything seems very focused and sharp. Thereafter, it is very difficult to see the world in black and white or out of focus and blurry. I can certainly soften down my annoying habits and shut up from time to time, I realised, but this was only the tip of the iceberg. Living with Charlotte meant more fundamental changes were required. I knew I wouldn't be able to turn back the clock and pretend things that had happened hadn't.

This was going to have to be on trial-and-error on a daily basis. I didn't fully understand what would be involved. It was an exciting prospect, but also a frightening one, and I knew it would go a long way to determining whether I would successfully wean myself off my medication. My time with Charlotte was going to have to be a profound learning process. I fully understood now that she was more accepting of me than I appreciated, but I had to realise that she was just a normal human being who had her own faults and foibles, and her own particular ways of doing things. I had to find an inner peace within me, otherwise Charlotte would always be on tenterhooks, and I had to develop the ability to listen to Charlotte in a more meaningful way.

Part Two

What actually happened – two hours ago

Loving someone was already making me feel like I knew absolutely nothing about anything. Thinking through what Charlotte had said was exhilarating, and I was soon incandescent. I was suddenly on cloud nine and couldn't sit still. It wasn't a claustrophobia attack, but every nerve in my body was suddenly on fire. These sensations had arisen from somewhere inside of me, and then spread instantaneously to every part of my body. I'd never felt anything quite like it before, and I was at a loss as to what to do. It was completely overwhelming, so I ran out of the house, and before I knew it I was looking at all the gravestones in the nearby church. I don't know why I went there, but in the graveyard, in a resting place for the dead, I'd never felt more alive in my life. I had attained a harmony in my body and soul and a beauty of spirit that was impossible to describe in words. I was utterly and completely smitten. I still didn't understand what would happen next, but I wasn't afraid any more.

The afternoon

It took a while, but I managed to find some equilibrium and breathing became easier. Lying on the settee and staring at the ceiling was therapeutic and my thinking became more recognisable and ordered. I realised, probably for the first time, that your enormous reach and influence over my life had ended. You'd ceased to matter in the way you once did. It was as simple as that.

It was then, whilst I was making myself a cup of tea, that a story I'd once written came into my head to reinforce this view. (Does the brain store every experience as a memory? When a certain chemical is produced, I wondered, does it then release it into the consciousness?) Anyway, I'd recalled a story I'd once written about you. It was a football analogy, and it was quite clever because it described the lengths I'd knew you'd go to if you felt your dominant position amongst your friends was ever under threat in any way. In it I imagined that you and one of your best friends had been invited for a trial with Arsenal. Mike was a brilliant prospect, whereas you weren't, so you were worried. Having a friend who might become a professional football player would be too much to bear. So, my story went something like this:

'Aaaahhhh!' After Mark's mis-timed tackle everyone heard the terrible crack as his leg almost snapped in two, and Mike's heart-wrenching scream as he plunged down to the ground. Then everyone went silent and watched in horror as he writhed about in agony. Mark stood beside him looking down, and only from a certain angle could a deliberately concealed smile be noticed. Everybody else was running in all directions: a few to ring for an ambulance, some in search of blankets to keep him warm, a lot to the toilets to be sick – whilst the rest seemed to be running around in circles, a little like Sergeant Jones did in Dad's Army, *because they didn't know what else to do.*

Later in hospital, Mike would keep saying to himself, over and over again, 'Football was your whole world – your whole world.' He knew he was doomed; his career was over before it had begun. He knew that once people's sympathy had run its course, everybody would forget all about him, also.

The next few years contained moments when he managed to pull himself together and stop feeling sorry for himself, but his decline was ultimately unstoppable. Barely recognisable now, he was observed by a dazed jogger in the park one pleasant Sunday morning screaming uncontrollably whilst reading the newspaper, perched on a park bench with his left leg dangling limply. When asked if he was all right, all Mike could do was continue screaming and point to the back page, and the main story, which began: 'TWO major triumphs in successive weeks. Is this the greatest Arsenal team ever? The present crop of brilliant youngsters have matured and are now playing to their full potential. There are no limits to what they can achieve.'

It was prescient, I thought. I was like Mike, of course (but without the talent). I knew you'd exert the power you had over me to its full effect. Until I started writing this diary, in actual fact, I always felt (using a chess analogy this time) that I was a pawn and you were the king. But I didn't any longer. It was devastating. I was not only in love, I wasn't frightened any more, or even angry. All the feelings of fear and anger that had always hung over me and been around me for so many years had simply vanished. I started to cry. Tears of joy started trickling down my cheeks.

Charlotte rang at about four. She was full of the joys of spring. 'I hope you don't mind,' she said, 'but I may be here for a while longer. I've painted my version of the Battle of Hastings, as shown on the Bayeux Tapestry, in a dizzying array of styles and formats, all over his bedroom walls. He's been kicking arses for so long; so one scene shows him sitting with Roger on a throne, and they are touching two shrines as they swear their allegiance to each other. Some people are acclaiming them, but many are afraid. These people are therefore standing with bowed heads and with terror in their eyes. In another scene I've painted myself as Goliath. I'm naked and with a sword above my head. Just before bringing it down on Mark with a downward stabbing movement, I'm saying, 'Look at me, I am the victor and your schizophrenic obsessions are over!'

I listened to her without interruption, wide-eyed, as she told me all this, whilst I wondered what was to come next. 'I've nearly finished,' she said, but then in a more refined tone of voice she added, 'but I intend adding some graffiti elsewhere, probably in the style of Jason Pollack, as I think drips of paint dropped onto the floor will provide a suitable contrast and add to the overall effect. After all,' she said, 'the sign of success is when the overall effect is greater than the sum of its parts.'

There was no doubt about it – we both thought that your main bedroom was the room that contained more personal embellishments than any other. It was therefore the room that surprised us the least, as it matched your personality, so even the translucent window shades added to our revulsion. We also thought the almost infinite variety of condoms, vibrators and sex toys (I never knew so many existed) summed up everything about you also. I once heard someone say, 'He was kindness personified' – but it was this room that indicated (to us both) that, in your case, an opposite characteristic applied. (But as I've already said that you had the manner of a snake-oil salesman, this description will have to suffice, even though it is quite clearly short of the mark).

Anyway, she finished by telling me that she still intended staying for another couple of hours. 'Tomorrow,' Charlotte said, 'you can see what I've accomplished when we pick up Mark's toys and games on our way to the Yorkshire Dales. Maybe we should consider camping or staying in a B and B over night – we won't get another chance, and it would be a shame to waste the opportunity.'

'I agree,' I said. 'There's also no need to hurry back on my account either. I've had a very relaxing day!'

Charlotte didn't come home until nine. I was at a loss as to what she'd been up to. 'I finished by sitting and contemplating, and two hours passed in a flash,' she said, and I was immediately struck by her very calm and gentle manner as she walked in. She possessed as ease of movement and a stillness of body that wouldn't have looked out of place in a dance studio, and when she came down after a bath, in her nightie and dressing gown, she looked like a princess who'd been kissed by too many princes and had simply spent the day pondering over which one of them to marry. She sat serenely in the chair opposite, her twinkling eyes and slight smile merely suggesting satisfaction with her day's work. 'I had the strangest feeling as I left and walked away,' she said as she looked at me through the steam that rose up from her hot chocolate. 'I felt a shudder as the whole house seemed to be collapsing in on itself in despair. But I didn't look back,' she said, 'because I knew it was folding in on itself, like buildings do in special-effect movies.'

Later, when she asked me about my day, I didn't go into any details. I simply told her that I loved her. She smiled and then sat next to me. We watched the television for a bit without saying anything more, and it is very difficult for me to give you an adequate description of how I felt. I am sorry.

I've also completely run out of time.

Conversation with a Literary Agent

'Hello.'

Silence

'Anyway, one of the things I try to do next is to compare and contrast two different childhoods – Nicholas's and Emily's – and in this part of the book, I hope I am able to show how important early experiences are. Emily's childhood is almost perfect, for example, so she has a good chance at finding happiness when she grows up. Nicholas hasn't. And even though Nicholas overcomes some of his early setbacks, and tries to become a virtuous man, his thinking still remained muddled – he can't change that! But being someone, as you know, who isn't virtuous, I liked the idea of inventing someone who is! So I enjoyed writing the diary. I know Nicholas was writing it for a purpose; nevertheless, he never felt he wasn't being watched, and this is ironic, I think. Too many of us behave as if we are being watched. This might be because we believe in God, but maybe we also do it because our minds are structured in this way. So what do I say to these people? I say look inwards – that is the place to start. And don't airbrush out any inconvenient truths, either, when you do. Never be a stranger in your own body. Unmask yourselves, I therefore say, and come to terms with who you are. I realise, of course, that in my case this means the ends justify the means, but it doesn't have to be the same for everybody. There will be pitfalls, but once you've started on your journey you too will find that there can be no turning back.'

Silence.

'The second half of the book also contrasts living in a small town with living in a big city like Bradford. Bradford, by the way, was once one of the richest cities in the whole world. Can you believe that! So I am convinced, though, that thinking about it, and what has happened to the city in recent years, will turn you into a better person. So please read this part of the book with an open mind. If you do, I think you might even enjoy the rest of the book. I've also read through these chapters, and found they were in need of a little tidying up. I also had to correct some elementary mistakes, so feel free to correct any further errors, but I'm sure most of the proofreading has been done for you now. I'd worry if I thought there were still serious errors; after all, in a panic championship you can rest assured that I'd win. Anyway, I might keep checking up on you, just to make sure that you're not messing me about, so don't be surprised if I ask you a few questions, as I'm sure you never read this far before.'

Regards. Joe

A Race Against Time

Capstan liked to encourage creative endeavour in his children. Earlier they'd all spent the day in Wharfedale. He watched them with pride as they explored and examined the world around them. It was as natural to them as breathing, and their enthusiasm knew no bounds. They were always well behaved and never needed to be told off. Whether observing crayfish in the gently rippling water at the river's edges, identifying trees in woods, experiencing the quietness of an abbey or the joy of paddling in the river, drawing pictures, asking questions, sitting in massive stone seats, or even filling in booklets, they had the ability to fashion appropriate responses and become almost spiritually uplifted. They'd even join in a game of rounders with lots of other children until all of the parents, who previously stood around the fringes looking awkward, joined in also, and remembered what it was like to be young again.

They'd started at Grassington, the main village of Wharfe. First they had a general look about, and then, as they walked through Grass Woods and beside the river, long shadows and strange shapes emerged and then disappeared as they walked past them. The drystone walls were cold, hard and dull, and turned the field into irregular shapes, whilst the barns sat in splendid isolation. The contrast between the grass, walls, sky and shadows made the views spectacular.

Afterwards they drove down to Burnsall – a picturesque village where the river sweeps in a gentle majestic meander – for a picnic. They watched as dogs chased sticks hither and thither and two boys turn simple padding into a water-splashing contest as their bemused parents looked on. Capstan then watched as one overweight and rather firm parent couldn't stand it any longer. He went up to the two children and said, much to Capstan's amusement, 'Enough is enough – just look at you both, you're soaked.

I don't know who's dafter, the two of you or the dogs!' This left the two boys bemused and dumbfounded for a while, but once they'd rediscovered their playfulness, they soon started arguing between themselves as who was the daftest, leaving their mother to look on in slight embarrassment, the father to turn red with rage, and Capstan to giggle slightly. The mother knew they were merely letting off steam – it was a nice day and no harm was being done – whereas Capstan thought the contest between the boys was irrelevant: the father had won – and at a canter.

A little further down the stream they walked to the Strid. Here, great boulders jut out and constrict the river to a very narrow channel so the water is deep and dangerous. It whirls around the underwater rocks, and they watched the water as it gushed and foamed. Natasha stood behind Capstan and peered out from behind him. 'I'm scared,' she said. 'It wants to swallow me up.' And they laughed because that was exactly what it wanted to do. Emily remembered being frightened herself when she was younger, especially at How Stean Gorge, a similar place in Nidderdale, where witnessing her younger sister's fear made her feel, for a time, more grown up then she really was, though she was soon running around in a carefree way once again.

Bolton Abbey was next on the agenda, and just a whisper away as the crow flies. Here they tried to work out which buildings were which, but it turned cold under the curved arches and stone walls so the two girls played hide-and-seek, whilst Capstan and his wife sat beside the river, which was now reasonably placid once again. They then finished off the day out with an ice cream, before going home. Later, Capstan even found time to go for a bike ride with Emily, and then made, as you know, a chocolate cake with his youngest.

So it was difficult to put into words exactly what he was feeling as he read Nicholas's diary. It too was filled with creative endeavour, and he'd become engrossed in it. An hour had flown by – in fact, reading it had made it difficult to believe that he was now dead. In some ways it was heart-rending and sad, especially when it delved into the murky depths of his past and his brother's character, but in another way it was fresh and alive, as he tried to fill his life with hope and optimism. He knew he found it difficult to step back and read it objectively as a detective should. So at one point he thought it was just as well he'd remained in uniform, but then later, and on the other hand, he thought that reading the whole diary had given him a more complete picture of Nicholas's life, and, more importantly, of his state of mind. On reflection, he knew he'd done the right thing.

Nicholas obviously had had great regrets in his short life; he'd clearly tried to correct them, but was doomed, it appeared, because he'd been stigmatised and was considered mad. Some children (those who answered questions wrong) once had to wear dunces' hats in a similar way, he thought. So Capstan realised that there was no way back for Nicholas, just as there probably wasn't for all those children who had to wear those hats. His mental-health issues were weaknesses Mark also exploited, and he used them as a soldier would once have used his gun against a warrior who only had a spear, and this was the thing that probably concerned Capstan the most. It had obviously gone wrong for him as a child, but he'd never been given a chance to recover, even though others in the family may have partly blamed him for his mother's death. Everybody should be given a second chance though, Capstan felt. As Jesus once said, 'Let he who is without sin cast the first stone.' So what did Mark do? Yes, that's right – he threw boulders at him. And although Uncle Alf came to the rescue like a knight in shining armour, the damage had been done. His young life was full of too many bad memories from then onwards.

Nicholas wasn't lacking in empathy for the plight of others either. His problem was quite the reverse, in fact, and he marvelled at how he'd merged fact and opinion together to create something that conveyed his true views, beliefs and feelings. Too many of us think too much and feel too little, he felt, but Nicholas probably cared too much for others, partly because he cared too little for himself. It really did appear that he empathised far too much, and Capstan thought that this as much as anything else may have crippled him. He was gifted, and he started to wonder if there were thousands of young people who were like him, who were living wasted lives in bedsits, without decent prospects. Were they, at this very moment, feeling that they were too helpless to be helped? Anyway, in one respect he'd seen a young man emerge, but that young man was now dead, and he still wasn't sure what action to take next either. And time was running out.

But then he put on his thinking cap, and he was suddenly able to see the problem in a different way. It concerned Mark's mental health. This was the real issue, he realised. It was a seismic shift and it created a whole new perspective, because he found that when he put himself in Mark's position, and focused on the events through his eyes, he was able to spot possible causal links, using the clues that had been there all along. So soon he'd formed a hypothesis, and if he was correct there would be a dramatic and very simple ending to the night's events.

He remembered an old film he'd seen which when it first came out caused some outrage. It was about a man who murdered women with a knife that was stuck on the end of his film camera. Basically he recorded on film the actual murder. Capstan believed he may also even have used a curved mirror of some kind, so that the victims saw their own distorted images in the mirror as they were killed. But murdering women didn't satisfy this evil man's warped imagination enough; he added an extra dimension for his own gratification, as he wanted to see the fear the women experienced over and over again. Animals kill to eat; he was killing for pleasure and then watching these gruesome events over and over again. The film was therefore an investigation into the nature of evil.

Mark seemed to enjoy tormenting Nicholas in a variety of different ways. It also gave him a buzz, Capstan realised, so he was convinced that Mark had tied Nicholas to the tree and that Roger had filmed the event on a video camera. And as Roger was at this minute travelling up from London, he wondered why.

It was, after all, a relatively simple procedure to secure premises that had been broken in to. Maybe filming their own version of *Lord of the Flies* was a precursor to a later more serious incident, he therefore wondered. Charlotte was convinced that she was being filmed while she was being raped, and Nicholas thought he was being filmed too, even though he was seeing visions at the time. Mark also reacted very strongly to this, as shortly afterwards Nicholas was sent to a mental hospital (and then into the arms of Uncle Alf and Auntie Gwen, who, by the way, are convinced, albeit in a diary that mixes facts and fantasy unquestioningly, that Mark is a bad 'un). It is, though, a defining moment in the lives of nearly everyone concerned; and even though the conversation in Scarborough between Auntie Gwen and Charlotte never happened, it is clear that Nicholas wanted some type of revenge, as both Charlotte and himself have suffered a great deal, so he created a situation where the two of them could get what they wanted.

Capstan at this point realised that the imagination is a powerful thing. He himself remembered being asked once at a dinner party if he'd ever wanted to kill someone – for example, someone who was in his way, or someone he hated – and he replied by saying that he'd never actually wanted to kill anybody, but that he often imagined smashing up things that belonged to them. He told them it was a way of trying to get to sleep! Anyway, thank God people aren't arrested for having evil thoughts, he thought, and for a few seconds he seriously wondered if he was capable of killing anyone. But he didn't dwell too long on this issue, because he knew that if someone harmed his family, even *he* might not be responsible for his actions.

Mark owned stunning home and cinema recording equipment; he also had a specially designed room. This was a fact. He also clearly remembered John saying in the diary that he was asked if he'd design an extension to the house. Mark had told him that it had to include a room for his film recording equipment, and Nicholas mentioned that some idiosyncratic features also figured in his plans. Capstan didn't know exactly how much of this was true. It was true that John was an architect and that John would have seen Nicholas a lot when he lived in York, but John wouldn't want to say too much to Nicholas about these plans as he'd be aware of how sore the wounds still were. He'd be careful what he said, or didn't say. Kindness would demand such a response. Of this he was sure. However, Capstan was certain John had been asked by Mark about designing an extension for him, and he was also sure that John despised Mark, so putting all the pieces together, he deduced the following:

He knew that Mark had definitely had another builder, or some other suitably discreet person he knew, alter the layout upstairs, and that the home cinema room had once been a fourth bedroom. This was a fact. Building work of some description had therefore taken place. A new layout meant a bathroom had been moved or removed, so walls had been knocked down or added, and putting himself this time in Mark's position soon enabled him to realise that some idiosyncratic features had almost certainly been added. As he recalled further details in the diary, he also realised that Nicholas had, albeit inadvertently, left behind a clue in his letter. When describing his feelings he said he often felt like he was living on the other side of a mirror, and this meant he felt he was looking at the world from a completely different perspective. On reflection, Capstan then immediately realised that this was precisely what Mark had done, but in a sordid and much more real way!

He'd moved his master bedroom across the landing and made it look stunning, whilst making the bedroom at the front of the house into a cinema room, that was much plainer and therefore far less memorable on the eye. He'd put in a false wall between the two rooms, thus creating a space where someone, almost certainly Roger, could film the events taking place. He was now certain that there was a hidden mirror situated behind those innocuous wooden wardrobes he'd seen on his tour of inspection whilst waiting for forensics to arrive with Chalkie. The mirror would of course be a two-way mirror, and it would be incorporated inside a frame that was on a hinge, so it would therefore open and close like a door. He prayed that he was right: if he was, he even promised himself that he'd recite the Jabberwocky poem that Nicholas sang whilst travelling back from Runswick Bay.

In the meantime, Chalkie had been very busy also, and although his more grounded and hands-on approach wasn't providing successful this time, he'd managed to accomplish a great deal in a short time. What he'd done was actually a little like that popular daytime television programme where a hundred designers, decorators and craftsmen of all kinds do up a house in an hour, while the owner is out shopping.

First, he'd told a mate on duty about the situation, and when his mate rang back to tell him that there were long tailbacks on the M1, so they had maybe an extra hour at most, he'd then told Capstan, and they'd both jumped for joy. Forensics were also about to leave when he arrived, so, using his boyish charms and tongue-in-cheek popularity, he'd managed to persuade a couple of them to stay on, and once he'd done that, he then rang his best mate from the station.

'Ed, what are you up to?' he'd asked.

'I was just about to make love to my wife,' his mate replied. 'Then I thought we'd have a—'

'Look, we need you; we haven't got much time left. I haven't even got time to explain – you're the only one who might be able to find anything dodgy or illegal on some computer hard drives – Ed, this fella is a piece of work,' he said.

Ed arrived within ten minutes. The two guys from forensics were already searching for clues, so he started trawling through Mark Torch's computer in the study, and even though Chalkie didn't think they'd find anything, at least they were trying, so the atmosphere was tense. Ed's head in particular was soon nodding like a pigeon's head does when it is picking up crumbs thrown to it on a pavement, as he altered between pressing buttons with his fingers and looking up at the screen, so Chalkie went into Mark's bedroom and started looking for clues, especially a DVD, whilst wearing gloves.

Chalkie was taken aback, it was fair to say, when he looked around with a discerning eye for the first time. He'd not really paid much attention before, and the room surpassed all expectations. The colour scheme was black, red and silver. It was undoubtedly unusual, but was nevertheless full of life and warmth, so it made Chalkie feel a bit sick inside as he took off his navy shoes. He didn't want to make any marks on the rich woollen carpet as he started searching through the silver wardrobes, cabinets, chest of drawers and dressing tables. Unfortunately, he found nothing remotely suspicious. Mark's taste in clothes consisted of the traditional and expensive, and the modern, trendy and expensive; so there was nothing surprising there. There weren't even any sex toys, condoms, or anything of that nature to be found, or even a television, for God's sake! It was in fact a very sophisticated room, and one where he probably drank champagne before and after making love to all the women he'd charmed, thought Chalkie, and his heart sank. Faint heart never won fair lady, it was true, but why, he wondered, did powerful men always seem to succeed? It was all Darwin's fault, he felt.

Anyway, once he'd looked under the bed and mattresses for good measure and found nothing, he looked in the other bedrooms, but as there wasn't anything that seemed to suggest further inspections would prove worthwhile, he then went to see if forensics and Ed had found anything. 'Sorry,' said Ed, 'I've found nothing illegal. I can keep looking, but I don't think anything will turn up.'

'Thanks,' replied Chalkie. 'You may as well stop then. I'll explain everything later. By the way, I think I should tell you that Carol wants a new kitchen. It'll only be a matter of time before Janice finds out you know,' he added as cheerfully as he could muster. He'd expected to find nothing, but was nevertheless disappointed with the result. Forensics also had been busy. They had everything to convict Nicholas of illegal entry and serious vandalism, but couldn't find anything to incriminate Mark. So once they'd left, Chalkie sat back and waited for Capstan's call.

He sat slumped in a chair and soon started to ponder. He was feeling dispirited, so he wondered what life would be like if everyone stopped caring for each other. Individualism seemed to be an end in itself, he thought, and like a domino effect, in essence. It would only take one person to start it all off, he realised, because everything would then trickle down. One person becoming self-obsessed would affect another, so he could foresee others following, and he then easily imagined a scene which was reminiscent of a Victorian mental asylum, where nobody is listening to what anybody is saying because everybody is busy talking to themselves. It was a vision of hell, and an extreme view of things becoming anarchic very quickly, but Chalkie was transfixed for a time. He'd read lots of science fiction books of this nature when he was younger, so you could say he was drawn to pessimistic predictions of this kind, but being a police officer also meant he saw many people at their worst. Mark seemed the most frightening man he'd encountered yet, and he'd only spoken to him on the telephone, so it was understandable why he was feeling deflated. But he soon realised that people like him were still a minority and that most people still did care for each other. It wasn't time for an end-of-the-world scenario just yet. And this thought cheered him up. He was also hopeful that Capstan would come up with something. He'd not rung yet, which was unusual, so some hope remained, he thought.

Capstan rang half an hour later. He was in buoyant mood and said, 'Chalkie, I think I know were the DVD is!' It was such a shock that Chalkie couldn't at first believe what he'd just heard. He was stunned.

'But I've searched everywhere,' he said, after a slight pause. 'Where is it, for Christ's sake?'

Capstan explained his theory, and even though Chalkie's first instincts were to not believe him, he was already halfway up the stairs before Capstan had finished talking, and he ran straight into the bedroom without pausing for breath. He didn't even take one while he pulled out the two larger wardrobes, nor as he probed further. But then his eyes caught fire and he took a deep breath. 'Fuck me, it's here,' he said. 'It's right in front of my eyes, I'm looking straight into it – Jesus, you were right!' he then said in a tone of voice that contained such an abundance of exuberance and disbelief rolled into one that he sounded like a little boy who'd just opened his first Christmas present. The tension he was feeling was therefore very clear, whereupon Capstan then jumped up and said with some impatience, 'Chalkie, smash the mirror with your truncheon – and do it now, for God's sake.'

'Okay,' Chalkie said, once he'd recovered his composure.

Capstan's heart missed a beat, but then he clearly heard a loud and repeated *thwack* as Chalkie's truncheon smashed into the mirror, and a delightful tinkle of glass as the shattered pieces fell to the ground like summer rain; the slight pause that followed seemed to last forever. 'I've found the fucker. It's even got "Charlotte" written on the front. Can you believe *that*?' he said soon afterwards, before going into the kind of verbal overdrive he was famous for. 'Mark, I bet you believed you were safe. Well, you're not. Well done, Capstan. Or maybe you should be called Columbo from now on? No, probably not. Daft thought, you'd become insufferable. I wonder what Mark will say when Roger rings. Jesus, I'd love to be a fly on the wall,' he said without pausing for breath. But just as Chalkie was building up a good head of steam, the wind was then taken out of his sails. Capstan had listened patiently, but he'd decided that he'd said enough, so he stopped him in his tracks.

'Chalkie,' he said.

'What?' asked Chalkie.

'Shut up, and get the hell out of there. And get someone else in, quickly. Roger will be arriving shortly,' he replied, and Chalkie immediately realised the implications and the importance of this intervention. He appreciated that the investigation wasn't finished, so he ran out to the car with some alarm and once again rang his best friend.

'Ed, what are you up to?' he asked.

'Oh no,' replied Ed. 'I knew I shouldn't have answered the phone. I knew it would be you. I was just about to make love to my—'

'Ed, we've found it. We need you and one of the forensic lads again. We need photographs of the broken mirror upstairs, and someone to greet Roger Goulding on his arrival. We need someone who will say nothing about what's happened so far. I'd love to be there, but Capstan wants someone else,' he said.

Aftermath

Capstan greeted Alf Turner as warmly as he thought appropriate. Both men looked and smiled at each other for a moment; they didn't speak, as words didn't seem necessary. Alf was a large, muscular man who was made out of granite but was about to break. He stood motionless with his hands by his side, and only very slowly lifted them as he shook hands with Capstan. His hands were huge and felt like tree bark.

Chalkie arrived shortly afterwards. He thought Alf looked like a man who had been out in the sun all his life. His skin was full of colour and tone, and he had a full head of hair which was silver and grey, and a full beard. Chalkie noticed how he stood completely upright and perpendicular to the floor, and how still he was too, but as they shook hands he was soon drawn to his eyes, which conveyed great sadness: they looked like empty holes. Both officers, in fact, could see that life had drained out of them. Alf Turner knew Nicholas was dead and all the officers could do was to confirm this with a nod of their heads. 'I'm so sorry,' Capstan said, as he held out his hand to comfort him, and Alf accepted the gesture and cried on his shoulder. Chalkie stood in silent awe at this moment. Capstan engendered such trust, even in a man he didn't know, and it brought a tear to Chalkie's eye. Human kindness suddenly appeared limitless, at least for a short time.

Once he'd got over the initial shock, Alf Turner rested in the chair and Chalkie made some tea. Alf sat upright, took a sip and after an appreciative nod said, 'It's partly my fault, that's the bit I'll never be able to forgive myself for. I knew it might end badly at some stage. I knew Nicholas so well.' His voice trailed off momentarily, and after a pause he then added forlornly, 'But to die alone . . . I can hardly endure the thought. I could have helped him; I should have been with him. The fact that he died alone will haunt me for ever.' Chalkie gazed at him and didn't know how to respond to this. He looked so kind and good that his own heart nearly burst. Capstan didn't say anything either. 'How did he do it?' Alf then asked.

It was difficult to know where to begin, but the two officers tried to piece together the night's events for him. They showed him Nicholas's letter, then, of course, the diary, then the envelope that contained the letter addressed to Alf, but they didn't tell him how he'd killed himself. Capstan halted proceedings at this point. All the events were too complex to take in, especially when you'd just been told that someone you loved was now dead. Alf Turner was a man who couldn't take any more bad news. Both officers could see this by the way his face was all crunched up and by the way he was clutching his stomach as he glanced around the caravan.

'Look,' said Capstan, 'the night so far has been the most extraordinary experience of my life. Chalkie will agree with this, but even he isn't able to put together all the pieces, as he hasn't read the diary. Alf, something very positive is going to come out of this tragedy, and a phoenix, as beautiful as a peacock and with eyes as bright as the stars, is going to grow out of the night's ashes! Trust me, and please bear with us. We can't bring Nicholas back, he's dead; there'll plenty of time for you and everybody else who knew and loved him to grieve, but right now we need to show you something. We have in our possession the DVD of Charlotte's rape. It was what Nicholas was searching for. It partly explains why he killed himself, after writing the letter and the diary, and why he broke into Mark's house.'

Alf then listened as the two officers each described their own personal experiences, and not only was he flabbergasted as he listened to the two versions, but so were Capstan and Chalkie when they heard each other's accounts. Chalkie had shown enormous initiative; whilst Capstan's deductive power highlighted just how remiss he'd been by not becoming a detective. Alf raised his eyes to the heavens at one point and almost felt the hand of God on his shoulders. He felt like he was a patient who'd been cared for and brought back to health in a hospital. His spirits lifted; he then broke down in tears, but this time they were tears of a different nature. Friendship takes many forms; Capstan and Chalkie were two men he didn't know existed two hours ago, now he felt they were men he'd go and fight with in a war, if necessary.

Charlotte and Roy were due back the next day, so after agreeing a plan of action, Chalkie said before leaving, 'You can identify the body tomorrow. Ring your wife, read the letter and the diary if you feel up to it, but try and get some sleep.'

'Yes,' added Capstan, 'we've all got a busy day a head of us. Oh, and if you have trouble sleeping, just imagine what kind of time Mark's having, probably at this very moment, and what kind of day he's going to have tomorrow, when he receives the diary in the morning. Even knowing Nicholas as little as I do, I feel it will have been sent by Special Delivery, and it will contain precise instructions as to who it must be given to.'

Alf smiled as he thought about this, and as he went inside the two officers drove off, then stopped in front of the main road. Chalkie rang Ed to find out what the state of affairs was at Mark's house.

'Oh joy of joys,' Ed answered. 'It was almost as good as making love to my wife. Almost . . . but, er, you won't tell Janice I said that, will you?'

'Ed, get the fuck on with it, will you?'

'Well, we first heard a screech of tyres, then we saw him storm up to the house. He looked around outside, and when he saw the damage, which is only slight, he started ranting and raving. He said, "Why, the rancid little toad. How dare he?" And then he really lost his temper, and even though his grammar remained good, his sentences contained more swear words than I'd ever heard before.'

'Capstan wants to know what he looks like.'

'I'd say he was tall, dark and handsome, unfortunately. He

looked as if he'd never done a day's work in his life. He's about six foot tall, has black hair, a square jaw and unblemished skin. He was a wearing a white T-shirt and an expensive two-buttoned casual jacket. He looked like the kind of man a mother would like to see her daughter go out with, if I'm being honest with you.'

'Yes, we kind of expected that.'

'But when we took him upstairs he shrank,' Ed said with some candour, 'he literally shrank. He melted, almost as quickly as a snowman does when the sun comes out about midday on a winter's day! And when he observed us looking at him, well, it was laughable. He tried to disguise the astonishment that was clearly visible all over his face, and in his glare particularly, with a look of innocent anger. His facial contortions were excellent. "The officer didn't mention this over the phone," he said. "I don't believe he told Mark about there being any damage at all in this room."'

'What did you say to that, Ed?'

'I simply told him that I'd arrived as cover. I said that the police realised that the owner was an important businessman who was coming to live here, so they requested that I remain here until he arrived. The two officers were called away shortly afterwards as it was a very busy night. I asked him if there was anything of great value or importance in there.'

'Outstanding! Even Capstan's laughing. Thanks, Ed,' Chalkie said warmly.

'But Capstan doesn't laugh,' Ed then said, as he waited for a response, but as there wasn't one, only a pause, he finished by saying, 'I enjoyed it, but don't ask me again for anything – especially when I'm just about to make love to my wife!'

Chalkie and Carol lived in a traditional house in a residential part of Harrogate. It was tucked off the main road and close to the shops. Surprisingly, Carol liked it because of the kitchen. It was of a good size and consisted of modern fitted units and ceramic tiled floors. They'd been married for four years, and whilst they still claimed to love each other, caring deeply for each other was probably a more accurate description. They'd known each other since they were teenagers, but there were signs that they were just starting to grow apart. Carol felt Chalkie was married to his job, and Chalkie felt Carol listened to her friends and colleagues at work too much; particularly when it came to home improvements. So it didn't help matters when Chalkie told Carol he had to go to work again at midday. 'But you didn't get in until the early hours,' she responded. 'I thought you'd have the day off. I thought we'd meet Andrew and Jill for lunch. I was looking forward to some time together. It's my day off,' she said.

Chalkie looked deeply and uncompromisingly into his wife's blue eyes and remembered the first time they dazzled him. She was studying in the school library. His legs were like long thin sticks of sugar cane, but they felt like lumps of lead as he walked towards her and sat down opposite her. He wanted to stroke her long fair hair and kiss her delicate lips, immediately, there and then. Even now that moment made him flush when he thought about it. 'You looked more beautiful than Julia Roberts, you know. I couldn't believe how beautiful you were when I first saw you, and I still can't believe I had the courage to ask you out,' he said. 'You are still a very beautiful woman. Sometimes I still can't believe I'm married to you.'

Carol then listened as Chalkie explained what had happened at work. She knew that talking about things really helped and she listened appreciatively. 'Capstan was unbelievable,' he said, and by the time he'd finished talking she began to understand what he was getting at. 'People change, I do appreciate that,' she said, 'I suppose we can't help it. I do understand that who you work with changes you, just as who you live with does. I suppose working in a library isn't as interesting as your job. I was just disappointed, that's all. Andrew and Jill are our friends. Jill's pregnant as well. She's so excited she can hardly contain herself.'

Chalkie once again looked deeply into her eyes, and appreciated that she had made an important point. 'Book a cheap hotel somewhere. Anywhere you fancy. Pick a place at random on the internet if you like. We'll go all weekend and make footprints in the sand. I do love you,' he said.

Alf had identified the body and sat quietly sipping a cup of black coffee. He was resting and desperately trying to regain his mental strength as a thousand thoughts went through his head. Mark hadn't rung from London, and nobody had any inkling as to what Roger was doing. Nobody cared. Chalkie and Alf had also read the diary and the officers knew that the initiative was in Alf's head now. They'd go along with his wishes where possible. But they were curious because they realised that Mark and Roger didn't know exactly what had happened, or, more importantly, what was going to happen next. Capstan knew they'd have realised that the police knew more than they'd told Roger. 'You can't complete a jigsaw with some of the pieces missing, or glue back together a broken cup and expect it to hold hot water,' Capstan said to Alf when bringing him up to speed. 'The two of them will be wearing out the carpets as they pace up and down wondering what to do though, I reckon. So Alf, have you had any thoughts on the matter?'

'I've read the diary and Nicholas's letters and had a delicious thought,' he replied. Charlotte is a lovely girl, you know, and utterly beautiful in an understated kind of way. She is fashion conscious, I suppose, but the clothes she wears are a cover – literally. Her real beauty comes from within. When you meet her you'll see this for yourselves. She's coming back off her honeymoon today and I don't think we need to bother her until the evening.'

'Okay,' said Chalkie. 'So what's on the agenda? What's that delicious thought of yours?'

Alf rang Mark an hour later, with the two officers in attendance.
  'Hello Mark, it's Alf. Sleep well?'
  'Er, this is unexpected. What do you want?'

'Besides roasting you alive, you mean? And as far as that glutinous piece of shit called Roger goes . . . even that is too good for him! Nicholas is dead, you know. But he's given us one hell of a goodbye gift. Now I'm either going to give it to the police, or—'

'What do you want?'

'Have you read his diary?'

'Yes'

'You should read the letter he's written too. So here's the deal, and it's not negotiable.'

The terms were harsh. Capstan and Chalkie nodded and smiled as Alf read them out in slow and methodical detail, making the conversation as difficult as possible for Mark. In one memorable moment he said, referring to Roger, 'And get that fucker out of Yorkshire *now*, and then out of *your* life. If my wife or I see or hear of him again, you'll be sorry.' They then listened as Alf carefully explained that these terms would be written up and witnessed, and that they were a contractual agreement between those concerned, and that they had to be followed to the letter. They included safeguards and meant in effect that he would no longer be a risk to the general public. The telephone conversation lasted nearly an hour.

Capstan and Chalkie both agreed with the general consensus: Charlotte was indeed beautiful. She had skin like soft satin and ginger hair that was long and elegant. Her face was graced by gentle curves and her cheeks were the colour of apple blossom. She revealed her true beauty, however, in the way she moved: she glided rather than walked, and, as Nicholas had noted, her stillness, when she was either listening to something or simply thinking, made her seem ethereal and not of this world. They both found themselves staring at her for long periods, and both had to turn their heads away with effort.

The two detectives had called around the following day to clear up any remaining issues, especially those concerning the DVD and the diary. Charlotte was still distraught of course. Roy told Capstan and Chalkie that she hadn't been able to sleep, which was hardly surprising. Her eyes still resembled black holes and she was still clearly filled with horror. This manifested itself in the way she carried herself, and they could both tell that she was enormously angry and deeply upset, though her self-control was a thing of beauty. Uncle Alf's planned resolution would hopefully help offset the pain, and in the days to come its full force would become more apparent, so the two officers were in an optimistic frame of mind.

'Mark's due up tomorrow. He's meeting Alf and his wife, and a lawyer,' Chalkie told Charlotte. He was happy that Alf had requested their presence as well, as both officers liked to see a job through to the end. 'So Capstan and myself will be there also, if that's all right with you two?'

Charlotte was lost for words. 'Of course it is – we are in your debt. Thank you,' she eventually said.

'Now you have a choice, believe it or not,' Capstan then said with a glint in his eye. 'Do you want the house completely destroyed? A wrecking ball can easily be arranged, and you can even start the ball rolling, if you catch my drift.'

'I'd like to see it knocked down, and I'm certain Nicholas would too,' Charlotte said, as the implications dawned on her – namely, that she was suddenly the mistress of all she surveyed. 'But I know what it's like to be homeless. So instead of destroying it, I'd like the house to be sold along with the land, and the money given to those institutions that need the money the most,' she said. 'Support workers and case workers are needed as well; it's not just a case of providing places to stay.' It was an impressive response and without any show of emotion at all. Roy immediately nodded in agreement as Charlotte sat back on the settee and held his hand. They then embraced and smiled at each other.

In a way they looked a strange couple – both officers felt this.

They'd also watched Roy carefully as he sat listening to Charlotte's answer, and it was noticeable how protective he was. He had a firm view on the matter, there was no doubt about that, but he'd said nothing. He was powerfully built and well aware of his own strength, but over time he'd developed a very gentle nature. Nevertheless, you still wouldn't want to rile him too much, and Capstan in particular wondered what would have happened if he had indeed met Mark. He was the eldest son of Margaret, so some of his genetical make-up must be similar to his mother's, yet he was carved with different tools and made up of much firmer features, both in body and in mind, it seemed. Destroying the house suited him too, that was for sure.

'The DVD is the next issue,' Capstan said as earnestly as possible. 'It has to be kept under lock and key. Uncle Alf wants to make the necessary arrangements. Is this all right? If you want you can have it destroyed, but I wouldn't advise it.' Chalkie nodded in agreement.

'Absolutely, yes that's fine too,' Charlotte said. 'I even like the idea that giving his house away is going to be publicised. Mark's companies are going to receive enormous compliments along the lines of "altruism is not dead", which will help the business recover from its loss; but what are the guarantees? Tell me again, what's to stop him raping someone else?'

'From now on Mark is going to be solely a figurehead. He's lost his power. Alf's wife is going to help run the businesses with the help of Mark's relatives. They have already been informed. They are being brought up to speed as we speak. Mark is to undergo psychiatric assessment, and any treatment deemed to be required will be compulsory. It is all part of the contract. I think we can therefore say that he won't bother anyone again,' Capstan said. 'I think it is a cast-iron certainty.' He said this with such conviction that all Charlotte could do was let out a giant sign of relief immediately afterwards.

'And lastly,' Chalkie said, 'Uncle Alf feels you should have this.

Capstan and I think you should have it too,' and he held aloft Nicholas's diary. 'Read it when you feel up to it.'

And as Chalkie walked over and gave it to her, she received it with their blessing and with a very heavy heart.

E-mail Sent to the Agent

Capstan's a clever fella – just like me, eh? I think his powers of deduction are as good as Lieutenant Colombo's – though they are not at the same level as Sherlock Holmes'. But give him time and you never know what might happen. After all, caterpillars turn into butterflies, so why can't something similar happen to Capstan?

Anyway, back to the matter in hand. I've even noticed that my mind also has become much sharper in recent days, and my thinking in particular has become much more analytical. Lights are brighter, and rainbows, when I picture them inside my head, are much more vivid. Even violet is clearly distinguishable from indigo. A remarkable transformation, I think.

Sometimes even my dreams seem real. Last night, for example, I dreamt I was a doctor giving a seminar on cocaine. 'Cocaine,' I said to my colleagues, 'should be legalised. It is the oldest local anaesthetic and lifts one's mood. And as it has similar characteristics to heroin and morphine it is therefore an effective treatment for pain relief, so these drugs should be available for patients, once they have been prescribed by doctors. Drug addiction,' I continued, 'is a medical issue, and should not be considered a political one.' Anyway, I thought it was amazing because I'm not a doctor and I'd never taken drugs in my life.

So I'm living in exciting times. And to think years went by previously when I didn't talk to anyone for days on end. Now, when I talk to Dennis at the pub, even he notices that my arguments are based on sound principles. And he should know. He's ninety years old and was a liaison officer on a French submarine in the Second World War, and in later life became an academic. 'I don't understand why Nelson is considered by so many to be their hero,' I said to him just the other day. 'Shakespeare I can understand, but not Nelson. In those days sailors were first press-ganged into service; then they were either smashed, cut to pieces, or even cut in half by shot fired from gun barrels only yards away in battle. Why, even Nelson himself died an agonising death, and I wouldn't like that to happen to me,' I said. 'Shakespeare, though, is a real hero, and so for that matter are writers of award-winning books.'

Anyway, it's time to go. But I think you'll agree, writing my book and talking to you has been very beneficial. Goodbye for now. Joe.

Day Out

'He's got the longest legs I've ever seen,' Charlotte said. 'It's just as well he offered to drive – he'd never fit in our car. Whoa, be careful with the garlic, will you? Yes, that's good, now cut it into slivers, and don't forget the olives either, and a little cheese.' Roy did as he was told, of course – it was pointless arguing. 'You know what they say,' Charlotte continued, 'if a job's worth doing, it's worth doing well.' She was walking backwards and forwards – to the cupboards under the stairs, to the spare room upstairs making sure she had packed everything they needed. She'd already put the buckets and spades by the door. 'I've never dammed a stream before, but I'm looking forward to it in a strange kind of way. What about you?' she asked, but before Roy could reply, she was gone.

Chalkie and Carol arrived bang on time. Carol was now pregnant and was sitting in the back. It was clear that Charlotte would sit with her. Roy was slightly awkward around women, though he wasn't ever out of his depth. He just said it as he found it. He left others to work out the nuances. Again, this was for a perfectly obvious reason – he worked with hardnosed young lads, who worked hard and probably played even harder. Polite chitchat wasn't a requirement on a building site.

It was a very pleasant autumnal day. The trees were turning and there was an early-morning chill, but no wind. The forecast was good for the whole day. 'I don't think even Nicholas would have foreseen the tumultuous events unfolding quite as they have,' Charlotte said as they set off. 'He'd liked his theses and antitheses, but I don't think he ever experienced a successful synthesis. The house raised a fortune at auction, and the money has already been earmarked. The local newspaper has reported the event, and Mark has been awarded almost saintly status. How ironic is that! Uncle Alf has written to various bodies also. It seems that the proceeds have been split three ways, with some of the money going to Harrogate and York, some to Leeds and Bradford, and the rest to London. It's just as Nicholas and I would have wanted,' she said without pausing for breath.

When Charlotte read the diary she cried for days. Roy read it too, and was deeply touched. He built houses for a living, but always thought demolition was more fun. Even Carol had read it. 'What was Nicholas like?' she asked, once Chalkie and Roy had started talking about football in the front. Charlotte was grateful, and was happy to talk about him.

'It's difficult to put into words, really. He was, I suppose, unique – yes, that's the only way I could describe him,' she said after pausing for a second or two. 'One minute he'd be laughing and joking, the next he'd drift into his shell. He'd sit, oblivious to his surroundings, for ages. I often watched him on these occasions,' she said. 'You could almost see the cogs turning inside his head. He never talked to himself out loud, but his head moved from side to side and his eyes rolled – one minute they'd be looking at the ceiling, the next at the floor; I felt that nothing ever could be resolved – he was always searching for something that wasn't there. I don't know if you know what I mean?' she said. Carol nodded, so Charlotte thought she did. 'I think he was a bit like the number three,' she went on. 'We see things in threes or twos every day, but never the actual number. Nicholas's thinking seemed to be like that. He was literally up in the clouds somewhere.'

They'd passed Thirsk, and Chalkie and Roy were having a debate about house prices, when Carol said quietly, 'He brought us back together, you know.' Charlotte was nonplussed at first, but once she'd told her how they'd been drifting apart for a while, she understood. 'Chalkie was ever so proud they found the you-know-what,' she said, 'and when they did I realised that I was lucky to have a husband who cared so much.' The two of them then talked about the baby; when it was due, and so on, until they passed Pickering.

'It nearly happened between us,' Charlotte then said, with a nod and a wink, but just then Roy interrupted their conversation.

'There's the train,' he said, and they all looked across as Chalkie pressed on the car's horn and waved – a sign of respect, apparently.

Meanwhile, Carol had turned to face Charlotte as she understood perfectly what she was getting at. 'On two occasions actually,' Charlotte said, 'and before I'd met Roy. The first time it nearly happened was after a trip to Whitby, and it was actually Nicholas who pulled away. I told Roy, of course, and he wasn't bothered at all.' Carol was intrigued.

'Why did he do that? He obviously loved you,' she said.

'Yes, it's strange, but I understood. People can go potty without love. I read somewhere that Cleopatra poisoned herself for this very reason. But the opposite was true in Nicholas's case. He knew he wouldn't have been able to cope with all of those chemicals, you know, the ones that swirl around inside of us when we are in love. Even in affairs of the heart he was rational!'

They were in the North Yorkshire National Park when they stopped beside a picturesque stream that sat in a hollow, just as Nicholas had described it, to stretch their legs.

'What's Capstan up to, these days?' Roy asked as they walked up the valley taking in the air.

'He's driving everybody batty, that's what,' Chalkie said. 'If he's not careful, he's going to end up with a new nickname.'

Charlotte's eyes widened as she considered this remark. 'How so?' she enquired.

'He keeps on going about drugs to all and sundry, and to anybody else who'll listen,' Chalkie said. '"They should be legalised," he says, "all of them." He goes on about it all the time. His new nickname will be drug-related, mark my words.' And everybody laughed at this.

Then on the way back to the car, sheep suddenly appeared, then a sheep dog and a farmer on his cart, on the road below. 'Fucking useless! You're fucking useless, Bess,' the farmer shouted in a deep voice – though the dog didn't seem to be paying him too much attention – and when he saw them walking towards him, he went quiet. Anyway despite the abuse the dog had received, it soon had the sheep heading in their intended direction, and so the farmer was pleased after all.

'Why didn't he become a detective when he had the chance?' Roy then asked.

'That's a simple one to answer,' Chalkie said. 'It's because he's a socialist, that's why. He's no good at grabbing the moment. He's an old whinge bag really. But he also likes wearing the uniform, believe it or not. He is, after all, our very own Dixon of Dock Green.' But as nobody knew who this was either, they let it pass, and they then walked back to the car in relative silence.

They listened to music for the remainder of the journey to Sandsend. They'd each chosen two of their favourite tracks, but as Charlotte chose two of Nicholas's also, it was *The Lark Ascending* that was playing as they reached their destination. Charlotte had grown to love it. She now listened to classical music a lot, and sometimes you could see her head moving and her eyes rolling from side to side too, as she did so.

Circus

A week later . . .

Natasha was as excited as a discarded puppy who'd found a new home. She was walking about the kitchen in a state of some confusion, not knowing whether to sit at the table and eat her tea, or to look out of the lounge window. 'What time is it? Where is he?' she said over and over again to nobody in particular. Then she drank her lemonade, ate her iced bun, shuffled on her bottom, and ran backwards and forwards to the window, repeatedly. Her mother and sister looked on in some amusement: her movements resembled those of Emily and her friends when they managed to milk a cow during the chorus routine of 'Thady You Gander', a country dance that Emily had once choreographed in a Christmas pantomime. 'Natasha, stop it,' Emily said whilst laughing. 'Behave! I'm trying to eat this sandwich, not spit it out all over the floor.'

When Capstan arrived home at the expected time Natasha jumped for joy. 'Daddy, Daddy, I've lost my red nose,' she said, 'will I still be able to go?' And after Capstan had nodded to say yes, she blew into his whistle and sang 'We're All Going to the Circus' to a tune that was unrecognisable. She'd never been to a circus before, so she was delirious, a little like old men are when they go for a ride on a steam train. Old men yearn for the halcyon days of their youth, so their excitement is therefore understandable, but Natasha was a still a child, and to her, what she was about to do was ten times more exciting than that, because her experiences were still brand new. It wasn't therefore surprising that she couldn't sit still. After a couple of laps of the rooms downstairs, she then went to talk to her mother, who was making her a witch's cloak for Halloween, leaving Capstan alone with his thoughts, for a short time at least. So Capstan sat down. But just when he was about to let out a large sigh, Emily appeared.

'Hi Dad,' she said. 'I had an interesting day at school today.' She spoke quite nonchalantly, and this surprised him into replying in a tone of voice which was, he quickly realised, inappropriate, for it conveyed a hint of sarcasm. He hadn't adjusted to being home as fast as he should have, so he quickly changed the mood of the occasion and sat up. 'Come and sit next to me,' he said as Emily showed him her homework. They first talked about Pythagoras, but this was in retrospect a ruse of Emily's. Capstan would only realise this later. She had listened to how Capstan talked to his friends, and had picked up one or two strategies from her own father, so after this initial discussion about Pythagoras, Emily then changed tack to the main event: 'The Winter of Discontent'. It was her English assignment.

'First I've got to present both sides of the argument,' she said, 'and then I've got to take a side and present a persuasive opinion.'

'Hummm,' he said as he thought about this for a moment or two, and liked the idea. Socialism wasn't dead, in his family at any rate, and as he knew that Emily actually shared these ideas, he decided he was looking forward to reinforcing one or two of her still-forming views. But Emily found it difficult to hold back, or to sit still, whilst she listened to her father speak, as she had an ace up her sleeve, but she managed to, all the same.

'It's a worker's right to strike,' Capstan said confidently, and rather like a politician. 'It should only be used as the last resort of course, but everybody has rights. Sometimes these rights have to be fought for,' he continued. 'Why, without the Suffragettes, women wouldn't have the right to vote,' he said as he sat back slightly and relaxed. He was pleased with his efforts and awaited Emily's response with interest, but even Emily thought he was being just a little too smug, and even conceited about his powers of persuasion, so she paused for a moment or two, and smiled pleasantly enough, whilst thinking like a chess master, or, more realistically, like a cold-hearted poker player.

He hadn't been exactly sticking to the point anyway, she thought, but Emily had caught his drift. Still, she didn't have the heart to tell him that they didn't study the early twentieth century until next year, because she had bigger fish to fry. She was growing up quickly, and when she could wait no longer she attacked with a movement designed to capture the king and win the game. And she did this simply by looking him directly in the eye. Then she told him what Susan's father had said about the matter. 'It should be illegal to strike. Sack 'em all,' he'd said. 'A worker's job is to provide a service. Without a demand for this service, workers wouldn't have a job. The consumer and the customer are master now.'

'She caught me off guard, that's for sure,' he said to his wife afterwards, as he looked for his own red nose (free with a donation to the homeless, the circus's charity for the night). 'Wow,' he said, as he looked longingly into his wife's eyes. Rosemary too was enjoying the moment, so she too poured more oil onto the flames. 'She's becoming like her father,' she said, and then, with mischief in her voice, added, 'It's a little frightening when you think about it.' Then she left, leaving Capstan to ponder the matter whilst he showered and changed.

So Capstan thought about the tactics his daughter had used, and as he did so he realised that he was going to have his work cut out keeping his 'Art of Rhetoric' medallion at the station, never mind in his own house, if he had more days like this one. And later, as he looked at himself in the mirror and brushed his hair whilst thinking about how fast children grow up these days, he even felt a touch of alarm in the pit of his stomach. It was a feeling that had arrived out of the blue, and for a time he thought he might even be transparent, but he was soon relieved when he realised that he still looked as opaque as ever.

The other tactic that had caught him out was of course entirely of female origin, and there was nothing he could do about it, he realised. He was able to see this later, too. He'd melted under Emily's glare and her innocent smile.

Otherwise, it had been a run-of-the-mill type of day, and nothing unexpected had happened, as far as he was concerned, at any rate. The weather and day of the week determined the behaviour of the general public. Revellers wait until they have swelled into a throng, outside nightclubs at midnight, for example, before even thinking about behaving badly, he realised, and usually at the weekend. During the week, these people are either earning or preserving money. So everywhere was quiet, and there was actually very little for the police to do.

Autumn was well set. The trees on the Stray were now mainly golden, and the leaves that were left hanging on tightly to their parent branches were fluttering in a brisk northerly wind. The schoolchildren too were in reflective mood, as they calmly walked home, or waited for their buses, without the usual cries and screams heard on a warm, sunny day. Capstan was pleased to see men wearing long trousers once again. He thought seeing a man's lower legs was ridiculous, but Chalkie wasn't so sure, so they talked about this for a while, as they went about their everyday business in a relative state of calm. As people walked by with fixed looks and rigid movements – a reminder of things to come, as it was nearly November, so the first blast of cold and blanket of fog would soon make the world outside look very different – the two policemen went about their daily business.

Chalkie had started off as talkative as always, of course, but Capstan wasn't listening. He was looking forward to seeing his two friends from the circus, so he had other things on his mind. He had, however, asked Chalkie how his wife's pregnancy was going, but merely out of courtesy, and when Chalkie replied, 'She wants me to be there, but at the busy end, where all the fannying about takes place. I'm not sure I'm up to it. I've already seen a DVD of a birth and it made me skirm.' Capstan simply smiled, having once again drifted off into his own private thoughts, leaving poor Chalkie with distressing images of messy childbirth inside his head. Chalkie realised that an unusual silence had suddenly descended on the proceedings, and this made him feel awkward, so he tried to focus on other things instead.

The fair had come and gone, fireworks were now on display, and the big top had been put up with surprising speed and ease. It looked impressive. The lights flashed, and already music was playing. All day long the clowns, with legs as long as poles, had been carrying balloons, juggling balls, and pulling things out of hats whilst telling jokes in various places throughout the town. The bright reds of their noses and their colourful clothing all added to the spectacle, and gave a touch of excitement and expectation to the town. Then exciting-looking modular capsules which fitted together like petals on flowers suddenly appeared, next to the large tent. They'd replaced the ubiquitous caravans, and they looked like buildings from a futuristic lunar landscape. When Capstan saw them they filled him with hope and optimism for the future, but Chalkie was confused.

'What the hell are those?' he asked eventually, once they'd passed them by for the umpteenth time. Capstan still hadn't spoken, and the silence was beginning to irritate Chalkie, so his tone of voice conveyed a mixture of excitement, foreboding and annoyance. Then, as he looked at them once again, he even wondered if he was about to see a strange three-legged alien appear from one of them, or maybe a large lizard-type creature.

Then Capstan suddenly said, 'I know the man who designed them.' He saw Chalkie's look of exasperation, and knew that his silent treatment had annoyed him, but with those few words, the enigma that was Capstan suddenly gained momentum in Chalkie's eyes.

'You've never mentioned that before,' Chalkie said slightly sternly, once it dawned on him that his partner may have a secret past.

'I know. It's my shadowy past catching up with me,' Capstan replied. 'It's who I'm seeing when you drop me off. They're the trapeze artists, a father and son – they come from Bradford. I've known them nearly all my life. The son has brains as well as brawn,' he said as his optimism took hold, so in the short silence that followed he pictured progress, innovation and an exciting future for the designer of the capsules, and his eyes glazed over thinking about it. Unfortunately the picture inside his head was cloudy, and he found this odd, but something in his bones was telling him problems lay ahead, and this made him feel uneasy. He didn't, though, expect to receive a phone call from Chalkie the next day telling him that Lenny had been run over, and that it had been deliberate. When Chalkie did drop him off, a little later, he merely watched as Capstan disappeared into one of the capsules, and wondered if he was about to disappear into another dimension in the fabric of time and space.

Sadly the problems that tomorrow would bring would bring it home to him that this view hadn't been that far off the mark.

'How are you?' Capstan said as he walked inside and greeted his friend with a hug. 'Lenny, has he been behaving himself?' he asked the younger man next to him. 'He's never going to take to retirement, you know. Flying through the air is something he'll miss,' he added, with a tinge of regret in his voice because he knew that retirement could be a killer of men. 'But we all get old, you know.'

The last time he'd seen Ronny was in hospital, he was badly battered and bruised, and his eyes were almost closed up. He was also suffering from the pain of a couple of broken ribs. 'You should have seen the other guy,' he remembered Ronny saying at the time. His jaw wasn't broken, but he'd lost a couple of teeth and was in need of some pain relief, not to mention some urgent dental treatment. 'Stop going on,' he'd replied once they'd embraced. 'That was my last fight. I've learnt my lesson. Once I could have knocked someone like that out with a couple of swift upper cuts and a punch,' he said. 'But not any more,' Lenny had said firmly, as his father nodded in agreement. 'I know son, I'm probably getting a little too old,' he had sighed. 'But having said that, you're pretty indestructible yourself, so even if I did drop you, you'd probably bounce and get up as good as new!'

Nothing had changed, Capstan observed, as they spoke now.

They were just the same as always: at each other's throats, because that was the only way they knew how to show their love for one another. He recognised the behaviour immediately of course, because he knew his own was sometimes similar at work, so as he sat down and looked around he felt a tingling in his stomach as Lenny made the tea.

The interior was comprised of the usual features, but the decor was in silver and black, and was in keeping with the futuristic shape and concept of the capsules. The sofa was very comfortable, and Capstan liked the open-plan layout, with everything radiating out from the central core: a fire with mock ducts, and an umbilical cord which provided the power. There was even a large LCD television attached to the wall. It was pleasantly warm also, solar panels adding a few degrees of heat, but it was the insulation that was most impressive: a cavity wall consisting of high-density polystyrene, apparently, which was very thick at the centre of the capsule, due to its shape. 'We don't even have the central heating switched on,' Lenny said with some pride. 'What do you think, Capstan?' he asked, as he could tell their friend was deeply impressed.

'It's fabulous. I don't know where you get the brains from, I truly don't,' Capstan replied, even though his words sounded a little trite to him, as nobody spoke like this in Bradford.

He stayed for about an hour and then called for Chalkie to pick him up. 'I'll bring my daughters around tomorrow,' he said as he left. 'Natasha, my youngest, is already deeply impressed. "Daddy, you know *who*?" she'd said, when I told her about you. I didn't tell her that you were reprobates though,' he said with a smile, as this sounded much better to him. Suddenly he was in a much better mood, and he was grateful to Chalkie as they set off in the car. 'If I were you,' he said, 'I'd stay well away from the fannying end when your baby is being born. Put your foot down, Chalkie. Let's go home.' With that, he looked at his watch and smiled.

The circus had a long list of exciting acts. Emily liked the budgerigars and the siege of Nottingham castle, which included cannonball acts, knife throwing, sword swallowing and tightrope acts; and Natasha laughed at the clowns and the poodles the most. His wife Rosemary liked the look on their daughters' faces more than anything else. Then the Master of Ceremonies announced the final act, and everyone hushed as spotlights lit up the silver poles, ladders and swings high up inside the black canvas that stretched way above their heads, and clapped as Ronny and Lenny entered the arena, and then climbed up, to begin their act. The drums rolled and the trumpets sounded.

   The gasps were real enough. The trapeze artists were defying gravity. They hurtled from bar to bar and into each other's outstretched arms. Then the drums rolled again, and the crowd went silent. Natasha's face went as white as a peeled coconut as the searchlight shone on the face of the older trapeze artist, who was hanging upside down in the air, and then on the younger man, whose muscular body glistened with sweat. He had a mane of black hair, and his stern features revealed little emotion. As the older man started to swing faster and faster the younger one stood poised and still, then suddenly plunged and turned three times in the air, as the crowd gasped one moment and roared the next. Natasha couldn't watch – she was convinced he was flying through the air towards certain doom. 'Oooh,' she said, with her eyes half closed, but then she heard the 'aaahs' all around and Emily's 'whoooah' and her 'yeeess', and she finally managed to join in along with everyone else, so she saw the moment when he was held tightly in his partner's arms. The crowd roared in approval, and when the two trapeze artists finally stood upright, safely on the ground, everyone stood up and roared again.

Heart to Heart

Lenny was in a critical condition. He was being prepared for surgery when Capstan arrived at ten. 'They have to release fluid inside his skull, otherwise the pressure will build and the brain would then swell or become damaged, and he would die or at the very least be brain damaged,' Ronny said. He was shaking and unable to look Capstan in the eye. A nurse came in shortly afterwards to say that there wasn't anything else they could do for the time being.

'Why don't you go home and try to rest for a couple of hours?' she said. 'We'll ring when we have any news.'

So Capstan led a reluctant Ronny out, and they went to meet Chalkie, who was waiting in the police car. Once they were back at the capsule, Chalkie made some tea, whilst Lenny and Capstan sat down. The conversation that followed was difficult to say the least.

'Okay, Ronny, start talking,' Capstan said, in a tone of voice that required serious and reflective answers. 'Chalkie has talked to two witnesses. Peter's very upset – not only because one of his poodles is dead, but also because he saw everything. If Lenny hadn't pushed you aside, he said you'd be dead. Another witness said something very similar. She was on her way to work when she saw a car jump the pavement and head straight for you. She shouted "Look out" and Lenny immediately turned and pushed you out of the way. She told Chalkie that Lenny had saved your life.'

'I've been a bloody fool. My boy's close to death and it's entirely my fault. I'll never forgive myself,' Ronny replied in between sighing, raising his eyebrows and hesitating, so both officers realised that there wasn't going to be one easy explanation. 'You'll remember Nigel from the early days,' he said at last.

'Of course I do,' Capstan replied. 'He's a serious piece of

work. The police in Bradford know all about him. But he's as slippery as an eel. Please don't tell me you've got mixed up with him. Jesus.'

The atmosphere was ugly, and Chalkie sympathised with his partner, who was struggling. 'You know he killed Richard?' Ronny said without hesitating. '*I* knew, but even so, I still had no choice,' he continued. 'I had to do something. The pain inside my head was getting worse, I'd had one fight too many and I also knew that I was getting old, so I knew I'd soon have to stop being a trapeze artist, otherwise I really would drop Lenny,' he said as Capstan sat without moving, staring directly at the floor. Chalkie sat down with the tea. 'We'd tried training an apprentice, but it was proving very difficult to get the right person. Anyway, to cut a long story short, I started taking amphetamines years ago to lift me up, but they weren't strong enough, so in recent years the only things that helped was first LSD, and then cocaine. Cocaine especially stopped the pain, it's like an anaesthetic, and Nigel let me have it cheap. He said it was an apology for him killing Richard, or so I was led to believe.'

'Don't tell me for fuck's sake that you believed him,' Capstan said, and then paused and collected his thoughts for a moment, amid much head shaking. 'Is this to do with why he tried to kill you? He wants his money back?'

Ronny was dumbstruck. 'No,' he replied. 'I'm afraid you've got the wrong end of the stick. I owe him some money – but the money I needed to help finance these capsules I didn't borrow from him. What do you take me for! That money's legitimate. I'd never risk my son's future with borrowed money from Nigel. You know me better than that,' he said as he looked Capstan directly in the eye. Capstan didn't reply, however. He'd already turned his head away.

'Nigel is blackmailing me,' Ronny continued, even though he knew these revelations were becoming ever more difficult for Capstan to grasp. 'He wants to bring drugs into Harrogate, by using me as his cover. Where there's money there's a need for drugs. He's just following the market and believes there is a lot of money to be made. He knows about Lenny's capsule ideas and promises to leave him alone if I work for him – although he wants to use some of them for storage, I believe. He's set up a network in York and has been reasonably successful there, but he likes to move around before the police can spot patterns and so on. He's very clever. But he had nothing to do with trying to kill me today.'

Capstan had been listening to Ronny's every word, but hadn't been able to put the pieces together, so he turned to Chalkie and said, 'What the fuck. Chalkie – can *you* make head or tail of this?' Chalkie had already worked out the situation perfectly, and was merely waiting to be invited to speak.

'Yes, a bit. As I don't know Ronny, I think I've been able to see it a little more objectively,' he said, feeling slightly awkward. 'Basically, I think Ronny's arranged to have someone kill *him*.'

Ronny was impressed. Up to that point, he'd hardly noticed Chalkie's presence. 'Fuck me. Who's the clever one?' he said, looking up. 'Yes, you're right of course. It was the only way out. I'd made the arrangement with Paul Cooper. You don't know him well, but the name will be familiar to you. Paul was the lad who was quite simply "strange" when I was growing up next to the lane. You'll know about him because everybody had an opinion about Paul. Some even think he was a paedophile. But it was those, including myself, who saw him roll two large lorry tyres down the lane and knock a motorcyclist off his bike that never forgot him. The man was in hospital for weeks, apparently, with two compound fractures of the leg. Anyway, from then onwards Paul had a reputation, and when he got older he became a "fixer". He'll do anything for money.'

Capstan stood up and paced about the room. It was all becoming too much for him. 'So, you're now telling me that you paid him to kill you? I don't believe I'm hearing this,' he said. 'What about Lenny? What about his feelings, never mind the feelings of everybody else? Yesterday even my own daughters thought you were Superman, for Christ's sake! What about the circus?'

Ronny's eyes welled up. He found the next bit especially difficult and could hardly believe what he was about to say. 'Yes, I'm afraid I am telling you exactly that,' he replied as he started to cry. 'My life insurance is the only thing I've got left. It was the only way to help Lenny. Don't you see this?'

Capstan went outside with Chalkie to think over these revelations, leaving Ronny to his own thoughts, as he waited on tenterhooks for news about Lenny. 'Ronny set up the youth club and gym. He was our hero in those days, and I suppose he always will be,' he told Chalkie. 'He married a local Latvian girl who had lived with her grandmother ever since they'd arrived in Bradford. The Russians had taken over their country. They were from a circus family, and as Ronny was a professional boxer and all-round athlete, he became a trapeze artist with a famous circus that regularly came to Bradford,' he said. 'There were plenty of rough diamonds in those days in the neighbourhood, but there were also people like Nigel about. Most of us, though, looked up to Ronny. I think he was why I became a policeman.'

Just after two the hospital rang to say that the operation had been a success. Ronny collapsed in tears. 'My boy, my beautiful boy,' he said. Then he looked up to the sky and thanked God. Such experiences make a believer out of many, Capstan noted, but he too was relieved and overjoyed. Though he and Chalkie had been busy during the last two hours, so their minds had been on other matters, the news about Lenny cheered them up. Capstan in particular looked skywards when he was told, and then he extended his hand in friendship as he and Ronny embraced each other.

'Come on Ronny, we'll take you to see Lenny now,' he said. 'Am I right in saying that Nigel doesn't know anything about what's happened today, then?'

'Paul won't tell him. He stays away. No one knows anything,' Ronny said as he climbed into the car.

'Okay Ronny, leave it with us for the time being. Just concentrate on helping Lenny,' Capstan said warmly, and he smiled as they set off. But Ronny interrupted him.

'Peter can take over on the trapeze tonight,' he said. 'He can't do a triple, but he can do a double. The audience will hardly notice. The circus must go on, of course, and our act brings everything to a close – we are the highlight, after all,' he went on as if nothing untoward had just happened, and for a second or two both officers couldn't comprehend what he was saying. But things gradually began to unfold, and the three men's opinions converged surprisingly easily thereafter, with the result that Chalkie then immediately rang Charlotte.

'What are you up to?' he asked.

'Oh, hello,' said Charlotte. 'You are now talking to the joint owners of a market stall,' she said.

'Hmmn,' said Chalkie. 'I look forward to your first million. Look,' he went on, 'can you go to Bradford straight away? Yes, this very minute.'

Once she had been given the necessary details, Charlotte set off immediately. She was pleased to help, and was looking forward to sitting in the best seat in the house later in the evening. She'd never been to a circus before.

The Kaiser had been informed of recent developments, and for the time being was leaving the two officers in charge. Lenny was definitely going to prison, that decision had been taken out of their hands, but with his cooperation, the sentence would be much reduced. Capstan and Chalkie also knew that action was going to be needed if a large influx of drugs into the town was to be avoided, and they'd already partly formulated plans that would change the way they lived their lives for the next two to three weeks. 'Carol won't be pleased, but as long as things are sorted in time, it should be all right,' Chalkie said.

He even felt Charlotte might be able to help. 'Charlotte could be useful, you know, and if she became involved, Roy wouldn't be too far behind. He can look after himself, and he could be quite intimidating, if required,' he said. 'Charlotte's had first-hand experience of taking illegal drugs after all, and she'd like to think that she was helping people like Molly in some way. What do you think?' he asked his partner. Capstan liked the idea. A sudden expression of light relief lit up his previously stern features. With characteristic clearness he considered the combination of Charlotte, Roy and two police forces to be a potent mix.

So it was soon decided. Chalkie was going to go undercover in Bradford. He would be a clown who was going to help Ronny and Nigel set up a drugs trade with Harrogate, and Capstan was going to be the link with both police forces. 'To see you pretending to be a clown will make my day,' the latter said with his tongue firmly in his cheek. But sometimes things can get very complicated very quickly, and Capstan then had a thought that changed everything. 'Fuck me,' he said. 'My daughter's already hit the nail on the head. I think our plan needs to be changed slightly. Listen to this,' he said excitedly. 'Chalkie, when you attend the meeting undercover, you need to turn one gang against the other. When they are sufficiently paranoid, they will do most of the work for us. They'll even show us where they've stashed all the drugs.' And whilst Chalkie looked on in a bemused fashion, Capstan continued. 'Absolutely, it's the only way. Listen, let me explain,' he said. And he told Chalkie all about his daughter's last weeks at primary school.

'Towards the end of her time there, she helped write a play called *The Sweetnappers*,' he said. 'They then turned it into a film at the school, and showed it to all the parents. It was about a group of children who, whilst finishing off some project work outside, sneaked out of school to pinch some sweets,' he said. 'Another group of children then distracted their teacher by asking him for help all the time, so the teacher was too busy to notice, but the second group became annoyed when the Sweetnappers didn't offer to share their sweets. The

Sweetnappers had become arrogant, in other words, especially once the police had checked the register, so they had a perfect alibi, and they felt untouchable thereafter,' he explained as Chalkie listened politely. 'Anyway, to cut a long story short,' he continued, once he realised that Chalkie didn't have anything to say, 'the second gang got their revenge. They waited until the Sweetnappers were about to enjoy eating their sweets in an old haunted cricket pavilion, and then one of them, dressed up as a ghost, appeared, and the Sweetnappers panicked. Unfortunately one of the Sweetnappers was run over (but wasn't badly hurt) whilst running away, so the story then moved on quickly and had a very moral outcome, where only the naughty children got their comeuppance, once their head teacher found out what they'd done.

'My daughter understands human nature, don't you see?' he then said as he looked into Chalkie's eyes, after taking a deep breath in the silence that followed. His heart even missed a beat, as he knew Chalkie was almost certainly wondering what a schoolgirl's play had to do with a real life drug story in a large city like Bradford, so he finished off by saying, 'Jealousy is one of the seven deadly sins, after all, and feelings of betrayal are very powerful too. Once Nigel feels he's being betrayed, he'll panic. With Ronny and Lenny's help on the inside, and Charlotte as a 'ringer' on the outside, it'll be a doddle. So, what do you think?' he asked at last.

Chalkie agreed. 'Yes, it's a good idea,' he said as he nodded his approval of the revised plan of action.

A policeman's job is a difficult one. Each day doesn't always end happily: there are always further problems and dilemmas to be sorted and resolved. Chalkie even wondered if Capstan always liked to get his own way too much, even though he approved of the changes his partner had made. Capstan had just shown him a copy of Emily's Sweetnappers script. 'She's a copper's daughter, there's no doubt about it,' Chalkie said.

'I think it should be entitled *The Nature of Being*,' Capstan said after nodding in agreement. 'I think greed and stories of revenge are universal. Without limits we are all doomed, so my views about legalising all drugs were probably wrong,' he admitted.

Joe's Second Note

Capstan's candour and plain speaking had actually made Chalkie confused, and he left wondering how he was going to tell his wife about the day's developments. He knew in his bones that life in the city wasn't as straightforward as Capstan liked to believe. He knew that over thirty tons of cocaine reached Britain each year, and that this was just the tip of the iceberg. Besides the more well-known Class A drugs, newer synthetic drugs were also coming onto the market all the time. There were therefore going to be criminal gangs involved. Nevertheless, he knew that they had to do something to stop Nigel, and the playscript, even though written by a child, did offer guidelines. He agreed with Capstan in this respect: feelings of betrayal are very powerful, and if it was possible to turn one gang against the other, they might be able to stop a large influx of drugs coming into the town; so he remained sure that the premise was a good one.

Emily was undoubtedly a very clever girl. Chalkie was certain about that. Nevertheless, what we think about our children can be biased, and there is, after all, a fundamental difference between their actions and the evil that some adults inflict on others. Anyway, whether Capstan's idea was wrong or right can perhaps be better gauged by reading the next chapter, which contains the script Chalkie had just read.

The Sweetnappers

Scene One: a classroom. The end of a school day.

MR WOPPIT: Today hasn't been a good day. I want this table *[he bangs his hand on the table]* and that table to stay behind. Your work hasn't been good enough. The rest of you can pack away and go home.
[These children leave whilst the remaining children bury their heads in their hands.]
MR WOPPIT: Now I'm just going to ring my wife. I don't want my sausages burnt. Sit still and be still. I won't be long.
[He leaves and the children digest what has just happened.]
CHILDREN IN GROUP ONE – *suggested speech:*
-He's always picking on me.
-And me.
-I never got a detention in my life until I came here.
-We've got to get our own back.
-Yes. I've got an idea. Whilst we carry out our survey work on the school, why don't we sneak out of school and pinch some sweets? We'll have our name on the register, so we'll have an alibi.
-That's a great idea.
-We could ask everyone else to cover for us by keeping Mr Woppit busy.

Scene Two: the classroom at the beginning of the school day. Mr Woppit has just taken the register.

MR WOPPIT: Now I'm not in a good mood. My wife burnt my sausages yesterday. So your work had better improve today. You only have two more days to complete your surveys and experiments. *[So all the children start to work.]*

[Child X from Group One strolls over to a child from Group Two.]
CHILD X *[whispers]*: We've got a private plan going on. Can you keep Mr Woppit busy?
CHILD A *[nods and smiles]*: Okay. I'll tell everyone in our group to ask for help. Mr Woppit won't know what's hit him.
[The children smile as they leave to carry out their 'survey'.]
CHILD A: Mr Woppit, my telephone isn't working properly. I want to see how it works when it is wet with thick string. I wondered if temperature makes a difference. Have you got a kettle?
CHILD B: Mr Woppit, my work needs marking.
CHILD C: The hairdryer's broken. I can't finish my experiment.
MR WOPPIT: What's going on today? I'm exhausted. I need to sit down for a minute.
[Meanwhile the children from Group One walk to the shop and pinch some sweets.]

Scene Three: the classroom at dinner time.

[Children from Group One enter.]
Suggested speech:
-It went like a dream.
-It was easy.
-Where are we going to hide them?
-My bedroom.
-No chance – you'll eat them.
-Where then?
-I know. We'll hide them in the cricket pavilion.
-But it's haunted.
-I know. No one will look for them there.
[Children from Group Two then enter from the room next door. They are finishing off their experiments.]
CHILD D: Hello. Can you hear me? *[She is talking into her telephone. She turns around and notices the other children. Her friends join her.]*

THE SWEETNAPPERS

CHILD F: What are you doing in our classroom?
[These children illustrate their annoyance at being disturbed with raised voices.]
CHILD Z: It's not *your* classroom. You think you're cool, don't you?
CHILD D: We're cooler than you.
CHILD B: *We* know you've got a secret. You're getting up to no good.
CHILD A: And we're going to put a stop to it.
[Mr Woppit then enters.]
MR WOPPIT: Why are you arguing? If you've got nothing nice to say to each other, say nothing.
[So everyone leaves the classroom. The sweets are hidden inside PE bags. The children in Group Two remain furious.]

Scene Four: the cricket pavilion. The children plan on eating the sweets the next day when they have plenty of pop to go around.

[The children from Group One bury the sweets.]
 Suggested speech:
-This place gives me the shivers.
-No one comes here.
-I know. The sweets are safe here.
-Bury them under that plank. *[They cheerfully do this and leave.]*

Scene Five: the classroom. The next day.

MR WOPPIT: Your work is getting better. It's been a much better day. Thank you, children.
[A policeman enters. Most of the children are excited but some are nervous. Nobody knows what to say.]
POLICEMAN: Can I have a word, Mr Woppit? Sorry to disturb

you. There's been a robbery at the local shop. A lot of sweets were pinched. Was anyone away yesterday?
[Mr Woppit picks up the register and the policeman walks over to look at it.]
MR WOPPIT: It can't have been anyone from this class. Look.
[He points to yesterday's attendance strokes.]
POLICEMAN: No, it can't have been. They were all here yesterday. Thank you, Mr Woppit. *[He leaves.]*
[Mr Woppit is slightly embarrassed. Some children whisper to each other whilst three or four children smile.]

Scene Six: the classroom. Dinner time.

[The children from Group Two are showing each other the ghost mask and clothing. They are really excited. They are nodding and joking.]
Suggested speech:
-This'll scare them.
-It will. I can't wait to see their silly faces.
-Yes. It'll teach them to muck about in school time.
-They'll be scared out of their wits.

Scene Seven: children from Group Two are walking to the cricket pavilion. They are talking to each other. One turns around.

CHILD B: Quick, they are coming.
[They run and hide behind the pavilion. One puts on the ghost outfit. They watch the children from Group One arrive. These children are very excited.]
CHILD C: This is the best trick I've played on anyone. The mask suits you, and it wouldn't scare me.
CHILD A: But it will scare them!
CHILD E: Come on. What are they doing?
CHILD D: They're talking about Mr Woppit, and the sweets. They are really pleased with themselves.

THE SWEETNAPPERS

[The children in Group One start sharing out the sweets.]
Suggested speech:
-This is wicked.
-Yummy.
-Opal Fruits.
-Wow.
-Share them out. I want a Picnic.
[The ghost appears and the children are scared out of their wits. Whilst screaming, they run back to school. Meanwhile a parent is leaving in her car. Whilst she is reversing out, Child Y is knocked down and all the children from Group One see what has just happened.]
CHILD W: Oh no, he's been knocked down.
CHILD U: We're going to get . . . done.
CHILD V: He's hurt.
[Two children from Group Three appear. They leave immediately and ring for the ambulance. Another two children tend and care to the child who has been knocked down. Another goes to find the headteacher – Mr Sunshine. The ambulance arrives and the ambulance man gets out.]
AMBULANCE MAN: What's happened here? What's your name? *[He inspects the wounds.]* It's not too serious. You'll be all right. I'm just going to put these bandages around the cuts. How are you feeling?
[Child Y then explains what happened as he is carried into school.]

Scene Eight: inside school. Mr Sunshine appears. He is dumbfounded.

MR SUNSHINE: What's happened here?
AMBULANCE MAN: I was called to help this little boy. He's going to be all right, but he's been up to a little bit of mischief. Some of the children in your school have been pinching sweets!
MR SUNSHINE: Pinching sweets! I've been a teacher for twenty-five years and nothing like this has ever happened before.
[Mr Sunshine immediately leads the children from Groups One and Two

into the school hall. The children walk in reluctantly with heads bowed low. They sit down where they are told.]

MR SUNSHINE: Come on, tell me. What's been going on?

CHILD A: It's all their fault. *[She points at the children from Group One.]* They had the idea of pinching sweets. It was nothing to do with us.

[Child X stands up and confesses.]

CHILD X: It's all Mr Woppit's fault. He's always picking on us. So we pinched some sweets when we should have been working.

MR SUNSHINE: Mr Woppit is a very good teacher. *[He looks down on the children.]* And you all should know that when you hurt someone else you also hurt yourself.

[Child B stands up suddenly.]

CHILD B: We didn't pinch any sweets. We like Mr Woppit. We tried to stop them.

MR SUNSHINE: Well you can all go home then. Straight home. Do you understand?

[They walk out cheerfully, leaving the children from Group One to moan and groan until they are told to shut up.]

MR SUNSHINE: We'll get to the bottom of this tomorrow. In the meantime I hope you will all think very carefully about what you have done. I shall be writing to your parents of course. Now you can all go home.

Scene Nine: the children from Group Three hold a court to determine punishment.

CHILD M: Silence in court. Bring in the accused. *[The children walk in silently.]* This court is now in session. The witness for the prosecution may now speak.

POLICEMAN: These children have been identified by the shopkeeper. I have here her statement. They are all guilty of pinching sweets. It's an open-and-shut case, I'm afraid.

CHILD L: Thank you. We also have witnesses from the class.

THE SWEETNAPPERS

So, you may sit down. What is the verdict of the court?
[All the children in court individually pronounce the children guilty.]
CHILD P: In all my years in court I have never come across such an unusual case as this. *[The children of the court then bow their heads to confer.]*
CHILD R: We have carefully considered all the aspects of this case, and our verdict is as follows.
CHILD S: All your privileges are lost. And you will all go on the last dinner sitting, where you will eat the scraps left behind by all the good children – until further notice.
[The children from Group One leave the court. They are stunned by the severity of the punishment. Mr Woppit enters and stands in front of the court.]
CHILD R: What is wrong with Mr Woppit?
Suggested speech from the children of the court:
-He's often in a bad mood.
-He always takes it out on us.
-I don't think he's a very good teacher.
[The children look at each other and each one turn their thumbs to the floor.]
CHILD Q: Mr Woppit, you have got the sack. The sentence is passed.
[Mr Woppit leaves immediately as the children watch impassively.]

Scene Ten: the dining room.

[As the children from Group One enter all the other children smirk and giggle as the children from Group Three serve them their dinner – scraps left behind by all the good children.]

THE END

One review may be of interest here to the reader, as it was the only speech Capstan and Rosemary could remember where the school representative fumbled and stuttered slightly, immediately after seeing the play with the parents. When she stood up she appeared uneasy, and even though this uneasiness only lasted for a short time, it was very noticeable. It made Capstan giggle (a little too loudly if the truth be known, as his wife had to prod him with her elbow in his midriff and tell him to hush). Capstan believed that it was Emily's use of Carly Simon's song 'Let the River Run' in the play which was the cause of the awkwardness.

'Well, er,' the representative said as she twitched and looked about. 'Firstly I'd have to say that the film was very well, er, made. It was also very imaginative; there was no doubt about it. But . . .' She continued, after pausing for a deep breath, '. . . I'm not quite sure what signals this passes on to the, er, younger children.' Capstan thought at the time, and also retrospectively, that she didn't regard this as one of Emily's finest moments. 'But we must remember,' and it was here that she started to speak with more rigor, 'that Emily and her class achieved outstanding SATs results, so we must congratulate them on all their achievements. They have, after all, been a credit to the school.' This was said wholeheartedly, and was appreciated by everyone.

It was true – Emily really had enjoyed her time in her primary school. She was grateful to all her teachers, as were her parents – but she was sure that the film wouldn't see the light of day again!

Joe

Defiance

Three days after The Meeting . . .

'How did you find me?' Paul asked as he turned to face Capstan. 'Oh I still have my moments,' Capstan replied as he gazed over his head so he wouldn't have to look at him directly, but Paul merely smiled scornfully, revealing uneven white teeth, and said, 'What are you drinking these days?'

Capstan ignored the question. 'Ronny's been detained for the time being and the bigwigs have taken charge. Kidnapping a police officer is, after all, a serious offence,' he said whilst trying to emphasise the word 'serious' and therefore making it clear that the police wouldn't be leaving until Chalkie had been found. 'Chalkie is my friend. You do know this, don't you? We investigated Lenny's accident together. It's why we came to Bradford,' he said. 'For your sake, you better hope that nothing has happened to him.'

But Paul knew all about the police, and the threat didn't particularly bother him. What irritated him more was the fact that he'd not completed the task he'd been paid generously for, for if he had, none of this would have happened, and everybody would be better off. And in the short silence that followed they could both sense each other's astonishment as they tried to comprehend what had happened to them in the years since their last meeting. They had come from the same neighbourhood, and both of them wondered how it was possible for two people to turn out so differently. Capstan wanted to tear off Paul's smug head, whereas Paul's thoughts were actually much more restrained, but no less meaningful. He knew that few people possessed the gifts he had at his disposal, so when he put two of his fingers in his waistcoat pocket a short smile developed, then quickly died, on his lips and turned into a grimace as he recognised that

Capstan's world had also been turned upside down, and he remained amazed that anyone could ever underestimate Nigel, so he whispered, 'You're a clown,' as Capstan stood there in the half light.

'Chalkie's been missing for three days now,' Capstan said at last, as boldly as he could, even though he knew that Paul would already know this. He'd be aware of the presence of the police, even though he had only been slightly inconvenienced by them, Capstan rightly thought. What was happening was, after all, just one of the hazards that came with the job, so he'd carry on as normal. All jobs have their little inconveniences, anyway. Just ask a roofer what he thinks of his job on a windy day, for example, Capstan would say when asked about problems associated with the job he did. So he knew it was the *idea* of the their presence, in a philosophical sense, which bothered Paul far more than their actual presence.

'What a fucking cheek – they try to take over, you know,' Paul said, as if to back up these thoughts. 'I don't understand why they do it, but their power is mere illusion. You do know this, don't you? They are simply a nuisance, but only at the level of flies in the summer,' he added as he looked into Capstan's eyes, as he wanted to see, as well as feel, the other man's displeasure. And when he sniffled and blew a ball of snot onto the floor, it was perfectly clear to Capstan what his feelings on the matter were. 'After all, the squeeze hasn't caused any pips to squeak, has it Capstan?' Paul said. He knew the gang at the Queen's pub were feeling the police presence far more than him; but he also knew that the police had no useful leads, so he was enjoying making Capstan squirm, and this tactic was clearly proving successful. 'I'd rather not drink with you if you don't mind,' Capstan said at last as he took a step backwards.

Paul's outward appearance had hardly changed at all, but by now Capstan's clearly had, and in the short time that had elapsed he was in fact suddenly feeling out of his depth, and this was a new experience for him: he wasn't capable of developing a certain detachment on this occasion, and this unnerved him. Paul, meanwhile, remained untouchable. Quite simply, he was a fixture in the neighbourhood, and someone who provided a service for anyone in need of specialist help, so his position was a very powerful one, and this was now clearly evident. 'Don't you realise that you don't belong here any longer? You are now seen as an intruder in this neighbourhood,' he said to Capstan like a weather presenter describing a sunny day on a Bank Holiday, as he knew this was the way to cause him the greatest unease and rub further salt into his wounds. Capstan, though, in a strange way, admired the way he was using the weapons he had at his disposal. I'd do the same, he thought, even though he knew it would be harder to insult someone like Paul, as the lesson he was being given continued unabated, and then he realised it was time to leave. But just when he was about to turn away, Paul said, 'As the police presence is a nuisance I will let you into a little secret. Nigel is a traditionalist, and once he'd acquired his status he resorted back to tried-and-trusted methods, and a personal approach which involved intimidation, his favourite tactic. The Queen's gang are more adaptable, so they are already developing new markets over the internet, using new drugs, whereas Nigel isn't. But this is his only weakness. He's still ahead of you lot,' he said.

This was an unexpected twist, and Capstan was slightly taken aback: Paul had surprised him. But immediately afterwards Paul reverted to his default position, and as he moved closer his facial features regained their gloss. Once again a slight smile appeared, so that he looked like King Arthur handing over a diamond-encrusted golden goblet in Camelot when he said, 'He's already left Bradford. He's flown the nest, in other words, so you'll never catch him now. And that's all I'm going to tell you. Now fuck off.'

Capstan stood his ground momentarily, until he quickly realised that this was merely adult posturing, so he simply left without saying a word.

CAPSTAN AND CHALKIE SAVE THE DAY

There were now many things on Capstan's mind. He remained in a cloud of melancholy, but feeling overwrought at the same time meant he felt he was in a state of flux too. It was his original intention to go straight back to his hotel room, in order to work out what he was going to do next, but he felt too agitated for that. So he walked to a bar in the town centre, and there he sat slumped on an old sofa with a pint and a whisky chaser by his side, as he'd been suspended from duties after telling his superiors to fuck off. Even so, it wasn't this that was weighing heavily on his mind – far from it; other matters concerned him far more, and time (which was running out) was only one of them. He'd even had to put his family on the back burner, and for the last three days they hadn't been the main focus of his life. When he started thinking about them, as he was doing now, he realised just how much he was missing them, so a weight started pressing down on his chest, almost stifling him, and even though he knew they were safe, this thought didn't prevent him from trembling slightly. Even so, other issues such as the look of terror on Carol's face, and the sense of disappointment she felt in him, were worse, and caused frequent terrible flashbacks and moments of panic – as did, of course, thoughts about Chalkie's safety.

So, in order to move forward and plan what he would do his next, he turned to drink. This wasn't, though, a *completely* nihilistic thing to do, because the first thing he had to do was get the look of pleasure on Paul's face out of his mind. If he couldn't do this he wouldn't be able to move forward. He also hoped that if he could assimilate everything that had happened in the last few days, a course of action might form in his brain. Seeing the whole of the last three days' experiences in one 3-D scene, and from every angle, was something he'd done before, so he hoped he'd be able to do it again. Once, that is, he'd gone through a period of feeling sorry for himself, as he wasn't used to things being his fault. So his mind soon began to wander.

He recalled the saying, 'It's wrong to have millionaires when you still have slums', and it was a tremendous idea because it changed the chemistry inside his mind, as the cogs and gears whirled into action. This and the quote 'Gain all you can; save all you can; give all you can', by John Wesley, were the first things he pondered as he began to relax slightly. *So, I'm just a cog in the 'market force' machinery* was his first thought, and the fact that it was therefore no wonder that the police were often helpless in so many ways was his second. What can I do, he then wondered, in a society partly based on selfishness, and on a desire for increasing wealth, where greater disparities between the rich and poor are inevitable? He knew he sometimes felt infinitesimally small, and if he did, it was more than likely others did also. But why, he wondered, did the gap in England have to be *so* wide? In America for example, the land of capitalism, many rich people put some of their money back into the community, but in this country this didn't seem to be the case. In fact, the only sign he saw of rich people giving something back in this country was when he saw some of them running in the London marathon, and this was a bizarre thought as he recalled also that he'd read recently that some people's wages were over eighty times the average wage. This seemed excessive, especially in difficult times, he thought, and he shivered slightly. As he finished off the whisky in one gulp he wished he'd studied these issues as a younger man.

With thoughts like these circulating around inside his head, he then started looking around, and as he did so he realised that he must look like a fish out of water in his present surroundings. Most of the people he could see around him were people who'd be described as of a lower social order, but when he looked at them with a more discerning eye, he saw how content and happy most of them seemed, and how incongruous his own feelings were in comparison. Two lads were playing around on a skateboard, most round there had tattoos and strange haircuts, but they were conversing happily with each other, and as they didn't appear to be talking about anything to do with money either, he realised that you can't miss something you've never had, even though he knew that seeing wealth all around them through adverts in the media and the like must have an effect on people. Aspiration was a good thing, he thought, but when there was no prospect of a job he could see that the gloom caused could be all-encompassing, so this depressed him, especially as the people he was looking at didn't seem to have a spiritual counterbalance either, so he thought that the views expressed by John Wesley shouldn't really apply to everybody. After all, it was only the rich who had choices.

Ideas were now appearing thick and fast. So why was it, then, he wondered, as the effects of the drink took hold, and as he looked outside at the blackness and thought about Christmas, that the richer some got, the meaner they became? 'Because they want to keep everything to themselves,' a voice called out to him from somewhere. He didn't have an answer to that, but felt that a weekly visit to church wasn't enough, as he reflected on the issue and wondered where the voice had come from. But as he didn't believe in God either, he put it down to an act of the imagination as he continued delving ever deeper into his consciousness, until the thoughts inside his head created moving pictures which resembled old newsreel footage. For a time, nothing seemed inaccessible to Capstan's imagination and the night's experiences were becoming even more of an ordeal than he had expected. He felt dizzy, so he sat up and breathed deeply.

Next, he wondered if he was a hypocrite. He certainly didn't consider himself selfish, but it would be remarkable if he was completely selfless. He knew he was still able to see beyond the undiluted views that had been emphasised since the 1980s, via the media and so on, on the importance of the individual, but he couldn't remember when he'd last done anything kind to anyone, within or outside his family, and this worried him as he stood up and started walking to the bar for another pint, with mixed feelings about himself buzzing around inside his head, like flies around a powerful light.

The room was actually a large rectangular one, on two levels, and with a layout common to so many pubs selling beer to the masses, but the bright lights inside weren't only doing their best to keep hidden. Whatever was happening in the world outside, they'd actually increased his own sense of isolation. He'd always known that egotistical desires were corrupting – they had spread through his mind as quickly as bad weeds in a garden – so it wasn't surprising to him that the world had turned out the way it had, so for a time he even felt he was a little like Travis Bickle in the film *Taxi Driver*. He felt lost in the big city, just like him, until he realised that he was simply regurgitating the same thoughts, but in a different order. Nevertheless, his mind was transfixed on them, so he turned around and started walking back to his seat, but then Paul's face suddenly appeared, and it seemed to grow and loom over him until he shivered at the menace of this vision. Whilst he was stuck in this way between two states of consciousness, another strange event occurred. This time he felt the soothing hands of his mother on his forehead, and it felt like a blessing to him. Her face was barely visible, but the warmth of her touch made all of his previous thoughts dissolve. It therefore wasn't long before he felt something emerging, like a flock of birds on the horizon at the start of a new day, as her face grew in definition and became visible, and as it did, all thoughts of calamity disappeared.

In Capstan's mind nothing moved for a time, but then something stirred, and he realised that his own vanity was only partly to blame for this, so it was time to trash all the sad thoughts that were inside his head, and with a slight sideward movement of his head, and with clenched fists, he acted. It was a brief and sudden event, but the effect was mesmerising. It was probably all very natural, yet something enchanting appeared to have happened. At first he even wondered if it was a vision of some kind, from God, but then he realised it wasn't. People often suffer, he realised, not because of their own imperfections, but because of how others treat them, and in that split second he realised that he wasn't responsible for the evil that Nigel was doing, so as the vision of his mother faded, his thoughts became more natural.

CAPSTAN AND CHALKIE SAVE THE DAY

He was once again a proud and decent man and he pictured himself walking through a rising steam cloud that hung over the streets, before the sun rises. He'd reached new heights and it was time to think like a proper policeman again. So that's exactly what he did. If Nigel wasn't in Bradford any longer, then where the fuck was he? If he could find Nigel he'd find Chalkie, he realised.

As he walked through his childhood neighbourhood, past Drummond Mill and Lister Mill – one of which once produced the finest mohair suits in the world, and the other the finest velvet and silk – pride swelled up inside him. He even remembered that a famous strike in one of them helped create the Independent Labour Party. Then he walked past the old swimming pool, next to where they used to eat the finest Cornish pasties, and he stood transfixed because it was there, in the swimming pool, that he received his first real-life lesson on the birds and the bees, and pictures of what once happened there were suddenly very vivid, as he recalled an incident that took place there all those years ago.

The doors of the changing rooms were situated on either side of the pool and they resembled the doors in the old Western saloons. They swung open and only covered a person's private areas, so heads and legs were visible, as bathers changed. It was in an end cubicle that Christine spread her legs. 'Eddy, you need to see what teenage girls are made of. You can look, but you can't touch,' she'd said. It had frightened Capstan, then much smaller, but he'd also been impressed at her candour, and walked into the cubicle; then, after looking at the sight which resembled a Martian landscape, he cheerfully walked away, grateful for an altruistic act he'd never forget. Her mother, Capstan recalled, was actually a prostitute; Christine herself had a lovely smile, and she was a really popular girl. Anyway, it had been a life-changing experience for him, and one, he realised, that even helped him when he told Emily about her own body, the differences between boys and girls, and where babies come from, when the appropriate time came. As he stood there with snowflakes fluttering down in the night sky, he did then wonder what had happened to Christine, but he didn't dwell on it for long because he knew fairy stories didn't often happen in tough neighbourhoods, so he moved on.

He walked passed his old school, and then passed all the places where most of the important things had taken place when he was a child. Even an old telegraph pole grabbed his attention and made him giggle. A rival gang set fire to it one year just before Bonfire Night, he remembered, when they'd foolishly left all their wood next to it prior to properly assembling it the next day, as building a bonfire required great skill, and only those with the training, acquired over years, were allowed to participate. The fire brigade, he remembered, had to be called out and none of the telephones worked for a week afterwards, but nobody got into any trouble, and even though their bonfire that year was a damp squib, they always laughed about it afterwards. Capstan even realised he was laughing now, too, as he walked passed it. The actual neighbourhood wasn't in fact very large, he realised. He hadn't really thought about it before, but as a child it seemed to stretch for miles, and buildings he jumped off seemed as high as skyscrapers, but when he sat down now, on a bench in Lister Park next to Cartwright Hall, he also realised that much of his life as an adult wasn't actually that much different from how it was as a child. No one truly escapes one's childhood experiences, he mused. But then he turned his thoughts to the matter in hand, and his heart suddenly felt cold.

He'd bitten his nails since he was a boy, but as there wasn't any biteable part of them left now, he chewed at any loose skin he could find, as he sat on the bench for over an hour. When he couldn't do that any more, he then bit at the corners where the skin met the nail, and he tore off small strips of skin, which he then ate. Biting his nails always helped him think, and soon a number of things then dawned on him, as he concentrated on the matter in hand. Paul telling him the truth was the first, he realised. So if Paul hadn't talked to Nigel, Paul's own role therefore in recent events was unknown to Nigel, because Paul remained completely independent of him. And if Nigel wasn't in Bradford, it was highly likely that Chalkie wasn't either. So, he wondered, how did Nigel find out about Chalkie? It was suddenly clear to Capstan that there were only two possibilities, and both were terrible to contemplate. The thought had probably been gnawing away at him all along in the background, he further realised.

He'd thus arrived at a place he'd probably been dreading all along, but one he knew had always been lurking at the back of his mind, and the cold wind, which be hadn't really paid much attention to previously, now made him shiver because of this unpleasant realisation. It was Lenny who'd talked. It was really obvious. He knew if Ronny had been threatened, and had been warned, for example, that his son's life was in danger if he didn't do as he was told, Ronny would have spilled the beans. He knew he'd do everything possible to save his son. He wouldn't care what happened to him, so threats against him wouldn't make him tell Nigel anything. But his son's safety would be his top priority, and Nigel would have known this. So it must have been Lenny who talked, he concluded.

Nigel had the characteristics of a germ in a foreign body. He was someone who could always find a weak spot, and this is what he had done. By moving quickly and unpredictably, he was well suited for wreaking havoc, Capstan realised. He was therefore sure that it was Lenny who'd talked, and the more he thought about it the more convinced he became, as Lenny would know that he was a man who always carried out his threats. Capstan also knew that it would take someone truly remarkable to say no to him, and even though it wasn't clear how Nigel had found Lenny (although he had a good idea), a course of action was now taking shape inside his head. So he felt both fed up and not fed up as he walked back to his hotel room, with thoughts about what he was going to do next whirling around his head like the snowflakes falling from the sky. He then lay awake for a time until his heavy eyelids soon forced sleep upon him.

His sleep was fitful. First he dreamt he was a miner digging for lumps of coal in a deep dark hole, then he was a man caught in the middle of a riot, but it was the night's developments, and dreams of those closest to him, that had caused him most distress. So when Capstan was awoken by the bleeping on his mobile phone, he came to in a panic, with his heart racing and the look on Carol's face was still ingrained in his mind. He felt more exhausted than he had done before falling asleep, but the bleeping then stopped and he realised that he'd received a text message, so he cleared his mind and turned his attention to what it might say. First, though, he wondered who'd sent it. He was baffled. He was fairly sure it wasn't from his wife, because she'd promised not to contact him unless there was an emergency at home, so he sat in contemplation for a while before looking at the message. 'Good morning, Capstan,' it said. 'Sleep well? No! Oh what a shame. Never mind. Get your arse over to Lenny's capsules in Harrogate ASAP. I think you will be pleasantly surprised. Now fuck off and leave me alone.'

His first reaction was one of surprise, which turned to anger when he realised who it was from. 'I'm not a fucking puppet, I'm not going to be pulled by one of your strings' was his first reaction, but then he wondered how Nigel had got his number. As he stared at the mobile he became intrigued. He placed his hand on the small wooden table next to him and raised himself up, and as he did so, he suddenly felt a burst of relief cascading through his body, like an enormous shiver. 'Why, we scared you into submission, didn't we, you fucker?' he said in a moment of overconfidence. 'But I'll deal with you later,' he added as he walked to the sink. Thoughts of seeing his own family again, and Chalkie, and telling Carol that he was all right brought tears to his eyes even though he'd decided that he wasn't going to do anything like that until he'd seen Chalkie in person first.

He quickly made himself a cup of tea, but after taking only a few sips, he walked to the door. Thoughts of how meaningless life was then permeated his brain as he grasped the door handle tightly and then turned it very gently As he deliberately looked around for one last time, he felt relief in his heart. 'I hope I never have to spend another night in a lonely hotel room ever again,' he said to himself. Then he walked through a short passage, down a steep flight of stairs and into the reception hall, where he handed over his hotel key to a very friendly young man. When he was outside he stopped and looked around again. He felt free, and as he took in great gulps of cold air, snowflakes fluttered down thick and fast, and the murmuring voices of people all around sounded like laughter to him.

He wondered what state Chalkie would be in, as he travelled to Harrogate. He knew his colleague would be badly shaken, but desperately hoped that that was all, and that further calamity wasn't round the corner. The nearer he got to Harrogate, though, the more uneasy he felt, and on his arrival there, feelings of trepidation were flowing freely. He remembered how he felt when they'd pulled up outside Nicholas's caravan, and by the time he was approaching the caravan park this time, the closer his thoughts resembled those earlier ones. When he saw that one of the doors to one of the capsules was slightly ajar, he became genuinely frightened, so he stepped inside as gingerly as if he was walking on eggshells.

He saw Chalkie straight away. He was sprawled across the sofa and was clutching his stomach whilst breathing heavily, and his long legs were curled up under him. Capstan noticed he'd been sick also, and then his worst fears were realised. 'I'm going to fucking kill you, Nigel,' he said as he rushed over to comfort his friend and feel his forehead. 'Jesus, it's red hot,' he said. 'How long has it been since your last injection?' he asked. But Chalkie merely looked up and said, 'Look what the fucker's done to me, Capstan. Don't let *anyone* see me like this!'

Capstan knew that after heroin is injected into a vein, a 'rush' is the first sensation the brain experiences as it is converted into morphine. It then binds rapidly to opioid receptors. He called his wife immediately. He knew she'd do exactly what he asked of her, as in emergencies she knew that Capstan's thinking often resembled a scatter gun. Rosemary knew he was always good in a crisis and she trusted him implicitly. 'Jesus' was the only thing she said after Capstan had told her what had happened. Then she went to tell their family doctor, who was a friend, what had happened. After that, she went to see Carol. 'Tell her,' Capstan said, 'that he's been found and that he's going to be okay, but don't do anything else. Tell her not to worry *too* much. She has a baby to protect, so tell her to be patient,' he'd said.

As Capstan waited for the doctor to arrive he paced up and down, in between stopping to comfort his friend, but he didn't have to wait long.

'Thanks for coming so quickly, Andrew,' he said, as the doctor set to work.

'My partner's covering for me,' the doctor said as he bent down to help Chalkie. 'I got here as soon as I could. I've been discreet, so there's nothing to worry about. Nobody knows what's happened to Chalkie,' he said. Chalkie's blood pressure was very high so he was given medication immediately to modify this and slow down his rapidly beating heart. Then the doctor gave him a sedative to help him sleep. 'As long as the needles were clean and there aren't any immediate bacterial infections, he should be all right,' he said. 'Anyway, we'll know in the next couple of days. In the meantime he needs to sleep. Withdrawal symptoms shouldn't be too severe, but he'll need someone to be with him at all times,' he told Capstan.

Once he had left, Capstan rang Ed. He kept his greeting short and sweet because he knew what the reply would be. So when Ed said, 'Capstan, you know I'm not allowed to talk to you,' he answered, 'Oh shut the fuck up and listen, I haven't time for any bullshit.' He added, 'Now get off your arse – Chalkie's here, and don't tell anyone at the police station just yet, either.' Ed was supposed to be meeting a head teacher at a local primary school with his partner, Christine (the woman responsible for giving Capstan his nickname), but once Capstan had told them about what had happened to Chalkie they sent their apologies to the school and swiftly arrived at the capsule.

'The bastard – is Nigel responsible?' Christine asked as she saw Chalkie lying there asleep.' Capstan nodded as Ed and Christine looked at each other with anxious glances.

'Yes, he fucking well is, but I'm going to get him and it's going to be sooner than he thinks! He's injected heroin into Chalkie. The doctor thinks he's going to be okay, but I've got things to do, so will you stay with him? I'll be in touch as soon as I can,' he said. 'Just make sure he doesn't choke, and if he wakes up, make sure he has plenty of water.' Both officers merely nodded. They knew that Capstan would do whatever needed to be done, no matter what.

'He'd knock down the Eiffel Tower if it got in his way,' Ed said once he'd left. 'He feels guilty, so he's best left to his own devices.'

Capstan drove until he was on a quiet road at the back of Rudding Park. Perspective is clarity, so sort out what you are going to say, he thought as he stepped out of his car and breathed deeply. Ronny was now tagged, so Capstan knew that he'd feel helpless, and that he'd be very restless also, and this was very evident when he spoke to him. Nevertheless, he wasn't in the mood to take prisoners, so when he said without beating about the bush, 'Have you spoken to Lenny?' the silence that followed told Capstan a thousand things.

Ronny feelings of unease had in fact been relentless, ever since Nigel's visit. He'd anticipated the worst, because he knew that Nigel knew that Lenny hadn't been dropped on his head in the ring. But as all desperate people do, Ronny had convinced himself that this wasn't possible. And even though Lenny's phone call had been peculiar, he'd tried to see it in a different light, even though he was certain that his son had been found by Nigel. It had been these thoughts that had given Ronny cause to feel anxious.

'It's strange you should ask, but I haven't heard from him for days,' he said as earnestly as he could, even though he knew that Capstan would know immediately that he was being disingenuous. So when Capstan replied, 'Enough is enough – when it comes to lying you're as useless as a chocolate fireguard. Remember who you're talking to.' Ronny knew that the writing was on the wall and he felt like jumping off a high building. But then Capstan made it much easier for him, and this time it genuinely surprised him. 'Look, I've already made a fool of myself,' the police officer said in a much gentler manner. 'I've learn that naivety is dangerous too, so I'll never underestimate people like Nigel ever again. I know he's got to Lenny. Now tell me what his mobile number is. I need to talk to him.'

Both men were still trying to make sense of it all, but as he stood beside the wall with the telephone in his hand, Ronny especially appreciated that a large part of him had died. He felt, once again, that it would have been far more preferable if Paul had succeeded in the task he had been paid for, for if he had the meeting wouldn't even have taken place. But he knew also that a lot of water had passed under the bridge, even in the last few days, and that the only course of action left to him was to avoid a moral dead end, and to hope and pray that Lenny wasn't aware of Nigel's subsequent actions. So he told Capstan all he knew, which actually wasn't that much. Nevertheless, he felt much better afterwards. And when Capstan then told him that he had anyway figured much of it out for himself, and that he wasn't surprised, the load he'd been carrying suddenly felt much lighter. 'I'll be in touch shortly,' Capstan said. 'Try not to worry too much. Lenny's a decent man, I'm sure he was only doing what he felt needed to be done. Now take care,' he said, as he put down the phone.

Ronny looked emaciated in the light, and he shuffled back into the shadows after the phone call because he was ashamed of himself. So it was only much later, and after much thought, as he went to make a cup of tea, that a new thought occurred to him. It was strange, too, because in actual fact the thought had been there all along. It had just been hiding away in the debris that was once a proud subconscious. He'd just not considered it before, even though it was really very evident. It was this: Capstan, he realised, was, in once respect at least, just like Nigel, being someone you'd not want to get on the wrong side of, especially when there was an important task to be done, as both men could be formidable. So, after smiling uneasily to himself in the mirror, he picked himself up and went for a walk. Snear to your heart's content, as you will undoubtedly do, he thought, as he considered Nigel's plight, but your time will soon be up. So if I was you I'd start running. I'd try to avoid corrupt habits and an immoral lifestyle, he thought as he walked into Starbeck.

Capstan had known Lenny all his life, so he appreciated that, whilst it was true that some people were stuck in a type of life they hadn't chosen, Lenny wasn't one of these people (even though some of his 'choices' were beyond his control). Lenny knew, for example, that all parents, whatever their merits or intentions, will always exercise (to some extent at least) some measure of control over their offspring. Even so, Capstan knew that Lenny had many reasons to be grateful to his father. Some parents, for example, say their children behave the way they do because it is in their nature to do so. Inherited genes demand nothing less, as the book *The Selfish Gene* shows; but the more discerning, and Lenny was one of these, knew that it was also a susceptibility to their environments that was just as crucial, and as this was clearly the major influence in Lenny's case, Capstan's primary thinking ran along these lines. So as he pondered the situation, Capstan knew that it was, by any standards, a difficult one.

'I hope there aren't going to be any unforeseen problems,' he said to himself as he flitted about nervously. He didn't want the telephone conversation with Lenny to be too uncomfortable, as he knew harsh words can do a great deal of damage, but he also knew he wasn't very good at beating about the bush at the best of times, so he was trying to formulate a fall-back scenario, just in case it was required. So as he thought about all the different possible permutations that could arise, he made sure sure he was properly prepared for all eventualities. It was all unnecessary, though, for Lenny was also burdened with guilt. He too had felt the heaviness of the black shadows that stretched throughout his body, causing him sleepless nights. So once the situation had been explained to him, he immediately told Capstan all he knew.

'Capstan,' he said 'there's been a large hole in my father's heart for a long time now. It's as if a maggot has been eating away at it, so I knew that there was something going on, and that Nigel was involved. So when Nigel threatened to kill him if I didn't help him, I panicked. I told him that I'd do whatever he wanted. It was as simple as that. I knew I was making a pact with the Devil, but I had no idea he intended kidnapping Chalkie. Honestly, Capstan, I had no idea about that. He never mentioned Chalkie at all.'

Some thoughts emerge slowly, others more quickly, Capstan realised as Lenny started telling him all this, but more was to follow, and soon he was talking so quickly that his outpourings resembled a stream of consciousness. 'It's his manner that's so scary, Capstan,' Lenny went on after a short pause. 'He appears so calm on the outside, but when things are bubbling away under the surface he's like a fucking volcano, and when he's like that he's capable of burying people in hot ash. He was literally bubbling with frustration and anger when he talked to me, so he scared the living shit out of me, I can tell you. He's also psychotic, so he makes everything personal. He's capable of anything if he doesn't get his own way.'

Once Lenny had finished speaking, Capstan told him about his father's arrangement with Paul, and his drug and blackmailing problems, which Lenny had only partly figured out, and Lenny then became incandescent with rage, sorrow and regret. Capstan at first listened politely, as he was appreciative of Lenny's candour, but as he continued pouring his heart out it wasn't long before he could take no more. 'That's enough,' Capstan then said. 'You're the son of my friend; none of this is your fault. You are not responsible for other people's actions. So let's move on. It's easy to see that Nigel is moving his centre of operations – so where have you been for the last few days?' he asked.

'All I did,' Lenny then explained, 'was pick up various parcels and boxes from a couple of dubious characters in Saltaire and Bingley. No questions were asked. I took them to one pub near York and one in Boroughbridge. The pattern was always the same. I knew I was carrying drugs, but I never asked any questions, and once I'd finished, Nigel even gave me a hundred pounds and told me to keep my gob shut. "Pass on my regards to those freaks in Scarborough," he said as he dropped me off, when he was finished with me.'

'Then what happened?' Capstan asked.

'Well, I asked him about my dad, and Nigel said, "You needn't worry about him any more, he's being taken care of." This worried me, of course. So once Nigel had gone I then rang my dad. It was a very strange conversation, but once I was sure he was okay, I felt much better. I was sure that Nigel was now going to leave us alone, so a great weight had been lifted. And that's all that happened, Capstan,' he said.

'Okay, now listen,' Capstan said. 'You're dad's going to be all right. He'll have to go to prison, but he'll be able to cope with that, won't he? It won't be a long stretch anyway. It'll be a piece of piss. Now Lenny, please be more specific. Which pubs and other places did you visit exactly?'

DEFIANCE

Lenny told Capstan that he had travelled to a pub next to the River Ouse near York, and the pub with a large car park near the centre of Boroughbridge. Capstan realised that he needed a map, and once he'd thanked Lenny and told him to stay in Scarborough for the next few days ('Don't worry about your father, either, we'll both be in touch shortly,' he said), he set off to the public library, with relief now flowing through his body. Everything was now clear and whatever doubts he'd had had vanished.

'God bless Lenny,' he said as he drove past the Stray and into town. Since all his hunches were proving reliable, he was becoming just a touch pleased with the morning's developments and he was grinning like a Cheshire cat as he entered the library, so if he'd had a tail it would have been held aloft, proud and still, like a scorpion's stinger.

'Of course,' he said, after studying the map in the library for only a short time. 'It's simple, the link is water. It's just as I thought.' All the places Lenny had mentioned were situated beside the Leeds and Liverpool canal, the River Ouse and the River Ure, Capstan realised. 'Why, you cunning bastard,' he then whispered to himself as he was aware the old man who was seated next to him was already taking an interest in what he was doing, even though this didn't worry him unduly. 'You keep your drugs on riverboats, and your new head of operations is going to be based in North Yorkshire,' he then said a bit too loudly, capturing the attention of all those sitting at the table. 'You've probably heard about the golden triangle, the area in between York, Harrogate and Leeds, and you think that's where there's money to be made. Wow!' he said exuberantly as his stomach rumbled. 'Thinking is not only good for the soul, it also brings on an appetite,' he muttered to himself as he nodded and bowed, and by the time he'd left his seat he was wondering if there was a link between concentrated periods of thinking which involved searching for causal links when in a tight spot, and appetite. As he left the building, his step was noticeably lighter. He knew as he set off for the supermarket with a plan in his head, that there was an element of selfishness involved, but it was a plan that pleased him. 'After all, we are what we eat,' he murmured.

At the supermarket he enjoyed thinking about what food and drink to buy as he ambled about between the aisles. He actually hovered around the sweets and chocolate aisles because he knew chocolate was close to many a women's heart, and he even started to whistle 'Hi ho, hi ho, it's off to work we go'. Then he asked the woman next to him if milk or plain chocolate is closer to a women's heart, as he thought she'd know something about the matter, as she was of generous proportions herself, but he bought both kinds, as well as the white chocolate variety, realising as he did so just how many different elements could be quickly and satisfactorily concluded at anyone time. Cooking would give him the time to talk to Chalkie, and the food would also help him recover. And once they'd eaten, he'd then ring Carol. Chocolate would be a good peace offering, he thought.

Chalkie was sitting up in bed drinking a cranberry smoothie when Capstan arrived. 'Oh, you've woken up at last,' he said with tears forming in the corner of his eyes, as he'd noticed the light of intelligence returning to his partner's deep blue eyes. 'Where's Ed and Christine?' he asked.

'Oh, I told them to go,' Chalkie said. 'They had an urgent call, but before they left, Christine gave me this to drink. It's called a smoothie apparently. I told them I was all right.'

'Look, I'm sorry,' Capstan then said. And once he'd finished by telling Chalkie how bad he felt, and how pleased he was to see him, and once Chalkie had done the same, the most difficult part of the operation was over for both men. Capstan then explained the position as it presently stood.

'Now,' he concluded, as he handed his partner a bunch of grapes and some fresh loganberries, 'I'm going to make a fennel and orange salad, followed by a fairly hot green prawn curry with fresh dill. I'm also making butterscotch bananas for afters. Those, by the way, are two more of your five a day,' he said, pointing to the fresh fruit. 'Don't worry if you puke either, because if they don't make you vomit the butterscotch bananas sure as hell will. The food should help clean out your system. The theme is sweet and sour. Once you've eaten something we'll then call Carol. I'll need to tell Charlotte that you're okay too. She's been worrying herself sick,' he said, as he went into the kitchen.

Chalkie fell asleep as Capstan cooked, and he dreamt of a field of wheat with rabbits jumping about merrily near a dry-stone wall. The scene was serene, until two large blackbirds swooped down and plucked two of the rabbits up with their giant claws, and he watched them as they wheeled high into the sky as the remaining rabbits squealed forlornly. Then sweet music played and the scene became calm once again, and he then awoke with a start because the dream was resuming its invasive feel. His stomach felt wretched, but when Capstan brought through the food, and once he had picked at it a bit, he felt better.

'We've got him,' Capstan explained as he placed his hand on Chalkie's shoulder. 'He's an arrogant bastard. He thinks he's untouchable, but I know what he's up to, and more importantly, where to find him. But I suspect we'll have to move quickly because he's very clever. So . . . are you up for it?' he asked.

Chalkie looked around the capsule and thought also about everything that had happened to him in the last few days. 'It was only a couple of weeks ago that I dropped you off, when the circus was here,' he said. 'You're now suspended, Nigel's tried to turn me into a smack head, and the police don't know that I've been found. Whatever we do is going to have to be done very quickly, so the sooner we get started, the sooner this whole affair will finish.' He stared directly into Capstan's eyes.

'Good man,' Capstan said. 'Now listen up. This is what we'll do.'

An hour later Carol and Rosemary arrived. Carol looked like a frightened rabbit in a car's headlights when she saw how pale Chalkie was, and she nearly cried, but she managed to show great restraint, even though her eyes looked unnaturally wide.

'Oh Chalkie, I was out of my mind with worry. How are you?' she asked, and Chalkie then did his best to reassure her. He told her in great detail how he felt and managed to convince her quite quickly that he was going to be all right.

'But things needed to be sorted,' he explained. 'It's not the time for a faint heart, so I won't be able to rest until Nigel has got his comeuppance.'

Carol understood the need for closure, so she was soon convinced that the plan formulated by Capstan was a good one, and when he handed out the chocolate and told Carol how sorry he was for letting Chalkie down, Carol hugged him tightly.

Comeuppance

It was a cold night but a clear one, and the moon was reflected in the lake beside Cartwright Hall, so as they sat on a park bench Chalkie imagined he was on a small boat sailing across a shiny ocean, to pass the time. He was making every effort to be optimistic, which was hard, as earlier he'd had another bad dream. In it, he watched as his wife gave birth and then, immediately after, as the baby died in his wife's arms.

'I'm glad we didn't linger,' Chalkie said. 'It's good to strike while the iron's hot.' Capstan agreed, as he recollected what Nicholas had once said about 'goodness'.

'I'm not sure what we are about to do is good, but I know this: some good will come out of it. Wheels turn strangely in the affairs of man,' he said. 'After all, events are merely manifestations of "what goes around comes around".'

Half an hour later Jason appeared and even though he was alone, both officers felt relieved. 'We're not completely happy about this – there is some discontent at the Queen's, but I've managed to convince them that this course of action is the right one,' he said. 'Everyone appreciates the irony though, so I think we can cope with the police presence for a little while longer. So we'll go along with your plan,' he went on as he nodded at the two officers.

Capstan and Chalkie were delighted, so when he walked away they knew that the most difficult part of their operation was now over, and their breathing became more regular as they drove to Boroughbridge.

Meanwhile Christine and her friends in York had been busy. They had succeeded in their efforts. 'It was a pleasure to help,' the policewoman said. 'There is such a thing as the greater good, after all, and everyone at York was pleased to have been able to offer assistance. The inspector believed me when I told him that my migraine was making it very difficult to see, never mind concentrate, so the operation is still secret.'

Capstan had always thought she was officer material, but when she'd explained what had happened he'd found it difficult to hide the admiration he felt for her. She'd spotted Nigel drinking in a pub next to the river in Boroughbridge with Plug and Johnny Handsome. She'd even tracked him as he walked into a local hotel, whilst her friends tracked Plug and Johnny Handsome back to a boat near Naburn Lock outside York. 'Gotcha!' she said, after finding their boat.

Early the following morning Chalkie rang Nigel and said in his Marlon Brando voice, 'Now then you wanker, did you think you were untouchable?' before holding up the phone so that Capstan could hear it go dead as Nigel threw it against the wall. They knew he was full of rage, but even they couldn't have anticipated how red his eyes would glow when he discovered that his feet were stuck, and how dizziness would overcome him when he suddenly realised he was trapped. This was a completely new experience for him.

'Who the fuck was that?' he said as he crashed to the floor when he tried to move.

Capstan and Chalkie meanwhile moved into position and waited as Nigel dashed to the window, once he could, to see if the street was empty, after deciding he wasn't going to stay in his room like a cooped-up hen any longer. 'There's got to be a way out of here without being seen,' he said aloud as he opened the door and looked to see if the corridor was empty, which it was. So once he was certain it was safe to do so, he scuttled like a frightened rabbit down the passageway, before running down the fire exit steps until he reached the bottom. He looked around to see if the coast was clear, but just when he thought it was, he was hit with a blunt instrument from behind.

'Gotcha!' Chalkie said, as Capstan immediately handcuffed him and put a bag over his head. Then both of them bundled him into the back of the car. 'Perfect!' Chalkie exclaimed, as Capstan turned on the engine. 'Fucking perfect. You were as predictable as a headless chicken,' he said to their captive in a voice that was low and harsh. Once back in Bradford, just as he was regaining consciousness, they handed him over to Jason.

'You've caused us a great deal of trouble,' Jason said. 'And to be perfectly honest, we're all pissed off with you. Now hold out your arm. It's time for *you* to appreciate what it feels like when things like giant bats whirl around your head in a dark sky where the wolves are always howling in the distance. This heroin is hot shit, and by the time we've finished with you all your nightmares will be real. You can trust me on this,' he said.

An hour later the first anonymous call was made. The Queen's gang were being true to their word and they told the police exactly what had been agreed. 'We've tracked him down, guys, to a flat nearby,' the voice said. 'Now get your arses over there. We don't want any thanks; all we want is to be left alone. We're doing this for Queen and country.'

The police burst into the room soon after, and they found Chalkie tied up. 'Is my wife, all right?' he asked immediately. 'Thank god you're here. Give me a phone. I've got to ring her,' he said as anxiously as he could. 'Nigel told me he'd hurt my wife if I attempted to escape. "We'll get her too," Nigel told me, so I've been here for days.'

It was an expertly delivered speech – he was, after all, a good actor, and the sergeant listened politely. 'Chalkie, relax. She's okay,' he said, as two other officers untied him. 'The police have already been in touch with her. She knows that you've been found, so relax. She's fine. Now, how are you?' he asked.

A short time later Jason rang the main police station in York and told them where a large amount of various illegal substances were being stored. 'All we want is for the police to give us some space. We've helped you, now return the favour; this is our last time of asking. You've all been pissing about in Manningham for too long, so leave us alone.' He said this in such an aloof and detached manner that afterwards even Capstan and Chalkie couldn't help admiring the way Jason had sent the police scuttling over to Boroughbridge and York, where they swooped once again, without hesitation.

And later, on *Look North*, the Chief Constable even said, 'This was one of the most successful operations ever carried out. These drugs were obviously intended to be sold over the Christmas period, so we are delighted that our streets will now be much safer places. This was a major find.' This was met with reassuring glances, both in and out of the television studio.

The last call the Queen's gang made was to the inspector in Harrogate. 'Sergeant Blake is a latter-day Sherlock Holmes,' a highly intelligent-sounding male voice said, referring to Capstan. 'You should take great care of him. He knows what's what, and he knows how to get things done. You should promote him. We'll be happy if you do. Just keep him away from our neighbourhood. We never want to see the likes of him round here again. That man has high expectations, and others around him seem to raise their game at his bidding. I bet his shoelaces never get tangled up when he's in a hurry,' the voice said, then rang off.

Joe's Last Note

Unfortunately happy-ever-after endings only happen in fairy stories. They don't happen in this story, so any thoughts of a dream ending are just a passing fantasy. Chalkie was in fact sitting in the station with Capstan, waiting to interview Johnny Handsome, when the previous 'comeuppance' was being written. He was just thinking about what the best-case scenario might be, and that's what the previous chapter was: merely a daydream of Chalkie's. In actual fact they'd searched everywhere for Nigel, but he'd scarpered off, and any help from the Queen's gang was merely wishful thinking; nevertheless, this daydream had pleasantly diverted him for a time.

'You'll never catch him, he's far too clever for you lot,' Johnny Handsome had told them as he was handcuffed after being found on a riverboat near York in possession of some Class B drugs, and he was right about that; but they'd managed to capture Johnny at least, and this was a positive result, one that had pleased their inspector. He'd been found with his pants around his legs, and what Capstan said at the time of his arrest still makes Chalkie laugh when he thinks about it. They'd swooped and found him in bed with a woman. 'Was it worth it?' Capstan asked him, once the woman had left. 'You're a stupid fucker. Did you know that? Stupid and a fucker,' he'd said.

So what was the nature of the prize? Well, it was bronze in terms of importance, nudging maybe towards silver, when both officers considered the matter in detail. The Class A drugs had disappeared, but they wouldn't be circulating in Harrogate, and neither, for that matter, would Johnny Handsome. Capstan remained annoyed about being worsted, and felt sore that he'd let his partner down, so this modest victory still left a bitter taste in his mouth. It was a hollow victory, but he knew that he could deal with it and learn from it, because he also knew that the outcome could have been far worse. Chalkie was due at the police rehabilitation centre for some peaceful recuperation, so he would be having a restful time and one devoid of anxiety; and Capstan's previously exemplary record meant that he'd only receive a written warning, and this was fair enough, he thought, even though he'd also have to go on an anger management course. He liked the irony though. 'If you think you're fucking Lieutenant Columbo, take the fucking exam and become a detective,' his inspector told him. 'Now take a couple of days off work and spend it with your family,' he'd said afterwards as he headed off down the corridor and into his office.

Christmas wasn't that far away, so this was something he was happy to do, but after a very relaxing and peaceful day spent with his loved ones, his competitive nature soon resurfaced, and the nature of its resurfacing was unusual. One task he could complete successfully, he realised, was to write a Christmas play for Natasha, his youngest daughter. After all, everything has a place, there is a time for everything, and as long as things stay in their rightful context, everything should be fine. He considered the proposal in detail, and the more he thought about it, the more he liked it, as he realised that it was another kind of role reversal. If his daughter could write a play, then so could he. So he set to work.

His first ideas involved viruses, germ-like creatures that invaded Toyland at Christmas, set to the *Pink Panther* theme song. The viruses then sent the toys topsy-turvy, and as the *Noddy* theme song played the children would create their own mad robotic dances. Other ideas then flowed freely. They involved a witch who could do anything except make children like her, and a journey through an enchanted wood as the good children set off to save Toyland. He decided to keep his ideas secret for now though, and he'd only ask Emily for help if all his ideas came to a dead end, which he hoped to avoid at all costs. At the same time he'd also read a few philosophical books, and recap on the some of the 'greatest ever speeches' reproduced in a book he once bought himself, because he was determined to keep his 'art of rhetoric' medallion for at least another year.

Ronny, meanwhile, was sent to prison for six months, but he would be released after four, and Lenny went to Holland. Dutch planning regulations meant that his capsules were ideal living quarters in areas of that country that were prone to flooding. They needed a little redesigning, but once they could be moved up and down, they would become very popular, and he would become a successful businessman. The language would always remain incomprehensible and 'double Dutch' to him, but he'd fall in love with a very attractive Dutch lady. Love, after all, finds a way, but he would always keep in touch with everybody.

Charlotte meanwhile would always continue to bewitch all those she met, and her market stall would expand into all sorts of bespoke holistic and astrological products which the public would buy because of her smile as much as anything. After all, the world loves a princess.

Epilogue

Bradford in the early 1960s was a diverse place full of interesting people from all over the world. By the time I was eleven I'd been to Scotland to watch Celtic play with Peter the Irish barber, been to a Latvian camp with a refugee and a teacher, and learnt to cook Jamaican food (and even eaten a scotch bonnet – a hot pepper – on April Fool's day which nearly burnt my mouth off). I'd watched Richard bowl in the Bradford League (he was faster than Freddie Trueman), and eaten numerous curries; I loved Italian food, knew a lot about Italian football and had fallen in love with Sophia Loren. I learnt that kindness was universal and felt privileged that I knew so many interesting people. Then, when the mills shut, everything changed and life was never the same again. My happiest days were over.

I don't know if everybody thinks about the past as much as I do, but for me doing so has always given my life meaning. My regrets, disappointments and so on are the foundations on which everything else is based, and this is the case for the characters in this story. I asked them when they were happiest, and their answers are given below. I think these responses help show the inner workings of their minds.

Capstan: What a question! Many memories spring to mind. I love watching *101 Dalmatians* with Natasha. Another memory that stands out involves Emily. At the end of Year 5 she helped organise a debate for parents during an open day. She knew that the Stray was protected by an Act of Parliament, so for mischief's sake she proposed the building of a factory on it, to see the reaction when I supported the motion. It was priceless! Finding that crucial DVD also stands out.

Emily: When reading *The Gruffalo* to Natasha.

EPILOGUE

Mark: My whole life seemed fucking fantastic. But I don't think I know what happiness is. Sorry, I can't help you further.

Charlotte: Passing my ballet and Scottish country dance exams as a child was great. I loved it also when the chorus started dancing in front of mirrors in the musical *A Chorus Line*. It was so beautiful. But, like Alice, who found the Red Queen getting further away the faster she walked towards her, I have found that happiness cannot be pursued. After overcoming so many obstacles in my life, it only occurs when I feel at ease with myself – and then only rarely.

Nigel: Fuck off. The question is irrelevant. Go away.

Johnny Handsome: Looking at me in the mirror each morning is usually the happiest time for me. 'Mirror, mirror on the wall,' I sing, as I stroke my hair, 'I am the most beau-ti-ful of them all.

Rosemary: The birth of my children was special. I love it when I also see the sparkle in my husband's eyes. They light up when he is with his children. It brings a tear to *my* eyes.

The Author: Making things subjective has always given a meaning to my life. Life otherwise would be unbearable. So I'd have to say that my childhood was my happiest period.

Lenny: Look, I'm sure that you're a very nice fella, but in my opinion it's sad that you have to ask. Therefore I assume that you don't know what happiness is. So I just say this: get a girlfriend! Please accept this advice with my best wishes. Your happiest period may be just around the corner.

Roger: Being with Mark, when I was his best friend, was a special time for me. When you wear a cloak of respectability (as we did), others saw only what we wanted them to see.

CAPSTAN AND CHALKIE SAVE THE DAY

Chalkie: Asking Carol out was nerve-racking. But it was great when we started going out together. Like Capstan, I was pleased when we found the DVD. I also love the banter at the station, especially when I am thinking up nicknames for new colleagues.

Carol: My whole outlook on life changed when I found out I was pregnant. I wake up with a smile on my face every single day. I've really enjoyed reading *Anna Karenina* by Tolstoy. Poor Anna's life was ruined when she had to leave her child, but I felt strangely uplifted when I thought about how our baby is going to change our lives in Harrogate.

Paul: Fixing things. What else!

Roy: Sharing my bed with Charlotte is always special.

Ronny: Ask me later – when I'm out of prison. I'm generally happy when my son is.

So there you have it. This is the end of *Capstan & Chalkie Save the Day*.

Joe

Author's Last Note

I wrote to all the publishers afterwards. No one had heard of Joe Boot. There were no plans to publish his book. When I asked Sarah, an attractive lady who works at the Blues Bar, if I could mention his book in Joe's story, she said I could, but asked me who Joe was. 'Joe's the lad I sit with,' I said. 'Really,' she replied, 'I've never seen you sit with anyone. You're always sitting by yourself reading the newspapers and looking out of the window when I've seen you.' Hmm, I thought to myself, I've got an alter-ego, how interesting. I pondered this and even though he wasn't someone who is particularly nice, I felt he might be under different circumstances. He was someone plainly desperate for some recognition; maybe he even felt he had something to prove and was simply trying too hard. The subconscious may even be something nobody can completely master, who knows? But I will try from now on to do it, I thought. Drink may even be partly responsible; if it is, that is something I can certainly do something about.

So Joe wasn't going to be famous; what a shame, I thought, but at least he wasn't going to go to prison. But what about the story? Well, I think I will try to have it published. Writing, after all, has really helped me, albeit in ways that haven't always been pleasant, and it's been a struggle that pushed me to the limits of my ability. Its even made me slightly mad at times – anxiety, after all, can be unremitting, for when I am not well I have discovered that it's either this or that, A or B, Sugar Puffs or Frosties, drink (to excess) or no drink at all; in other words, the middle ground doesn't exist for me – whereas when I'm operating normally, life experiences involve, for example, a little bit of this, more of that, and loads of the other: experiences, after all, create chemicals that operate on the brain like a tap, and their effects can be modified where necessary. So writing has been especially good for me in this regard. Writing a book isn't like programming a computer: sentences are not based on ones and zeros; sure they can be cruel and hard, beautiful or sad, but they don't have to be black or white.

Finding the links was the key, and I know that 'blackmailing' a publisher gave me the confidence to proceed. Without it I wouldn't have tried, and once I'd invented Capstan and Chalkie, not being a policeman didn't stop me from writing about being one, either, because when I was a teacher, creative writing was everything, and finding links between things was more important than the thing in itself, so I still cling to the belief that there is a place for 'pretend' – so much so, that even now I still like this approach to learning. After all, an idealistic stance isn't possible without an imaginative leap! And this can't be a bad thing, can it? Anyway I just hoped, in my case, that it wasn't all a giant leap in the dark!

But it wasn't. I asked Sarah out, there and then, and soon after we became lovers, friends, and partners all rolled into one. Writing the book had given my confidence such a boost. It was certainly surprising to me, when I thought about it afterwards, because once I wouldn't have dared do such a thing. Anyway, the next five years were the happiest of my life. But then one day Sarah didn't come home. I'd heard an ambulance passing down Knaresborough Road whilst I was on my way to the shop for some bread for our fish and chips, but thought nothing of it until the hospital rang later. 'I'm so sorry,' the voice said, 'but there's been an accident.' Anyway, to cut a long story short, she was dead. She'd been knocked down by a hit-and-run driver and left to bleed on the pavement.

Later, I wrote 'Staring at the walls, when there is nothing to do, is like being on a road to nowhere' when I was full of despair. I think it adequately illustrates how life once was (when I was ill), and how it has remained, ever since Sarah died.

AUTHOR'S LAST NOTE

Staring at the Walls

Staring at the walls, when there is nothing to do, is like being on a road to nowhere. I'd see it stretch out across empty fields where nothing lives. The picture in my head is in sepia tones. It is a desolate scene – but also strangely beautiful. There are no weeds growing on the roadside, and there aren't any shadows, and in the distance a ruined church lies – it is the only point of focus. It has a square tower and only plain glass windows, and these are cracked and broken. So I approach wearily and my eyes turn to the graveyard – which is desolate and overgrown with weeds. On closer inspection I then notice that the gravestones lie at strange angles and the engravings on them are worn and cracked. Then a black hole suddenly appears, so I walk towards 'the event horizon' and look down into nothingness. But this is no ordinary black hole and I jump. Suddenly I am weightless. And as I hover in midair I realise that I have a choice, apparently. So do I brake or fall?

Unfortunately there's never really a choice. People go on and on, even when there seems no point, and in a way I suppose this is even admirable, but to me my life was a slow and painful existence from then on. Partly this was because I was a man. Women create support networks, whereas men don't, and this meant, in my case at least, that people soon stopped calling round, so loneliness envelops you in its own black cloud, where even changing your clothing can then become one effort too many, especially when it all leads to the realisation that friendships between fellow males is a myth, a farce, and a pathetic one at that.

So I left my house and moved into a caravan. I bothered no one and no one bothered me. I think the following newspaper report I wrote, a short piece imaginatively set in 2026, but based on a real report in the local newspaper, adequately describes my feelings on the matter and my thoughts about the changing nature of this country. Goodbye.

CAPSTAN AND CHALKIE SAVE THE DAY

North Yorkshire Herald – Online
(www.northyorkshireherald.co.uk)
Voice of the Region Since 2015

July 4, 2026
Paupers' Funerals Soar

New figures released today shed a disturbing light on a subject that isn't often talked about – even in these distressing times. They show that various local NHS organisations have cremated over a thousand people who had no family or friends willing to pay, in the past year. They have an obligation to undertake the funerals themselves when there is no one else to do it.

One spokesman said, 'We haven't the time or the resources to deal with each case individually, but we provide a minister, and they are all given a basic service. As long as they don't have a criminal record we do our best to make sure that this is done in a dignified way, but our resources are stretched. The figures are shocking and it's a sad state of affairs.'

'Why are you reading the local news?' Smidge had asked.
'Because the national news is even more depressing,' Jug replied. The national news had been full of plans for means-testing the poor. This meant that if babies couldn't be afforded, having one would be banned. 'Jesus,' Jug said to himself, when he saw the headline 'The State will soon cease to exist.' The final pieces of the jigsaw will soon be in place, he thought. 'Mark my words; there'll be no turning back now,' he'd said.
Meanwhile, Smidge had just received a call after a local caravan owner had discovered a dead body, so the two officers were soon on their way, and as they left the roadside police station, next to the container park where the jobseekers lived whilst working in the local area, Jug watched as some of the worker's were returning back early to watch the final of the World Cup on giant 3-D

screens. And as he himself was looking forward to watching the match himself, with his son, he hadn't really paid much attention to what his partner had told him. The virtual stadiums had worked really well across the country, so he was looking forward to seeing an actual 'virtual match' on the Stray. Already they'd watched giant screens being erected around the pitch which had already been accurately measured to the last millimetre (so it was an exact copy of the original). 'She broke into the caravan,' Smidge had said. 'The dead man hadn't paid his month's rent. The caravan site holder told the operator that he always pays on time, so he knew there was something wrong. Jug, are you listening?' he'd asked. But his words had continued to fall on deaf ears.

But as incidents like this were increasingly common, if the truth be known, neither police officer was perturbed as they drove off on their electric bikes, in the police lanes set aside for quick and easy response times, which were always monitored by central control.

The person had been dead for about five days, but as Chris Haxby had died of natural causes the case wasn't unusual in any shape or form. There were no known friends or relatives, but money was available for a decent cremation, and the remaining spare cash went to the regional authority. And that was all there was to say about the incident, which barely registered on the consciousness of most present. But Jug's attention had been grabbed by copies of a book he'd written called *Capstan & Chalkie Save the Day* that were lying around the caravan. And when he looked inside one of them, there was a copy of part of a letter he'd written to a politician over fifteen years ago, and this had caught his attention because one sentence was outlined in capital letters. It said: 'It is the rich and powerful people who are to blame for the ills of this country, not the poor. Jesus, will the meek never inherit the earth!'

Why, he was a Socialist, Jug realised. He was one of a dying breed probably, and someone who would believe that he was the last of his kind, so this intrigued Jug. He therefore collected up all the books and took them home with him. On his day off he'd read the book. It was set in Harrogate, and reading it would while away a couple of hours, he thought.

A week later

'The State distorts the market, so get rid of it' had been the orthodoxy since as long as Jug could remember. And honing their skills, so that entrepreneurs could extract maximum value from any exchange, had allowed many people to become very rich. But the philosophy was flawed, Jug realised, and many people lived in abject misery. Rich people were building higher walls then ever to protect themselves, but tricky discussions with people responsible for the caring for others were always put on the back burner by the politicians, so any momentum for change was lost. But civilisations have their own entitlements too, he realised, and as his training, with its emphasis on objective thinking, suddenly dominated his thoughts, he even appreciated that knowledge can be a dangerous thing. It can even destroy the 'knower', especially when such knowledge can't be used (even when it would be for the benefit of the general good), he realised. Individual liberty had been repressed, cruelty and injustice existed, but this now didn't worry him unduly. It was true that some people (like Mark in the story) now dominated public life, but it was also true that the underlying reality has always been thus. Utilitarianism was now the new utopia, and as affirmative action benefited most of the population, to some extent at least, he knew a left-wing philosophy was still out of the question. He knew that there have been short golden periods in the country's history, but as something was needed that was even more serious than the threat of global warming to shatter the complacency that undoubtedly existed, this was his last view on this matter. And as he had no views on how this could be achieved, he turned his thoughts to the part of the book that interested him far more: drugs.

AUTHOR'S LAST NOTE

Jug realised, as he read about Capstan's views and Chalkie's experiences, that little had changed in terms of the law, so it was probably true that most of the older drugs were entering the country undetected; but fierce custodial sentences were a deterrent because a life afterwards was almost impossible for anyone with a conviction relating to illegal substances. It therefore meant that most people either became indifferent to these consequences or very clever at avoiding detection. So he was pleased with the inroads the entertainment industry had made, in terms of the development in artificially induced dreams. These could be bought, once the state had given its approval, and even taken in the privacy of your own house. Engrossing virtual fantasies emerged, once the new synthetic drugs had broken the barriers between the subconscious and conscious parts of the brain. There were rumours of psychotic after effects, but just when he was starting to retrieve the memory of his virtual journey his wrist phone vibrated, so he closed the book and turned to the matter in hand.

After kissing his wife goodbye, he was soon on his way. There had been serious flooding in Pickering. Reading the book had passed a pleasant couple of hours, so just like the virtual stadiums and the virtual journeys, escapism too, he quickly appreciated, was only a temporary release from the realities of everyday life. And once past Helmsley, his last thought on the book was this: Chris Haxby spent the last 25 years of his life doing very little. Crikey. How was that possible?